S   little
kiss…

"It's OK," she whispered, fascinated with the darkening of his grey eyes. Tillman wanted her every bit as much as she wanted him. *Dangerous territory,* her mind whispered. *Remember what happened to your mother when she fell in love with a human.* Shelly squeezed her eyes shut, determined to drown the demon voices of doom. She had wanted to get close to him for so long, had fantasized about this moment for over a year.

His lips were upon hers, hot, demanding and probing. She was drowning in sensation, her bones and blood liquefying in pools of desire. The sweet, fierce hotness made Shelly's toes curl into the warm sand. The pounding of the waves matched the pounding in her blood.

SIREN'S SECRET

DEBBIE HERBERT

First published in Great Britain 2013
by Mills & Boon, an imprint of Harlequin (UK) Limited,
Eton House, 18-24 Paradise Road, Richmond, Surrey TW9 1SR

© Debbie Herbert 2013

ISBN: 978 0 263 90419 2

089-1113

Harlequin (UK) policy is to use papers that are natural, renewable and recyclable products and made from wood grown in sustainable forests. The logging and manufacturing processes conform to the legal environmental regulations of the country of origin.

Printed and bound in Spain
by Blackprint CPI, Barcelona

Debbie Herbert writes paranormal romance novels reflecting her belief that love, like magic, casts its own spell of enchantment. She's always been fascinated by magic, romance and gothic stories. Married and living in Alabama, she roots for the Crimson Tide football team. Her oldest son, like many of her characters, has autism. Her youngest son is in the US Army. A past Maggie finalist in both Young Adult and Paranormal Romance, she's a member of the GA Romance Writers of America. Debbie has a degree in English (Berry College, GA) and a master's in library studies (University of Alabama).

To my parents, J.W. and Deanne Gainey,
my biggest fans.

To my husband, Tim,
who believes and supports me in everything I do.

And to our two wonderful sons, Byron and Jacob.
I'm so blessed to have each of you in my life.

Chapter 1

Under autumn's moon-blood red
Beneath a foam-tipped wave
The unseen mermaid spies the dead
Sink to a watery grave.

With a flick of her mermaid's tail, Shelly surfaced from the deep coastal waters holding the dead body of victim number two.

Black garbage bags, held together with yards of duct tape, wrapped around the dead human like a macabre gift package. A cement block dangled from the rope attached to the body. Shelly removed a knife from the leather pouch belted at her waist and sliced through the rope, releasing the block. She plunged her long, sharp nails into one end of the garbage bag, ripped open a layer of plastic and stared into a pair of empty eye sockets.

The killer's signature calling card. News of the previous dead body with missing eyes, dumped weeks earlier in the bayou, still dominated the news media as an unsolved case.

From the tip of her fin to the top of her scalp, an electric surge of fear blazed through her body like a burn. *This could have been me.* Whether she was on land in human form, or at sea as a mermaid, both worlds were filled with danger.

Miles from shore, she kept afloat by swishing the tail fin beneath her torso. Her gaze froze on the maimed body as her heart pounded in time with each rise and fall of the waves. Seawater pooled in the victim's empty eye sockets like wells of tears. The placid mood of the ocean shifted, as if it resented the violent encounter it was asked to hide. Shelly's arms ached as she struggled to hold the slippery plastic-encased body in the turbulent water. Against the waves, the plastic wriggled and slithered like a monstrous black eel.

The abrupt rumble of a boat engine sliced through the humid night air. Shelly jerked and the victim's body skated from her grasp and bobbed beside her in the water. She thought the killer had left, but panic and surprise at the unexpected encounter during her swim had made her careless.

Earlier, she'd been close to her human home, finishing her evening's swim, when a sudden splash sent screaming vibrations rippling through the sea. She'd heard the boat above her on the ocean's surface and watched as the long, cylindrical object sank like a torpedo not twenty yards away. She should have left at once. But she had suspected the foreign object was human, and hoped the human might still be alive.

So Shelly had watched and waited at first. Through the dark ripples, the full moon illuminated a man peering over the side of an old johnboat. She couldn't move as he'd stood there, waiting. Probably making sure the weighted-down corpse wouldn't pop back up, and then the boat had sped away.

Now he was back.

The boat gathered speed and headed directly at her.

No! I can't be seen. Stupid, stupid, getting caught. Got to get the hell away. He would be on her in seconds. Shelly reached for the body and her hands slid off the slick plastic. She took a deep breath and forced her panicked mind to be clear. Her fingers, then palms, grabbed a handful of plastic and she pulled it close enough to circle her arms around the victim's center. But the now-waterlogged body was so heavy it slipped through her arms down into the sea.

Yards away, the killer stared at Shelly with the eyes of an intense predator. With the light of a full moon, she made out the curly dark hair peeking out from under a baseball cap, a hookish beak of a nose, glittering dark eyes with gold flecks and a short, wiry body tensed in fury.

Her eyes burned as she strained to adjust her vision from water to air, the sudden beam of a flashlight blinding her for a moment. Judging from the way his mouth gaped open, Shelly knew he'd seen her inhuman pupils do their wild thing, shine with the bioluminescent glow of deep-sea marine life as the irises swirled like a miniature aurora borealis. Her muscles seized and locked, refusing her mind's screaming command to flee.

Damn. Wait until he sees my tail.

The boat stopped next to her and the man's face contorted with rage. He pointed at Shelly. "What the hell?" he screamed in a tight, shrill voice. He reached into his pants pocket and drew out something. Silver flashed as moonbeams reflected off a thin metallic surface.

A long-bladed stiletto knife.

The sight broke Shelly's paralyzing stupor. She somersaulted, momentarily flipping her tail fin in the air before diving down to the ocean floor. Despite a mysterious, searing pain in her tail, Shelly swam to the bed of sand, knowing he couldn't come after her this deep down.

The foreign odor of dead human wafted through the usual smell of marine life. As her eyes adjusted to the absence of light in the deep sea, Shelly located the body and swam over to it.

A few long strands of black hair escaped from the torn garbage bag. Shelly ran her fingers through her own honey-colored locks. She had never come so close to evil and death. It wasn't right to leave the body this way. Too disrespectful. Unable to resist, she touched the victim's forehead, noting the heart-shaped face and delicate, arched eyebrows above the gaping wounds.

I am so sorry this happened to you. So sorry.

She tucked the long black strands back into the plastic, trying to bestow some dignity and kindness on the dead woman. *I'll come back for you,* she promised as she placed the body in a wedge between a large outcropping of limestone rocks.

The sharp pain from the tip of her tail fin broke through the shock and grief. She looked down and saw a small stream of blood oozing out in swirling, crimson eddies. The killer's knife had stuck into her fin. Damn. In the split second her tail had been exposed, the killer had managed to stab her. She pulled out the knife and this time the pain was excruciating. Had this been what he used to kill his victims?

I have to stop him.

She forced herself back up through the black depths of water, gripping his weapon in her right hand. Nearing the surface, she found the rusty boat still rocking from her downward dive. Flat-bottomed and only fourteen feet long, the rusted aluminum boat was not the best choice for anything but the calmest of waters. Although the style was popular in the bayou for leisure fishing, and easily navigable in the winding backwaters threading along the bayou shoreline, the killer was out of his element so far from land and with the increased wave action of the sea.

His engine sputtered as the killer tried frantically to restart the old worn-down motor. He was on the scrawny side, but his biceps bulged as he yanked the pull cord over and over.

As the boat's motor sprang to life, the waters churned and roared around her. Too late to knock him overboard now. The motored blades could slice her to pieces if she came too close.

Her fingers gripped the knife's handle in frustration as the boat raced off.

She fought against the instinct to fling it away and leave it on the ocean floor. Maybe the killer's identity could be traced through the weapon.

Certain he was gone, Shelly lifted her torso higher out of the ocean and spotted a dingy white baseball cap floating on the boat's wake. She grabbed it and submerged undersea again.

Home. There she could think, form a plan. And get her cousins' advice.

"Anybody out there?" Shelly pushed air out of her lungs, sent the vibration of her voice in a compressive wave motion, similar to the high-frequency elocution of dolphins but minus the clicking sound. *"Lily? Jet?"* If they were anywhere near, they'd pick up her message

and respond. Underwater sound traveled twice as fast as on land and four times as far.

Shelly strained to hear an answer but only caught the snapping of crab claws and a few toadfish whistles.

She swam home, each flick of her fin sending shooting sparks of pain through her body. *Please, no sharks.* She focused on keeping an eye out for opportunistic predators attracted by bloody smell—a mermaid's worst nightmare. She feared hungry sharks more than the killer returning. No way could that man get near her so many fathoms deep.

At last she swam through her home's undersea cave portal with its narrow tunnel climbing upward, and broke surface. The tunnel led to land, the opening covered by a hurricane-proof steel structure shed erected after Hurricane Katrina. It replaced the dilapidated tin building that had stood in this exact spot ever since Shelly was a teenager visiting her cousins on summer vacation. Some such structure had stood for decades at this portal, providing cover for her ancestors as they came and went to the sea.

Dark, humid air rushed into her lungs and she paused at the portal's slender opening, about the size of a city-street manhole. Arms clinging to the edge of its sandy surface, Shelly braced to raise her tail fin out of the water.

This was going to hurt like hell.

The transformation from tail fin to legs usually lasted about thirty seconds with only minor discomfort as oxygen bubbled through her veins. But tonight's stab wound was a bitch. Already tired and in shock, it took all Shelly's energy to pull her body out of the sea. When her breathing slowed a bit, Shelly stood on her left foot and cautiously put weight on the injured right one. It was bearable. She limped to the left wall of the shed and fumbled for the flashlight, kept for these late-night swims. Once she shifted from mermaid form, her night vision decreased to that of an average twenty-nine-year-old.

The halo of light revealed a deep puncture wound, but the bleeding wasn't as bad as she'd first feared. She hoped that was a good sign. She removed the sporran always belted to her waist during swims. It contained her knife, useful for cutting her way loose from fishing nets and as protection against dangerous predators.

Shelly had thought the human world a much safer place.

Until tonight.

The moonlight made her feel exposed and vulnerable as she hobbled to the house. Once inside, she quickly locked the door behind her and leaned against it. Home. It had never felt so good to be home.

The smell of grilled seafood and the musical babbling of her cousins in the kitchen hit her with such relief it made her knees wobble.

She meant to call for her cousins, Jet and Lily, but she was too spent for her voice to carry. She stumbled into the kitchen and leaned an arm against the table. Her long hair dripped, forming a puddle on the Spanish-style tiled floor.

Shelly drank in the domestic scene. Jet put down a platter of extremely rare grilled shrimp and crab claws while Lily rolled up chopped fish in seaweed for sushi rolls. From the back, Lily's long blond hair, so similar to her own, fell in graceful swirls down to her hips. Jet noisily pulled out knives and forks to set the table. The colored glow from an antique Italian chandelier cast variegated prisms of light dancing across the walls.

"It's not like Shelly to get home so late," Jet said, running a hand over her cropped black bob. "And she's the one who insisted on grilled shrimp tonight, too."

"I'm here," Shelly said weakly. Neither could hear her over the kitchen rattling and a small TV playing the evening news.

"It's a full moon," Lily said. "I'm sure the tug of the tide called her. I plan on a long swim myself after dinner. Care to join me?"

"I said I'm *here*," Shelly managed, louder this time.

They turned as one to look at Shelly standing there, dripping and shivering from a combination of fear and cold. Jet strode over and shook her arm. "Shelly? Are you hurt?"

Shelly gazed at her injured foot and pointed a trembling finger.

Jet knelt down for a look. "Holy shit, girl. How'd you get this?"

"Kn-knife wound," she stuttered.

Lily gasped and dropped a handful of the seaweed wrap. A glob of raw fish plopped against her pedicured toes.

"How'd you manage that?" Jet asked.

Lily hurried across the kitchen. Stepping over the dropped sushi, she grabbed a chair and set it behind Shelly.

She sank into it gratefully and stared at the worried faces of her cousins, the only family she had left in the world and the only ones who truly knew and understood her. Being mermaids, the trio pretty much kept to themselves and protected one another from outsiders.

The enormity of what she had just witnessed hit Shelly like a tsunami. If she was in danger, so were her cousins. So was every mermaid, few as they now were in the Gulf Coast. The toxic oil spills had chased away most of those lingering in the area.

"I saw a body being dumped about three miles out in the ocean, near the mussel beds."

"You mean—a dead body?" Jet asked, eyebrows furrowed in confusion.

"Yes." She took a deep breath and spoke again, the bottled words tumbling out. "I felt the pulse of the water change and when I looked to the surface I saw a tall object falling. And…and there was a boat, too, but it left." Her mouth quivered violently and Shelly clamped her jaws, trying to still her chattering teeth.

Lily laid a gentle hand on her shoulder. "You're okay now," she murmured in a voice that held the echo of an ocean wave.

Shelly nodded. "I knew, as soon as it dropped, that it smelled human even though it looked all wrong. You know? Just a long, cylindrical object with no arms or legs moving.

"I dragged the thing up and realized the plastic had interfered with my sense of smell. When I tore open the bags, the human smell overpowered me and I saw…" Her whole body convulsed. "I saw a face with missing eyes."

"Just like the body found a few months ago," Lily whispered. "Oh, honey, no wonder you're so upset. How awful."

"That's not the worst part," Shelly confessed. "I was seen. In mermaid form."

A stunned silence settled in the kitchen.

"Don't tell me the killer saw you," Jet demanded.

Shelly hung her head. She'd screwed up big-time. "He got close enough to stab me in my tail fin as I tried to get away. The damn thing stuck."

Jet's hands fisted at her sides. "Son of a bitch. Wish I'd been the one who killed him."

They thought she'd killed him.

"Don't be upset." Lily stroked her arm. "You did what you had to do. It's over now."

"It's *not* over," Shelly confessed. "He got away."

Jet slammed a fist down on the kitchen table. "He can't know our secret. I'll take him out myself." She took a determined step toward the back door. "Just tell me what direction he went and I'll find the bastard."

Lily stood. "Let me do it. I'll sing to him. No man can resist me when I sing. It'll be easier that way, and less violent."

"But he's gone." Shelly stood, grimaced at the shooting pain in her right foot and sat back down. "Besides, you don't know what he looks like."

Jet faced her, hands on hips. "So. Describe him and the boat."

Shelly shook her head and lowered her lashes. "It's too late to do anything about it now."

"So…what? Are we supposed to sit around and chance that he'll find us?" Jet paced, running her hands through her short hair.

Lily's musical voice interrupted. "He doesn't know who we are. It was dark. A human's eyesight isn't as good as ours. We should be safe."

Shelly again felt the killer's fierce eyes boring into hers. "Maybe," she said doubtfully. "But Bayou La Siryna is a pretty small town and he got a close-up view of my face. What if I run into him on the streets? Will I have to watch my back every day for the rest of my life wondering if he's recognized me?"

"We'll find him first," Jet said. "Find him and kill him."

Shelly regarded her cousin warily. Jet's bloodthirsty nature surfaced at the first threat of danger to her family. Once aroused, Jet was more like a tiger than a mermaid. She didn't resemble a typical mermaid anyway with her tall, athletic body and bold brown eyes.

Lily, on the other hand, was all feminine grace and mystery. A petite but voluptuous body, golden hair to her waist and large ocean-blue eyes that could be kind with her family, coy with the men and a bit calculating with everyone else.

Lily's eyes fixed on Shelly as she tapped her full lips with graceful fingers. "We don't have to find him ourselves. We'll let the police do it for us."

Jet snickered. "They didn't catch him the first time. What makes you think they will now?"

The first stirrings of hope warmed Shelly. "Because we'll lead them to the killer," she said slowly, with a slight smile at Lily. "I know where the body is and I know what he looks like."

Jet was already shaking her head. "We can't go to the police. No way. They'll either think we're the killers or that we're some kind of accomplices. Besides, what can you tell them? Hey, I was out swimming miles from shore, alone at night, and—guess what?—I found your killer for you."

"We can do this," Shelly said, with more enthusiasm. "I haven't told you the best part yet. That knife he stabbed me with? I've got it. Along with a hat that blew off his head. Maybe with all that, the police can find him."

"Those local yokels? Don't bet on it." Jet folded her arms across her chest and sighed. "I guess it's worth a try. But I'm still going to do some searching on my own."

"Don't. Please don't," Shelly begged. "I've got you both in enough danger already. This is my fault. I have to fix it." She pictured Sheriff Angier. Remembered his intense aura and tall, lanky body that moved slowly but with deliberation and controlled energy. The few times she'd run into him at the YMCA, picking up his brother, she'd been reluctantly intrigued by him. "Besides, you're not giving enough credit to our local law enforcement."

Jet interrupted Shelly's thoughts of Sheriff Angier. "Where are this hat and knife?"

"The shed."

"I'm going to get them." Jet dashed off, ready to take action.

"Don't get your fingerprints on anything," Shelly called out. "Bad enough mine are already on there."

Lily placed a hand on top of Shelly's head. "I'm going to get a towel for your hair, fix you a cup of chai tea and then see to that foot of yours."

Lily's image blurred from unexpected tears. Shelly was overcome with exhaustion as the adrenaline rush left her body. "You and Jet have been so good to me since I came here."

"We're lucky to have you, silly." Lily bent over and gave her a quick hug. "If you haven't noticed, Jet can be a real pain to live with sometimes."

"Yeah, I kinda noticed." Lily's kindness lifted her spirits. "I don't know what I would do without the two of you."

* * *

Ten minutes later, hair wrapped and sipping chai tea, Shelly watched as Lily finished cleaning the knife wound.

"It could really use a couple of stitches, but if you're dead set on not going to the E.R., it ought to heal okay with the butterfly bandage," Lily said, sitting down at the table with Jet and Shelly, each wearing yellow Playtex gloves.

"I'm fine." Shelly lifted the soggy hat Jet had placed on the table. "'Trident Processing and Packing.' Terrific. That's not going to help us find him. Half the people who live here either work in the plant or have relatives who work there."

They stared glumly at the white baseball cap with the blue Trident logo emblazoned on the front.

"It may give the police something to work with," Lily said.

Jet picked up the stiletto knife. "This won't. The make is mass-produced. And thanks to being in the water, I'm not sure there's going to be fingerprints. Was he wearing gloves?"

Shelly closed her eyes and pictured the killer, seeing again those burning hate-filled eyes. That was the first thing she would always remember about him. She forced her mind to roam the larger picture, trying to pick up details. She opened her eyes abruptly. "Yes, he wore those heavy rubber gloves up to his elbows that fishermen sometimes wear when it's cold. But I say the knife could still be a clue for the police."

"Don't see how." Jet examined the blade. "Don't see any markings."

Shelly watched the metal blade flickering under the

chandelier's light and shuddered. He had used this at least twice now to gouge out the eyes of his victims.

"Sick bastard." Jet dropped the knife back on the table. "So we're in agreement. I'll retrieve the body and put it on shore for the cops to find."

"No. You're not doing it. *I* am. I'm the one that got us into this mess. If he comes back I'll take care of him like I should have done in the first place." Shelly hoped her voice sounded convincing. She couldn't kill a human but she could, if necessary, injure the killer and help the police capture him.

"I'll do it," Lily said, rising to her feet. "It will be easier for me since I've got the voice that can mesmerize if we run into him. Most useful in sinking a boat."

Shelly was startled. Lily sounded as if she had experience in doing just that. Long ago, there were a few pockets of mermaids known for violent protection of their sea territory, but the decrease in the mermaid population coupled with human advances in science and sea travel had forced mermaids to abandon such bold, public tactics. No, Shelly shook her head slightly, she was wound up tonight and reading too much into Lily's words.

"Guess it's going to take all three of us," Jet reluctantly agreed. "Drive the car to Murrell's Point and park around the bend. This time of night, teenagers will be making out in parked cars, too busy to notice us. By morning at least, a fisherman will discover the body. When we poke our head out of the water, blink the headlights once if the coast is clear, twice if not. We'll put it on shore with the knife and hat."

"Okay. I'll tell you exactly where to find the body. It's secured undersea between two large rocks in that huge limestone outcropping three miles southwest from our house. The dead human smell will lead you right to the victim." Shelly hesitantly picked up the weapon by its handle. "Maybe we should keep the knife."

Her cousins stared at her in surprise.

"Why would we want to do that?" Jet asked.

"Say the police are suspicious of our guy, but there's no physical evidence to tie him to the murders. We could plant this on him."

Jet shook her head. "But I told you, there's nothing special about this knife. Even if they found it on him it doesn't prove anything."

Shelly smiled—they were buying into her plan to frame the killer instead of tracking him down on their own and meting out their own form of mermaid justice. "Not yet it doesn't," she said softly. "But if we learn his identity we could carve his name and the victim's initials on the blade and plant it for the police to find. They'll think it's some kind of sick trophy."

Jet blew out a whistle. "That would be some damning evidence."

Lily ran a long, manicured fingernail across Shelly's cheek. "Now you're thinking like a true, full-blooded mermaid."

A tiny prickle of chill ran down Shelly's spine at the words. She suspected her cousins could be quite ruthless when it came to preserving their secrets. Just how far would they go to protect their hidden mermaid heritage?

As far as necessary, whispered a tiny voice in her mind.

Chapter 2

Close your eyes, all is well
Seal your mouth, don't ever tell
For if you do, shame will come
Mama's Boy falls all undone.

Shelly rolled her shoulders back with determination. Even with no sleep last night, she couldn't allow fatigue to interfere with her clients' therapy. And staying focused on her job helped keep the terror at bay when she pictured the killer she'd encountered the previous evening.

Eddie made a beeline for the water, eyes focused straight ahead to their objective, ignoring his mother three steps behind him, stumbling in designer sandals.

Shelly moved between Eddie and the pool steps, holding up a vest. "First, we put on our vest, then we get in the water," she reminded him.

Eddie reluctantly let Shelly strap it on.

"He's too fast for me," his mom panted as she caught up to them. Mrs. Angier wore black pants and a frilly high-necked white shirt accented with a striking coral necklace. While the rest of the locals sported shorts and T-shirts, Eddie's mom stood out with her inappropriately elegant attire. The blood-sucking Alabama humidity that had everyone else sweaty and defeated never seemed to affect Portia Angier. "I can't keep up with Eddie," she whined, rubbing her temples with a slight wince.

"No problem," Shelly assured her.

It had taken a whole month of once-weekly sessions to get Eddie to accept the water jacket without it being a major ordeal. He was extremely sensitive to the texture of anything against his skin. And it had taken about the same amount of time to stop Eddie from stripping off his bathing trunks the minute he stepped out of the pool.

Suitably strapped in, Eddie walked down the pool steps and waded around the shallow end, splashing and laughing.

"Too bad we don't have an indoor pool at home," Mrs. Angier said, still rubbing her temples, Donna Karan sunglasses dangling in one hand.

"Headache?" Shelly asked, getting into the pool with Eddie.

"The worst. If it's okay, I'll head on home and have his brother pick him up."

Shelly's heart did a little flutter. Tillman Angier had a way of making her feel like a lust-crazed teenager. *Get a grip.*

"Fine." She turned to Eddie. "Ready to get started?"

He was already a step ahead of her. He picked up the kickboard from the side of the pool and began kicking his long legs. Water shot up around him but for all the exertion and noise, he only swam a few feet. "Good job," Shelly said anyway, and they high-fived.

Eddie jumped up and down, laughing and spraying water over the side of the pool. Shelly held his hands and they jumped together in mutual delight. The buoyancy and feeling of weightlessness in the water was good for the soul. Besides improving coordination, flexibility and muscle, the warm water provided healing benefits. Shelly speculated that people with a special affinity for water were long-removed descendants of mermaid blood—so far removed they knew nothing of their heritage but were inexplicably drawn to water, especially the ocean.

She was rewarded with two seconds of eye contact before Eddie looked back down to the clear aqua depths swirling around his body.

"Time for the ball toss," she said. She took a twelve-inch beach ball and tossed it to Eddie. Without aiming, Eddie threw it back, the ball landing a good six feet behind her.

Shelly swam after it and returned to Eddie. "Let's try again. Throw it to me this time."

Eddie slam-dunked the ball in the middle of her face.

Ouch. Well, she wasn't specific enough.

Shelly threw it back and waved her hands in front of her. "Throw it at my hands, Eddie."

He did. But after less than half a dozen throws he started humming. A sure sign he was growing impatient. Shelly quickly moved on to another exercise. During the next hour, she alternated coordination tasks with social play. Afterward, she'd return to her office and make notes on his progress. Few things gave her more satisfaction than celebrating clients' progress.

"Shoes," Eddie suddenly called out.

Shoes was one of Eddie's code words—it meant someone was here to take him home and he needed to put on his shoes, get dressed and go. She searched the room with more eagerness than necessary.

Sheriff Angier, in his neatly pressed brown uniform,

headed toward them in long strides. His presence filled
the room and she was acutely aware of every detail of
his strong face…the prominent jaw, the sharp planes of
his cheeks and broad forehead. He was as unlike his sib-
ling as much as Jet and Lily were polar opposites. The
only common feature of the brothers was the same light
brown, slightly wavy hair. She knew Eddie's age was
twenty-eight and that Tillman was several years older
than him. Where Eddie was shorter and more compact,
and prone to softness in his stomach, Tillman was tall
with a well-defined musculature. Unlike Eddie's vague,
unfocused blue eyes and dreamy expression, Tillman's
slate-gray eyes were sharp and penetrating—as if he
could see down to the hidden depths she didn't allow
anyone to know about.

Shelly took a deep breath and hurried after Eddie,
who could be pretty darn quick when properly moti-
vated. She reached him just in time. At the last step
out of the pool, his hands were already at the top of his
bathing trunks.

"Wait," she said. "Put on your robe."

No sooner had he fastened the robe than the trunks
came off.

Shelly bent to pick up the wet trunks at the same time
as the sheriff. His large tanned arm brushed against her
smaller, paler arm. Prickles of heat spread from the point
of contact to all parts of her body.

"I've got it," he said in a deep husky voice that
warmed her insides.

They rose together and Shelly fought to control her
rapid heartbeat. Here she stood dripping wet with him
so polished and sharp in his uniform. She judged him
to be in his early thirties, only a few years older than

herself, and yet he exuded a natural authority and confidence that befitted his position.

Shelly sighed inwardly. He had not caught her on her most flattering day. Her huge green eyes, what she considered her most striking feature, were red-rimmed from lack of sleep and her honey-colored hair was nothing but a sodden heap of tangles at the moment.

"I'll be right there," he called to Eddie, who was already halfway to the locker room.

"Your mom left Eddie's tote bag of dry clothes over here." Shelly went to the bleachers, acutely aware of the sheriff following behind. Damn, she should have wrapped a towel around her waist. Toned or not, wet flesh in the light of day made her feel vulnerable. The one-piece bathing suit she wore was modest, but it was still a bathing suit. And her hair was flat and clung to her back in wet chunks. She'd given up on makeup at work. Even the waterproof stuff didn't hold up to hours in the pool.

The edge of her bathing suit rode up the cheek of her left buttocks. Terrific. Shelly fought the urge to pull it down. If she was lucky and left it alone, maybe the sheriff wouldn't notice.

She picked up the bag and forced herself to remain professional as she faced Eddie's brother and held it out.

His eyes jerked up from her derriere. Oh, crap. She could tell by the darkening of those gray eyes and the ghost of a smile on his lips that he had definitely been checking out her ass. But perhaps that was progress, since he hadn't paid her much attention before. "Hope your mom is feeling better," she said with a self-conscious smile.

His lips thinned and a flicker of annoyance lit his

eyes before he slid back into his cool, confident persona. "You're limping." He pointed at Shelly's foot. "An accident?"

"A minor cut." She shrugged. "Kitchen mishap."

He jerked his head toward the locker room. "I better see if Eddie needs any help."

Shelly stared at his back as he walked away, a tiny bit disappointed. The man was definitely not a conversationalist.

The sheriff whirled around and caught her staring. His lips twitched at the corners.

"I watched you working with Eddie. You're doing a great job."

"I love working with your brother. He's my favorite— I know I shouldn't have any, but he is."

"How about you let me take you to dinner Friday in appreciation for all your hard work?"

Shelly fought not to sound too excited. "Sure." *Please don't invite your mother,* she thought fervently. *Don't let this be a family thing.* Nice enough woman, but she wanted the sheriff all to herself. It had been too long since she'd felt any interest in dating again.

Lurlene Elmore and others from the senior water aerobics class, the Water Babes and Buoys, emerged from the ladies' locker room.

"Eddie's stark naked in our locker room," Lurlene called out in way of greeting.

A tinge of red crept up the sheriff's neck. So he wasn't perfectly composed at all times, Shelly thought. What a relief.

The sheriff tipped his hat to Mrs. Elmore. "Sorry. He doesn't know the difference between the men's and ladies' rooms. I'm on my way."

"Don't apologize." Lurlene let loose a honking laugh. "For God's sake, it's not like any of us have reached our advanced ages without seeing a man's talleywacker a time or two."

Shelly followed her ribald senior clients to the shallow end of the pool. "Talk to you later," she said with a wave at Tillman.

Lurlene pointed at Shelly's legs. "I tried to find that lotion that makes your legs sparkly but I didn't see it anywhere."

Not that again. Lurlene had been hounding her for what she used to make her legs glitter. Shelly glanced down discreetly. They weren't *that* noticeable. The skin had a faint opalescence, like silver-and-pink mica particles freckling the legs. Lurlene would freak if she knew the glitter came from the faint residue of her tail fin when she shape-shifted.

Shelly shrugged. "Just put some powdered pink and silver eye shadow in a jar of baby oil and shake it."

Lurlene nodded as she sank her massive frame into the pool. "Saw the sheriff checking you out." She winked. "He's a handsome devil."

It occurred to her these senior women had probably seen more action in the past two years than she had.

Friday night couldn't get here soon enough.

Melkie roamed the downtown shops, avoiding eye contact and blending easily with the crowd. Even in early September, the air was thick with humidity and his shirt felt sticky from perspiration. He smirked as he passed the quaint shops. The town was nothing but a fucking Mayberry R.F.D. perched precariously on the edge of a continental shelf. Hurricane Katrina had almost swept it entirely away.

A fat woman in spandex bike shorts and an oversize fuchsia T-shirt exited the soda parlor and brushed against him. Her triple scoop of blueberry ice cream narrowly missed plopping on his chest.

"Excuse me, darlin'," she said with an apologetic grin.

Melkie pulled away and shot her a furious look. He fought back the urge to growl. The woman's smile faded and he registered confusion, embarrassment and fear in her fatty pig eyes.

He lowered his head and kept going.

She was like everyone else in this stupid, stinking backwater. They had no idea who he was, what he was capable of doing.

Three blocks away, he entered the Bayou Seed and Feed to get a bag of Rebel's favorite dog biscuits. Several old men in denim overalls stood around the counter, bullshitting. Melkie plopped the bag on the counter where an old fart with rheumy eyes winked at one of the customers. "How's that ol' mutt of yers gettin' along?"

Melkie threw down a ten-dollar bill on the scratched Formica, ignoring the jibe.

The cashier handed back the change, which Melkie stuffed in his pocket. As he headed to the door, one of the men muttered, "Ugliest damn dog you'd ever want to lay eyes on."

Snickering ensued.

Melkie slowly turned. All of them fell silent and looked away. He wanted to say *Fuck off,* but he wouldn't give the cashier an excuse to ban him from the store. Instead, he settled for banging the door shut behind him.

The attached bells gave a satisfied clanging at the violence.

He was in a crappy mood today, when he should have been calm and in control. That's how he had felt after the first hooker, anyway. The second one...well, that was a problem.

What the hell had happened out there? That—that *thing* had risen up from the sea. She—it, whatever—had seen him, knew who he was and what he had done. Somehow he had to find her again. He couldn't let a witness live. Big mistake dumping that second bitch at sea. He thought no one would ever find the body. Unlike the first one he'd left in the shallow salt marsh. That had been clumsy and ill-planned.

Images from the night before consumed him. Sure, he'd had a few beers before getting on the boat, but he wasn't stinking drunk. He knew what he saw and that was no scuba diver. When the woman disappeared with the body, he'd seen a giant fish tail emerge.

Melkie threw the bag in the bed of his rusted-out Chevy truck with his other recently purchased supplies and drove out of town, onto the white sandy roads leading home. In the past, he would have taken Rebel with him, but he got sick of the ugly jokes. Ignorant hicks.

He'd found the dog abandoned on the roadside years ago and had taken a shine to it. At first, Melkie thought the stray resembled an overgrown rat, but he checked the library's internet and found it was a full-bred hairless Chinese crested. Try telling that to people in the bayou.

His thoughts turned again to the woman at sea. Either he was crazy or that woman was truly a mermaid. He brooded over the mermaid possibility.

Bayou La Siryna had as many mermaid tales and

sightings as some places had their resident ghost haunt-ings. A few locals claimed to have seen strange creatures at night, half human and half fish, swimming deep at sea. Some scuba divers once claimed they'd seen a top-less mermaid with long blond hair swimming close to the marsh grassland savannas that lined the shore. All stories Melkie never believed.

Buildings changed from redbrick structures to clap-board shacks with dirt floors that smelled like a com-bination of ripe soil and mice droppings. At last, his neighborhood was heralded by a faded hand-painted sign reading Happy Hollows, nailed to an oak tree.

There was nothing happy about Happy Hollows. He flipped off the sign, as was his custom. Tired shotgun-style houses lined the streets, in various states of disre-pair. He pulled into an unpaved driveway on a dead-end street. Rebel yapped excitedly by the peeling handmade picket fence slapped together from scrap wood.

A smile tugged the corners of Melkie's thin mouth for the first time today. Rebel spotted the biscuit bag and ran in circles, delirious with joy.

"Shut that ugly mutt up," a neighbor hollered from a front porch crammed with broken kids' toys and other unidentifiable junk.

"Fuck off," Melkie hollered back. He didn't have to pretend to be nice around this place. Niceness got you nowhere with these folks; instead, it was viewed as a sign of weakness. Melkie had learned early on not to take anything from anyone. Ever.

Melkie stomped up the rotted steps and onto the porch, arms laden with bags and boxes, carefully avoid-ing spots where pieces of boards were broken or missing, exposing sand and weeds four feet beneath the foundation. He opened the screen door, but Rebel pushed up underneath his feet and a cardboard box fell out of his arms. An explosive noise of crashed glass erupted in the box like a miniature self-contained bomb. Rebel whimpered and ran away, skinny tail tucked between his legs.

"What the hell was that?" his neighbor screamed from across the street.

"None of your business," Melkie yelled, kicking the mess to one side of the door. The box of broken Mason jars, used as insect-killing jars, joined the cast-off collection on his porch—a broken washing machine, plastic beach chairs with missing slats and who knew what else.

Melkie perked up at seeing the brown package tucked between the screen and front doors. As he checked the mailing label, his mouth curved upward.

He whistled for Rebel and the dog followed him inside. Melkie headed straight to the fridge and pulled out a beer. His unemployment check was running low, but he always had a cold one for himself, a biscuit for Rebel and his ever-increasing insect collection.

Only ten steps from the den, he entered the cramped kitchen with its battered pine cabinets. Another eight steps and Melkie would pass through a tiny bedroom, leading to a bathroom with only a toilet, a rusted-out tub and sink. Another ten steps led to the final cramped bedroom, barely large enough for a mattress and dresser. This pathetic, rotting dump was all his. Mom's last legacy. The sisters were long gone, escaped as soon as they'd found some pussy-whipped dope to take them away. But he was still trapped here. For all its miserable worth, the house was a way to live rent-free.

"I don't owe nobody nothing, do I, boy?"

The dog leaped on Melkie's legs, clawing for his treat.

"Coming right up," Melkie promised. He peeled off his sweaty T-shirt. Opening the kitchen drawer, pulling out a dull knife with a cracked wooden handle, he cut open the bag and threw a biscuit on the ripped linoleum floor. Normally, he liked watching Rebel tear into the treat with his buck teeth, the few remaining ones jutting out at crazy angles. But today he stared at the knife gripped in his palms.

His knife.

Anger rose in him, fierce and hungry. Melkie tamped it down, refused to let it interfere with the gratification in his latest package. Pulling up a chair to the table, Melkie cut open the box and spread its contents onto the scarred Formica. A hurricane of colors lay hodgepodge before him, but he focused on the largest specimen— a black spicebush swallowtail with a robin's-egg blush fanning its hind wing and the forewing bordered by white dots. Beautiful. The butterfly's delicate antennae and proboscis had survived shipping intact.

He dug out supplies from a plastic container and set to work, pinning the specimens with stainless-steel insect pins against a white styrene foam board. Rebel barked and whined, but Melkie shushed him with an impatient flick of his hand. At last pleased with the arrangement, Melkie slipped the foam under a shadow box frame.

It took a good twenty minutes to find the perfect location amongst the den walls covered with similar arrangements, mostly butterflies but also mountings of praying mantises, grasshoppers and dragonflies.

As soon as Melkie drove in the nail and hung his latest creation, Rebel barked and ran to the kitchen for another treat. Melkie tossed him one and Rebel gobbled it up with his yellow misshapen canine teeth.

The anger returned as he palmed the kitchen knife. His prized knife was gone. He'd seen it stuck in the tail fin of that thing at sea. He grabbed a six-pack and settled into the den's old recliner with its ripped turquoise vinyl upholstery. He gulped his beer in long swallows, brooding over the lost knife. It was what he had used to cut out both bitches' eyes. It was special. It also happened to be the only gift he ever remembered getting from his mother.

A big beautiful knife in a worn leather case.

"Here, kiddo," she'd said, casually tossing it in his direction one Christmas when he'd asked her where his presents were. "It belonged to your dad. He told me it was a gift from his father."

Melkie had grinned, fingers closing over the family heirloom. Violent vibrations hummed in his hand as he held the knife.

It had been the best Christmas ever.

Rebel jumped in his lap, jolting Melkie from the memory, and dog and owner stretched out to watch a police drama on the twenty-inch black-and-white TV set with a rabbit-ears antenna. No cable in this backwater hellhole.

Melkie petted Rebel's mottled skin before raising an arm to flip on the window air conditioner. Between the loud hum of the AC and staring at the fuzzy speckles on the TV screen, Melkie sensed the tension ease out of his lean body. He'd just relax a bit, not sleep. If he took short dozes, Melkie found he was less apt to dream or, at least, remember them if he did. He avoided sleep, but after days of only ten-minute naps snatched here and there, his weak, treacherous body would rebel and go under for hours at a time.

Most people welcomed sleep, sought refuge and refreshment in the mysterious, suspended state of being. Not for him. Nighttime was when his mother used to slip into bed beside him. She'd creep past the first bedroom, which she shared with her two daughters, and seek him out.

But most nights she didn't creep, she stumbled, a result of too many gin and tonics, trying to wash away the taste of customers. Then she staggered and often fell as she went through his sisters' room to get to him. Not that his older sisters gave a damn. They conserved their energy for their own survival—for those nights Mom brought a customer to their sorry shack.

When he slept now he still fought against the groping, the sucking, the humiliation that rolled over him in waves, leaving him powerless and frightened. Even when it had happened, he knew it wasn't right. By day he was her whipping boy and at night...

The old bitch had been dead ten years now and she still haunted his dreams. But he had found another way to fight the memories, to punish someone and take back control.

Melkie flexed his large hands with its long fingers, so out of proportion to the rest of his smaller physical frame.

Oh, yeah, he loved taking control.

Jolene Babineaux. Age thirty-four. Caucasian.

Tillman studied the photographs for what had to be the hundredth time. In one, provided by a family member of the deceased, Jolene sat on a sofa, cuddling a couple of children. A second photo was a grim mug shot of her arrest for prostitution a year earlier. She wasn't smiling in that one. The last photograph was of her battered, skimpily clad body, sans eyes, which had been discovered last evening.

Even though Bayou La Siryna was a relatively small town, Tillman had never run across the victim. And he was pretty good at remembering names and faces. All part of the job. But a large part of the population, at least a third of the county, lived in a squalid, poverty-ridden area with the unlikely name of Happy Hollows. Most of the families there were a tight-knit community of shrimpers—people who lived for decades fishing on family-owned boats.

Evidently, Jolene had resorted to the world's oldest profession to supplement that meager income.

Tillman snapped the file shut. Despite door-to-door interviews in Jolene's neighborhood and surrounding area, Tillman's officers had no leads.

Tillman shoved the file to the side of his desk and opened the second folder with photographs of the second victim, China Wang. Age thirty-seven. Vietnamese.

She had the same missing eyeballs as Jolene. But there, the similarities ended. Where Jolene had been a big-boned, redheaded woman, China was petite and exotic-looking. Never married, but with three young children, now farmed out to relatives, she had spoken broken English and never made it past the sixth grade.

The only obvious similarity between the two victims was their line of work.

Because of the festering pockets of poverty in the bayou, it wasn't unheard of for women to use their bodies. Often to drum up enough business, it was necessary for them to ride into Mobile, about twenty miles east, and walk along the port city's shipping docks for johns.

Even in bad economic times, customers could be found if you priced yourself competitively.

He tapped his fingers on his lips. Jolene's body didn't have a rope around it and it was discovered by Old Man Higginbotham who'd been out boat riding in a remote swampy area.

When China's body had been found on shore at Murrell's Point, there was a thick rope around the victim's waist that frayed at the ends. The body hadn't been submerged in water long enough for the rope to have disintegrated. He dialed the coroner's office, anxious to see what forensic evidence had been unearthed.

Jeff Saunders was the Englazia County coroner. A retired doctor, Tillman bet Saunders thought being coroner in a small town would be an easy gravy train. But that had all changed.

Saunders confirmed sperm was found in China's body, but the sample would have to be sent to the state crime lab in Montgomery to know if it matched the sperm sample from Jolene Babineaux. "We did find a curious thing with the second body. I recovered a couple strands of blond hair, thirty-one inches long, interspersed with the strands of China's black hair."

Tillman sat up straighter. "Can you determine if the hair came from a male or female?"

"Probably not. Unless the hair was yanked out of the scalp, there won't be enough follicular matter to run a DNA test."

China's family all resembled her, olive-skinned with dark brown or black hair. Tillman hung up. He tilted back in his chair, feet on his desk, and speculated on the news.

It could be the killer didn't act alone. Perhaps he had

a female accomplice, Tillman thought, remembering the small footsteps they'd found leading from the body into the water. But the psychological profile from the first case indicated the perp had a deep hatred of women. If true, a female accomplice seemed unlikely.

How had the body been moved to shore? And why?

The plastic bags covering China had been coated in sand, leaving patterns consistent with dragging. A thorough search had not turned up any evidence other than a baseball hat with Trident Processing and Packing emblazoned on it and footprints. Had the killer decided against leaving the body in the ocean and left it out to be found—either a subconscious wish to be caught or as a kind of sick bragging trophy that he had gotten away with murder twice now? And what was that damn rope around China supposed to be for?

Carl Dismukes rapped sharply on the door before entering.

"A little brain food," he said, plopping a box of glazed doughnuts on the desk.

"A little cliché, don't you think?" Tillman asked. "But I could use the sugar and carbs right about now."

They dug in, Tillman studying China's photograph, his deputy opening the first file and reviewing Jolene's photographs. Carl threw it back on the desk after a cursory examination. "I ever tell you I knew Jolene?"

Tillman gulped down a mouthful of doughnut in surprise. "No. I think that's something you might have mentioned long before now." He struggled to keep his censure mild. Carl was thirty years his senior and his dad's right-hand man when he'd served as sheriff. When Dad died from a heart attack two years ago, Carl had been the one to break the news to him. And it was Carl's suggestion that he come home and fill his father's position until the next election.

Tillman had been torn. He loved being an investigator with the Mobile P.D. and thought he'd been falling in love with Marlena. But shortly before Dad died, she'd moved to Atlanta to further her interior design business. Mobile was plenty big enough; he had no intention of moving to Atlanta. Besides, after he'd taken her home the first time, he'd known it would never work. Mom had been tipsy and asked pointed questions about Marlena's family pedigree, while Eddie had taken an immediate dislike to his girlfriend. "Bye-bye," he kept telling Marlena, taking her arm and leading her to the door. In the end, Tillman knew his duty and he'd come home.

The doughnut settled heavy on his stomach and Tillman pushed the box in Carl's direction. "Just how well did you know Jolene?"

"Not that good." Carl held up a hand and rolled his eyes. "Never been a customer. Your dad and I went to her place a time or two over the years. Typical domestic violence stuff. Her latest man would beat her, but by the time we got there Jolene would refuse to press charges." Carl ran his fingers through his close-cropped silver hair. "I felt sorry for her little ones."

Tillman had his share of those calls when working the beat in Mobile. It was always the kids you remembered most. Scared and hopeless before they graduated elementary school.

"How much longer on that forensics lab report?" Carl asked.

"Another two weeks at the earliest." Tillman filled him in on the blond hair discovery.

"Doubt much will come of that. Damn salt water kills everything."

"But it could answer how the body got back on shore." Tillman mulled over the hair. "It didn't come from the teenagers that found her. They both had dark brown hair."

"It's possible someone else came across the victim before our lovebirds. She—or he—was unsure what was under those plastic bags and tore into it to look. When they saw what was inside they panicked and ran away."

"I've called my old partner at Mobile P.D. to see if they have any missing person cases for known prostitutes. Just in case our killer has spread a wider net."

Carl shook his head. "Something tells me our perp hasn't stopped at two victims." He clapped Tillman's back. "Damn shame it's happened on your watch." Carl hesitated. "But at least your dad was spared this. He had enough on his plate without chasing a serial killer."

Not to mention taking care of his wife, Tillman silently added. But if Dad didn't want to break their family's code of silence, then he wouldn't, either.

"Here's something I whittled for Eddie." Carl set a three-inch wooden block on the desk.

Not another one, he inwardly groaned. Eddie's room was overflowing with Carl's creations. He opened a drawer and placed it in a bag filled with about twenty similar blocks. As his deputy meandered away, Tillman put in a call to Sam, his old partner, to talk things out.

"You've got a disaster brewing," Sam commented. "Thought moving to Hicksville would be a bore. One more body surfaces and the FBI is on your doorstep. Good luck with that."

Most law enforcement officers were territorial and

hated outsiders coming in. But if the manpower would help catch a killer faster, he was all for it.

Tillman hung up and closed his eyes, wanting to erase the violent images. The investigation had been eating at him, long days and nights of nothing but working the case or helping out Mom and Eddie. Damn it, he was tired of living like a monk, all work and no play.

Unbidden, he pictured Shelly, the way her wet bathing suit had clung to her smoking body, the friendly green eyes and long hair plastered around her hips…a hot angel of deliverance.

Chapter 3

A mermaid—really? Can this be?
A creature of part land, part sea.
Mustn't let a siren's call
Make me falter, make me fall.

Melkie cruised the back roads, Rebel drooling and snorting by his side. He had no particular destination, but after hearing on the local television news that a second body had turned up on the beach, he'd been going increasingly mad at home. He kept waiting for a knock at the door, his paranoia growing with every second enclosed in the shotgun house.

How had that body gotten to the shore? That woman—*that thing*—must have put it there. Melkie found himself on a road leading to Murrell's Point. Rounding a bend, he spotted half a dozen police and sheriff's vehicles gathered on one side of the road.

Right there. That must be where they'd found it.

He was suffocating, the truck's interior closing in on him. The old truck's dying AC was no match against the pepper-hot heat. Maybe the cops were here waiting for him to return to the crime scene. They already knew he was the one. His life was over. He'd rot at Holman prison on death row. His breath came in painful, jagged spasms and his body knotted with tension.

The wet sensation of tongue on his right forearm broke through the paralysis. Rebel licked and whimpered, attuned to Melkie's panic. The dog's eyes, despite their disarming milky haze, pierced Melkie with pure love.

He caught his breath and patted Rebel's hairless flesh. What would happen to his dog if they took him away? He had no friends or family. And everyone found Rebel repulsive, even though he was worth more than the rest of that sorry-assed lot of humanity.

Melkie turned his head from the cops and kept his eyes focused on the road ahead. The azure-blue of the sky met the gray-blue of ocean in a horizontal line. The moment passed, and he looked out the rearview mirror at the uniformed police scouring the area.

Fucking pigs. Where were they when he was getting punched around as a kid?

The familiar rage tamped down on the residual panic.

"How about you and me getting a little treat?" he asked Rebel, who yipped in excitement.

He pulled into the drive-through at the hamburger shack in town and ordered cheeseburgers and fries for both of them, plus a chocolate milkshake for himself. The fat-and-sugar rush sated his gnawing anxiety. Why had he been so freaked out? There was nothing that could tie him to the murders. He was safe.

He was contentedly gulping the last of his shake when a purple-and-pink sign slammed into his consciousness.

The Mermaid's Hair Lair.

What the hell?

Mermaid. The word was a red neon light burning in his brain.

He'd lived here all his life, been down this main street forever, but had never paid much attention to the beauty parlor or the large water fountain in the court square with a figure of a mermaid sculpted in copper.

The image of the thing in the water arose. Melkie slammed on his brakes and parked at the first empty spot. Rebel gazed at him quizzically, panting onion breath.

Wouldn't hurt to look in the window. Melkie put a leash on Rebel and knelt down to whisper. "We'll just walk real casual-like, okay?" He stood, took a deep breath and sauntered by the shop. The ever-present smell of bilge and shucked oysters assaulted his nose.

In the salon window he saw old ladies in chairs, gray hair tightly bound in perm rollers, with bubble dryers over them, a few younger clientele getting bleach jobs. The interior was painted in shades of coral, with paintings of mermaids hung all over the walls.

He knew just how it would smell, the stinky ammonia fumes and peroxide in the air so strong it would make your eyes water. His stomach rumbled and he was back in that dumpy house, Mom and her whore friends dyeing each other's hair and preparing for the night's work.

"There's little Melkie," one of them would coo, beckoning him over with long red nails.

His face aflame, he'd have to go into the gaggle of whores. Nine years old and the stupid bitches would pull down his shorts and giggle.

"Let me feel that cute little pecker." They'd grab him and fondle and laugh at the predictable response.

Especially dear old Mom.

She'd refused to allow him to cut his hair. She and

her posse of bitches teased him about his thick, wavy hair and would put rollers in it and paint his face. A few years later he decided it was worth the ass whupping to disobey Mom and cut it short.

Even now, the memories churned his stomach. That cheeseburger wasn't such a hot idea, after all.

The sight of a woman with long blond hair caught his attention. She stood behind a chair, wielding a pair of shears with grace and authority. Her hair was unusual, a thick honey-gold confection with streaks of the palest pink and lavender. On her, the highlights looked natural, not like on the phony Goth teenagers you saw in Mobile these days with bold colors against black hair.

His mermaid that night had long hair, but impossible to make out the color other than it was light. It had hung down the front of her torso like a second skin.

What if…what if this was *her?* Maybe she had the ability to be on land and sea. It wasn't such a stretch to think the thing had some kind of mutation abilities. He recalled those eyes of swirling colors. Melkie peered intently at the woman's reflection in the mirrored walls. The eyes were a perfectly human shade of blue, not that freaky cat-eyed glow he'd seen.

He would seek out Tia Henrietta. The hoodoo witch down in the boondocks might know something. He'd never placed any faith in the old woman's tales but his mother and sisters and all their buddies swore by her occult powers.

If anybody knew something about mermaids or sea creatures, it would be her.

Shelly leaned back in the beautician's chair and let Lily massage her head and neck as she washed her hair.

It was after hours at the shop, but when Lily had heard about her date, she wanted Shelly to come on in and get gorgeous.

"Your neck muscles are tight," Lily said. "Relax."

Lily's soothing voice failed its usual magic. As did the varying shades of coral, rose and ivory on the walls that a local artist had painted to their specification. The effect of the pearly tones usually soothed Shelly—it was like being enveloped in the shelter of a giant conch shell.

Shelly opened her eyes and met Lily's in the mirror. "How can I relax?" The half-moon dark circles under her eyes and the faint lines of worry on her brow were new. "I'm scared to death that psycho will find one of us."

"You're here with us now." Lily pressed her strong fingers on a trigger point at the base of Shelly's skull. "Nothing's happened."

Jet looked up from the desk. "Good thing you have a date tomorrow night. Nothing like a man for distraction. Just don't let it get serious." Her fingers resumed their clicking on the adding machine. Thank goodness Jet actually enjoyed working with numbers, since Shelly and Lily avoided it as much as possible. At the shop Lily was in her element and had earned a reputation for her talents. Jet handled the business end of things and filled in as shampoo girl when needed.

Shelly groaned. "I haven't been on a real date in two years. I'm a nervous mess."

Lily laughed. "Just have fun. A man's attention will get rid of a funk every time."

The adding machine's clicking stopped. "Attention, hell," Jet said. "We're talking sex."

"You're almost thirty years old, in your sexual prime," Lily continued. "I couldn't go without it more than a couple of weeks myself. And it's been *months* since I've been with a merman." A dreamy look clouded her eyes. "Nothing like sex with a real merman."

Shelly eyed Lily curiously. As a full-blooded siren, her cousin responded instinctually to the call of an annual spawning ritual. Mermen and mermaids gathered at a remote South Pacific island for a week of orgies. Those inclined to produce a litter of merchildren built undersea nests in beds of coral for fertilizing and hatching their newborn.

Shelly had no desire to attend a reproduction ritual. Not that she would be allowed—that right was reserved only for the full-blooded. Raised as a landlubber in a human family, the whole thing sounded bizarre and unappealing. Regular sex, right here in the bayou, would be exciting enough. She shut her eyes, imagining Tillman's naked body against hers. It had been so long since she'd desired a man.

"Little cuz is blushing," Jet said wryly.

Lily rinsed Shelly's hair. "No teasing," she scolded. Lily placed a warmed towel over Shelly's head and rubbed. "Any special style requests?"

"I leave it all in your hands. Even if I don't like it, it will grow out in no time."

"Our hair is a pain in the fins," Jet said, her eyes still on the numbers. "Easiest thing to do is just keep it hacked off like mine."

Lily and Shelly shared a secret smile. Their mermaid hair grew at a rate of nearly an inch a week and their nails grew so fast weekly manicures were a must. "I like the long layers you have in it now," Shelly said. "Just give it a good trim and blow-dry it."

Shelly relaxed as the warmth and noise of the blow-

dryer eased her tension. Everything was going to be
okay. They had done what they could to help the police
identify the killer by putting the body on land. Well, almost everything. She still had the knife.

Her mind drifted to the date. She'd had her eye
on Tillman for quite a while. But she didn't think he
even noticed her. He was always so remote and professional the few times he'd picked up Eddie. Shelly imagined those gray eyes darkening with desire for her and
squirmed.

*Stop it. You're way past the age to be so nervous
about a date.* It's just…sex and companionship. That's
all she could hope for since that was all she could offer.
No man wanted to love a freak; it could only end in disaster. Her parents' stormy marriage was proof of that.
All the tears, the shouting, the fundamental differences
that stifled her mother's mermaid desire to be at sea and
frustrated her human father, who resented that his love
wasn't enough to make her happy. The answer lay in a
long-term affair of mutual affection. Sure, she risked
him finding out her secret. But she was tired of being
alone. She knew her cousins were there for her, but it
wasn't the same. It could never be the same. She was
part human…they weren't.

Jet interrupted her thoughts. "Tell us about this guy.
How did you meet him?"

"He's the older brother of Eddie, one of my clients
at the Y."

Jet crossed her arms over her chest. "Could be awkward if you break up and you have to keep running
into him."

"Always the pessimist," Lily murmured. "Just think
of having a good time for as long as it lasts." A smile

tugged her lips. "In fact, pass him on to me when you're done with him. I cut Gary loose a couple days ago."

Jet yawned and headed to the break room. "I need coffee."

"You've only been seeing Gary a month and you're already bored?" She shouldn't be surprised; Lily went through men like crazy. A wonder there were still men left in town she hadn't already had an affair with and then dumped. An unexpected burst of jealousy reared its head. "Is a man named Tillman one of your exes?"

Lily patted the top of Shelly's head. "I prefer the bad boys, not Boy Scouts who take care of their little brothers."

Jet returned, coffee cup refilled. Lily turned to her sister. "Learn from Shelly. Get yourself back out there and find you a man."

"Don't need 'em," Jet said, settling back down to the books. "There's always a one-night stand if I'm in the mood for sex."

Shelly and Lily eyed each other with a knowing look. Jet had never gotten over Perry and his betrayal. Almost three years had passed since he'd been put in some South American prison for stealing sea treasure and Jet still ached. She'd never admit it, but Shelly suspected her cousin's life was on hold until Perry showed up again. *If* he did.

But who was she to judge her cousins? She'd made a mess of her own past love life. Never again would she tell a man her secret and be called a freak. That college experience still rankled. She'd passed off her confession as a drunken fantasy but Steve had dumped her shortly afterward.

Her cousins—and their attitude toward men—was what it was, just as she was a product of her parents' mixed genetics.

Melkie drove the endless stretch of sandy back roads that seemed to be never-ending paths to nowhere. Finally he rounded a corner and found Tia Henrietta's shack.

A scraggly orange tabby came out from behind a bush, arching his back at Rebel. The dog barked and jumped out the truck window before Melkie could stop him.

A screen door banged open. "Call off yer dawg."

The old woman glared at him with eyes dark as midnight. Under the purple turban her olive skin and faintly almond eyes made her something of an enigma. Melkie wasn't sure if she was distantly related to the many Vietnamese who worked in the fishing industry, Creole or black, or perhaps a mixture of several races.

He whistled and Rebel slunk to his side, tail tucked between his legs. Melkie patted his head in reassurance.

Tia Henrietta approached. "What you doing way out here?"

"You're the psychic. You tell me."

She turned and walked back to the house, surprisingly spry for her age. "You always were a smart-alecky little 'un. C'mon, then."

They walked to the porch, Melkie motioning Rebel to stay before he followed the old woman inside. For all the unkempt appearance outside, the inside was neat, if shabby.

The place hadn't changed in the past two decades. Dozens of Jesus and saint candles glowed atop several mini altars of seashells, crystals and peacock feathers.

Small pieces of folded-up paper were tucked among the altars. People seeking divine help for their problems. What bullshit.

The same mysterious, earthy scent of smoked herbs pervaded the sitting room.

Tia Henrietta snapped off the small black-and-white TV in the corner.

"Sit." She gestured to a grandma floral-print sofa that looked like a 1950s thrift shop throwaway.

Melkie carefully sat on the edge. Even with his wiry five-foot-eight-inch frame, he wasn't confident the crappy furniture would hold. His eyes darted to a glass globe on the end table.

Still there.

He remembered coming here at age eight with his mom and two of her drunken whore friends. They'd stumbled in with their high heels and teased hair, dragging him along like a rag doll. Anita, his mom's closest friend, had downed tequila shots all morning before deciding it would be a hoot to have Tia foretell her future.

Melkie had picked up the globe. Instead of the usual plastic orb with a trapped Santa Claus and snow swirls, this glass object had a mermaid figurine suspended in blue-tinted water. He had picked it up and shaken it, sending white-and-pink sand swirling around the mermaid.

Whack. A burst of pain had slashed hotly against a cheek.

"Put that down," Mom had screamed. The globe slipped from his grasp onto the cheap linoleum and rolled. The wooden base broke off.

Could this really be the same one? Melkie picked it up and squinted at the pedestal.

"I hot-glued it back on," Tia said. "That hot glue gun was the best damn thing I ever bought. That, and duct tape, pretty much holds everything together around here."

He carefully placed it back on the coffee table. "You remember that day?"

Tia shrugged. "Yer mama is not an easy woman to forget. Heard she died of the cancer a few years back."

Amen and thank heavens for that.

Tia sat across from him, folded hands in her lap. "So what brings you back here?"

Her eyes were smoldering coals, even beneath some weird kind of film at the corners. Probably cataracts, he guessed. Melkie shifted uncomfortably under the direct gaze. He hated anyone looking at him, especially close up. His fists tightened. Why, he ought to cut out those eyes.... He forced himself to focus and pointed at the globe. "They real? Mermaids, I mean."

"Oh, they's real awright." She clicked her tongue. "Saw one when I was a teeny girl. I was picking up sharks' teeth on the beach when somethin' made me look up. And there she was. A beautiful redheaded siren not far from shore. Nekked from the waist up. When she caught my eye she winked and flipped her tail fin up in the air afore she dived back in the sea."

Tia closed her eyes, a dreamy smile on her wrinkled face. "I ain't never forgot her, neither." She opened her eyes. "You seen one?"

"Maybe."

"Where at?"

"None of your business," he snapped. Nosy old woman.

"You've turned into a bitter, angry person," she said

after a moment of silence. "You've got a red aura with black streaks in it." But there was no real bite in her voice, more a dispassionate observation. "Can't says that's a surprise. Given yer background and all."

Melkie scowled. "Never mind my background, witch."

"That's no way to talk to an ol' woman. 'Specially if you want information."

Melkie reached in his wallet and slapped a twenty on the table. "Talk."

"You a real smooth one," Tia said, scooping up the money and stuffing it into her bra. "Whatcha wanna know?"

"Everything you know about mermaids."

"That won't take long." She settled back in her rocker and took a dip of snuff. "Lots of folks 'round here claim they done seen mermaids. 'Course, not nearly so much over the last ten years. What with the increase in shrimping and the oil spills."

Melkie frowned. "Don't see why shrimping matters none. There's always been family shrimping boats trolling the bayou."

"Think about it. All those nets in the sea bother more'n just dolphins. Could be trouble to any sea creature afraid of being trapped."

"And you think the oil spills out here can harm them, too."

Tia spit into a plastic Coke bottle that served as a makeshift spittoon. "Been killin' all kinds of wildlife out here including birds and crabs. No reason for nothing to hang around the Gulf no more."

So why would a mermaid hang around? he wondered.

"Could be they's done grown attached to this place."

Time to get to the real matter at hand. "Is it possible for them to come on land? You know, grow feet or something?"

"I done heard a such. Usually 'cause they think they's fallen in love with a human. Love's a powerful thing." She stopped rocking and leaned forward. "Have you fallen in love with a mermaid? That why you here?"

Melkie snorted. "Love? You really are crazy."

Tia picked up the mermaid globe and pressed it into his hands. "A little something to remind you of yer mermaid."

He scowled but kept it. "Tell me more. Ever hear of a mermaid living on land?"

"Used to be when I's a little girl, some sailors claimed to have got them a mermaid, brought them home, and made them their wife. Usually didn't end up so well for the husbands. Mermaids may leave the sea, but it always calls to them. Sooner or later, they'll go back."

"But they're half human, too, and must have human needs." Melkie ran a finger over the cold mermaid globe. "Maybe they wouldn't have to leave. Not if they lived close to the shore. They could split their time, have the best of both worlds."

"I suspect you're right," Tia agreed. "Back in the old days, locals believed mermaids lived amongst them, 'specially beautiful women new in town were looked on with suspicion. One of my papa's friends, he was a fisherman, said he once saw a woman jump off a boat and turn into a mermaid. She swam away and never came back."

"And you believed him?"

"Why not? I done seen plenty a strange things in my lifetime." She stopped rocking and tilted her head to one side. "I think lots of folks done forgot why the bayou's called 'La Siryna.'"

"Thought it was some French word."

"I don't know if it was *Frenched* up, but it's named for the sirens."

Melkie wrinkled his brow. "But you said the bayou was named after mermaids."

"Same thing. Folks used to say the mermaids—sirens—could sing so's a man would fall instantly in love with her."

Melkie pictured the mermaid at sea. He couldn't deny what he'd seen with his own eyes. He'd better face up to it and find her before she got him in trouble.

Tia lashed out weathered hands, scarred at the base of every finger, and caught his right one in hers, exposing his palms. He flinched at the contact and tried to pull away, but the old woman's hands were surprisingly strong. Tia moved a callused finger over his palm lines before letting go. Those perceptive eyes blazed at him.

"Yer filled with hatred and rage," she warned. "Learn to control yourself or the anger inside will be yer death."

"And you're full of crap." Melkie seethed with resentment. He didn't like being touched, especially when it was unexpected. He slammed the door on the way out.

He would have to find a way to test the waters himself with the mermaid. Try to fish her out or scare her into admitting she was the one who saw him dump the body.

Halfway home, inspiration struck.

Chapter 4

Purloined coins and copper vases
Portraits of striking female faces
Antique swords and silver spoons
Artifacts filling every room.

Shelly picked through the seafood platter of sautéed shrimp and clams, scraping the baked potato, corn and bread sticks off to one side.

"I see you're not much of a vegetable person," Tillman said after a bite of his potato.

"'Fraid not." She forced herself to take a bite of corn. Truth was, her diet consisted almost entirely of seafood. Anything else pretty much tasted like sawdust. Besides, she was too nervous to eat much. Which was ridiculous, really. Yeah, her dates had been few and far between since she'd moved to Bayou La Siryna three years ago. But part of it was because she didn't relish the thought of dating any of Lily's leftovers. The beautiful siren mercilessly enthralled the opposite sex. Lily had pretty much used and discarded the best the bayou had to offer, and Shelly wasn't interested in being a consolation prize for Lily's lovesick exes.

"Eddie's enjoying your sessions together at the pool."

"He's come a long way. At first, he wanted nothing to do with me. Splashed around and did his own thing with minimal interaction." She smiled, enthusiastic about her work.

"How'd you win him over?"

"Patience. I have lots of experience with special-needs persons. They need time to know you're safe and that there's a predictable pattern in what you ask of them."

"He needs predictable routine, all right." Tillman nodded. "Any little change in his routine throws him out of whack."

She stared at him thoughtfully. "It must be tough dealing with Eddie on a daily basis."

He shrugged. "It can be. But Eddie's also my best friend. We go fishing at least a couple times a week and he never laughs at my off-key singing or rolls his eyes at my bad jokes."

"And I bet he's an excellent listener," she added with a grin.

"The best."

"Let's hope others appreciate his good qualities, too, because I hope eventually Eddie can move to a group session. Socialization skills are important. Of course, I'd start him off slowly, just add one or two other people to his session and then gradually add more."

Tillman frowned. "It's hard for him to be around groups of people. Too much noise and he gets over-loaded. I'm not sure that's such a good idea." He reached in his pocket as his cell phone went off. "Angier speaking."

Shelly ate a few more clams as Tillman carried on his conversation.

He half rose from the table. "Excuse me, it's work. Let me take this outside a few minutes."

She waved a hand. "No problem." She watched him head across the restaurant, noting the way his jeans hugged a very nice-looking ass. She hoped his invitation tonight wasn't just to thank her for her work with Eddie.

A middle-aged woman decked in polyester approached. "Lily," she said, "what are you doing here all alone?"

"Lily's my cousin—I'm Shelly."

The woman lifted a well-manicured hand to her mouth. "I'm so sorry. The resemblance is uncanny."

"Happens all the time."

"My apologies. I'm Lulu," the woman said, extending a hand. "Be sure and tell Lily I said hello. Your cousin is an absolute genius with hair."

"She is," Shelly agreed. "I'll tell her I ran into you."

Tillman returned, worry lines creasing his brow. "Sorry about that. Occupational hazard. One of my deputies had a question about a due process hearing at the jail."

"Sounds like you never really get away from your job."

He shrugged. "Comes with the territory. Does that bother you?"

"No. I know what it's like to put your heart and energy into a job. I care about my clients." She gave him a pointed stare. "And I won't push them to do anything I don't think they're ready for."

Tillman held up a hand. "I believe you. No harm in trying out the group thing with Eddie."

"If I see it's a problem, I promise I'll back off." Shelly took a long swallow of wine, curious if he had any news about the body she'd found. Maybe he could tell her something to ease her fears. She was *not* pumping for information. Well, perhaps a little…but what was the harm in that?

"It can't be easy for you, what with the latest body turning up a couple of days ago."

His jaw clinched almost imperceptibly. "This will be the last one."

"Really? That's good news."

"No such thing as a perfect crime. We're closing in on the sick bastard."

Shelly's heart pounded. The sooner the better. She waited for him to continue but he concentrated on his shrimp platter.

"Any good leads?" she prompted.

"A couple."

"I hope you find him soon. It's nerve-racking knowing he's out there. If I leave work after dark, I'm looking over my shoulder in the parking lot."

He frowned. "Our office is working hard. We're doing everything we can to end the fear in our community."

At his grim face Shelly touched his hand. "Nobody doubts that."

"Give me your phone."

"What?"

"Just let me see it a minute." He grinned. "I'm not going to read your texts."

"I didn't think you were." She retrieved it from her purse and handed it over. Tillman punched in some numbers before giving it back.

"I put in the number to my office and my personal

cell number. Call if you feel threatened or see anything
that makes you nervous."

"Thanks, I appreciate it." Probably one of the nicest
gestures she'd had from a man in ages. Uh-oh, she'd
better guard her heart with this one.

Tillman touched the ring on her right hand. "Nice
emerald."

Shelly knew he was evading specifics on the case.
Mata Hari she was not. She only hoped he was right
about finding the killer. She glanced at the ring. "This
belonged to my mother. She died while I was in college
and I've worn it ever since." Mom told her she'd recovered it from a shipwreck somewhere in the Baltic Ocean.
Shelly liked to think it might once have belonged to a
Russian princess. The gem quality was truly that rare
and magnificent.

"I'm sorry about your mother. How did she die?"

A sharp pang cramped her stomach at the concern in
his warm gray eyes and she had to fight past the lump
in her throat to speak. "Car wreck. A drunk driver hit
my parents as they were returning home from a movie."

He nodded. "That had to be tough, losing them both
at the same time."

She managed a small smile. She doubted the fierce
pain would ever ease and she'd feel like an orphan even
as an old lady. She imagined rocking on the front porch,
alone, gray-haired and forgotten, staring at the vast expanse of the ocean while her only blood relations were
out there somewhere frolicking under the sea.

"My dad died two years ago, I guess about the same
time you came to this town. It was tough, we were close.
I looked up to him," Tillman said.

"He couldn't have been that old. What happened?"

"Heart attack. I'm sure the pressures of work and home contributed to it."

"I'm sorry, Tillman." She touched his hand and felt warmth travel up her arm at the brief contact.

"He was sheriff here. When I got the news he died I left Mobile and came back home. They wanted me in the Sheriff's Office, and Mom and Eddie needed me, too."

Shelly's heart clinched. "Do you plan to stay in Bayou La Siryna or is this assignment temporary?"

Tillman hesitated. "There'll be an election next year for the job. I don't see things changing on the home front."

"What do you mean?"

"Eddie's a handful."

"True, he's on the severe end of the autism scale, but I've seen worse."

"You haven't seen Eddie at his worst. And Mom…" His voice trailed off and he shifted in his seat. "She can't deal with it."

Shelly recalled Portia Angier's pale, delicate face, the way she rubbed her temples, how she often dropped off Eddie and called Tillman to pick him up from the Y. Probably suffered the classic Fragile Southern Belle Syndrome. "You're a good man to help your family."

He shrugged his broad shoulders. "I'm no saint."

Shelly smiled inside. She certainly had no use for saints. Her fantasies of Tillman were far from saintly.

It had all been so easy.

A quick search on the internet at the public library to find her photo and name, and then one click for her personal address. Their names were listed on the hair salon's business license. There had even been a picture of them at a ribbon-cutting ceremony for the shop years earlier. Lily Bosarge had long blond hair and the other, Jet Bosarge, was taller and had dark short hair that barely covered her ears.

Lily was his target.

Melkie parked his car down the road, careful not to be seen, before approaching the large Victorian home with its wraparound porch. The silent darkness of the house reminded him of a cemetery. He peered through the windows and listened for the faintest sign of life inside. Convinced they weren't home, he searched and found, behind some dense hawthorn shrubs, a small unlocked utility window. Donning latex gloves and a black skullcap to prevent loose hairs from falling, he squeezed his wiry body in the small opening and landed in the basement.

Melkie crept upstairs, entering the living room. He stopped every few seconds to check for sounds or the beam of approaching car headlights from the driveway. Taking out his penlight, he explored. He'd never seen anything like it. Coins and clutter oozed in every cubbyhole, spilled over the tops of pricy-looking furniture, and lined walls were stippled in rich tones of burnt umbers and corals. He stuffed his pockets, indiscriminately shoving handfuls of coins and little doodads that gleamed in the dark. That couldn't be real gold, could it? What little hope he had of finding his knife vanished. Needle in a haystack, baby.

A laptop computer lay on the kitchen counter, the monitor asleep. Melkie jiggled the mouse and the screen came to life. He clicked on the email icon, grinning at the thought of leaving a message. He'd keep it short and succinct.

Die, freaking mermaid bitch. Boatman.

That should scare her out of hiding.

He headed upstairs, the pine steps creaking like a coffin opening in the midnight emptiness of a morgue. Portraits of strikingly beautiful women in old-fashioned dresses from different eras lined the walls on both sides. The old house had six bedrooms and three bathrooms on the top level. The three stale bedrooms with no signs of life he quickly dismissed. He wanted *hers*.

One bedroom definitely had a lived-in look. Clothes, mostly jeans, shorts and T-shirts, draped the bed and antique dresser. Melkie opened drawers, found more T-shirts and plain underwear and poked around papers and books on the nightstand. Nothing useful there—used tubes of ChapStick, old yellow-stained maps. Probably the short-haired Jet's room, although he couldn't rule out that it might be the bitch's room.

The next bedroom was slightly neater, although its dresser was littered with expensive-looking glass perfume bottles and an elaborate silver comb and mirror set atop a mirrored plate. Its closet was jammed with sundresses and lacy negligees in pastel hues that shimmered like ghosts in the darkness. Melkie fingered several—their soft, feminine fabric gliding against his callused skin like the promise of sex, of tangled bodies in twisted silk sheets. He imagined fashioning a length of that silk, wrapping it around a fragile neck, jerking and pulling until she lay broken, that neck red-welted and raw from the smooth fabric. His erection was immediate and painful; all mixed with outrage that she had seen him and knew who he really was.

Focus.

He turned from the closet and went to a huge dresser stuffed with lacey things, little slips of panties with matching bras. No knife. Melkie opened the silver flask on one of the perfume bottles, breathing deep its scent, both musky and floral, complex notes scrambling his brain with lust. He put the top back on it and stuffed it in his pants pocket, too. As he left the room, possibly *her* room, he saw an Oriental jewelry box by the nightstand. He crossed the room and greedily swiped gold rings lined up against black velvet, sparking like midnight rainbows. Sweet. These pickings would help supplement the state of Alabama's measly unemployment check.

This could be her room—but he'd seen nothing to know for sure.

The last bedroom was pristine, and he'd almost passed it by. But a faint citrusy scent gave him pause. He entered, checking out the closet and dresser drawers. Perhaps an overnight guest of Jet and Lily Bosarge?

Light bounced off a photo on a nightstand. Melkie picked it up, pocketing the black pearl necklace draped on its abalone-shell frame. The corners of his lips twitched as he stared at the photograph of the mermaid with her long, blond hair.

Gotcha, he whispered in the stillness.

He set it back on the table, reached in his back pocket and pulled out the mermaid figurine from the globe Tia Henrietta had given him. Breaking it into two pieces, he laid the broken mermaid under the pillow. That message should be clear enough. Melkie lay on her bed, pulling out the other present he'd bought for her—one of his mom's old hooker panties. He'd intended to just leave them where she would find them, knowing someone had been in her room. But now—the scent of woman, the lingerie, the photograph of her smiling at him as he lay there—now he had another gift for this mermaid.

He'd show her who was boss, would make her scream in agony as he ripped out those sea-witchy, freaky eyes. Melkie unzipped his jeans and began rubbing Mama's panties on his crotch.

By the time they got out of the restaurant and drove to Murrell's Point for a walk, Tillman's phone had rung twice more. Shelly wanted to toss the device in the ocean. How could he stand being tied to it all the time?

One disconcerting moment occurred when they had exited Tillman's car and a half-dozen cats gathered around her. They bristled and hissed, their alien eyes flashing fluorescent in the moonbeams. Clearly they sensed she was the mother lode of a fish dinner. One had nipped at her legs experimentally until Tillman gallantly shooed them all away.

The ocean was calm with only an occasional whitecap in the distance. Even though the moon was beginning to wane and not at its peak, Shelly still felt a strong urge to leap in and swim, to feel the undercurrents tugging at her weightless body as she played and swam among kindred creatures. She breathed in the briny air, rife with the scent of algae and seaweed and wet driftwood. She sighed in longing, doubting she'd ever feel safe out there again.

Tillman regarded her curiously. "Smell something good?"

"I love the smell of the ocean." Shelly grinned, slipping off her sandals.

"You mean that stinky odor produced by bacterial gas?"

She lifted her hair from the back of her sticky neck and let the ocean breeze cool the clammy skin. "I see you're quite the romantic."

Tillman took her hand and led her closer to the water.

Her sudden pleasure at his touch disappeared. Being in a pool was fine, but if her feet contacted the ocean's salt water her body would automatically transform. The bare skin of her feet, when mixed with the alchemy of the sea, caused webs to form between her toes. All it took was an unexpected splash around the knees and both legs would fuse into a single tail. Iridescent scales would burst forth, coating human skin, completing the metamorphosis from legs to fins.

She hung back. "Let's walk here where the sand is dry and warm."

"Guess this means my fantasy of a skinny-dip together is not going to happen?"

Shelly laughed. If he got her in the sea, it would be beyond any fantasy he could ever imagine. Her laughter choked at the sudden hot ache as she pictured Tillman swimming naked. Her cousins were right—it had been too long since she'd had a man in her life. Probably explained why she was so drawn to Tillman.

He must have caught the drift of her errant thoughts. Tillman pulled her to his side and she snuggled up against his hard body, her head against his chest. The fingers of his right hand traced the outline of a wicked scar on her shoulder. A nasty souvenir from an encounter two years ago when she'd swum too close to a charter fishing boat and a hook had sunk into her flesh. Those fishermen almost got the surprise of their lives.

"Where did this scar come from?"

"Childhood accident from swimming too close to a pier." Only a half lie.

"Ouch."

His hand explored further to a smaller scar by her collarbone. "And this?"

"I don't remember," she lied. She could hardly tell him it was from struggling to get out of a tuna net last summer. Her torso bore several such scars, especially since returning to live in the Gulf. She hung her head, wondering what he would make of a close examination of her body.

He tilted her chin up with a firm hand.

"I'm too curious," he said gruffly. "Another occupational hazard. Great for my job, not so much with people."

"It's okay," she whispered, fascinated with the darkening of his gray eyes. He wanted her every bit as much as she wanted him. *Dangerous territory,* her mind whispered. *Remember what happened to your mother when she fell in love with a human.* Shelly squeezed her eyes shut, determined to drown the demon voices of doom. Surely there was no harm in a little kiss. She had wanted to get close to him for so long, had fantasized about this moment for over a year.

His lips were upon hers, hot, demanding and probing. She was drowning in sensation, her bones and blood liquefying in pools of desire. And when his tongue explored, she eagerly met it with her own. The sweet, fierce hotness made her toes curl into the warm sand. The pounding of the waves matched the pounding in her blood.

Tillman pulled back first and cupped her face in his

large hands. "I've wanted to do this for a long time," he said in a voice husky with desire.

"Thank God. I was beginning to think maybe this date was only your way of thanking me for my work with Eddie."

"Not a chance."

His fingers caressed her scalp, then traveled through the length of her hair. He paused, a thoughtful look on his face.

"What is it?"

"The length and color of your hair reminds me of something else." He shook his head and dropped his arms. "Never mind." He appeared to hesitate a moment before clasping her hand and continuing their walk on the shore. "If you'd like, we can go to a club in Mobile for a little dancing."

Shelly thought fast. From what he'd told her at dinner, Tillman must live at home with his family. Not exactly conducive to privacy. The thought of loud music and crowds of people was the last thing she wanted. "Let's just return to my house for a drink. We can sit on the porch with a glass of wine. Or a beer, if you prefer."

"Beer sounds good." He turned a curious sideways glance her way. "I was going to suggest we go back to my fishing cabin, but I'm sure your house is much nicer. From what I understand, not many around here have been invited inside the Bosarge home."

Shelly followed him nervously back to the car. What had she done? Her physical desire for Tillman made her reckless. If she had been a little more patient, he would have invited her to his cabin where they could have been alone.

If she was lucky, Jet would be off for a swim, or in

her bedroom immersed in her old undersea maps and shipwreck books. Her cousin could be tricky with humans—short-tempered, suspicious, condescending. No problem with Lily, she was all sweetness, unless someone bored her. Besides, Lily would be out on another flavor-of-the-month date.

Shelly drew steadying breaths as they drew nearer. Everything would be fine. Sure, they had valuable treasure scattered throughout the place, but a casual observer wouldn't realize their china was from the Ming Dynasty or that the pottery on display was from ancient civilizations or that the various knickknacks lying about were rare maritime relics.

But when they walked in the den, Jet was sprawled on the sofa watching a Jacques Cousteau documentary.

"What are you doing back so early? Thought you'd—" She broke off at the sight of Tillman.

"Jet, this is Tillman Angier. He's our sheriff, by the way." Shelly waved a hand in the direction of the sofa. "Tillman, my cousin Jet."

"Pleasure to meet you." He crossed the room in three long strides and shook Jet's hand.

Jet wasn't the siren her sister was but was still a stunner with her tall, athletic frame and unusually dark irises that gave the impression her eyes were solid black pupils. Those eyes now flashed in irritation.

Tillman either didn't notice or didn't care. Jet shook his hand with the briefest of human contact.

"Surprised we haven't met before." He surveyed the room and let out a small whistle of appreciation. "Someone around here's a collector."

He crossed to the dozens of swords, mostly Confederate, which hung over the mantel. "Where'd you get all these?"

"Jet used to be an antiques dealer." Shelly shot Jet a pointed look at the coffee table, its surface strewn with dozens of cartographic and monographic maps of known shipwrecks.

"Here in Bayou La Siryna?" Tillman asked with his back still to them. He strolled over to a mahogany étagère storing their better pieces of seventeenth-century French, Italian and English pottery and ceramics they couldn't bear to sell on either the open or black market. The pieces were shipwreck finds of several generations of Bosarge mermaids from all seven seas.

"My business was wholesaling to other dealers," Jet said, turning the treasure maps facedown on the table. "I didn't have an actual store." She stuffed her magnifying glass and cartographic measuring tools under the brown leather recliner.

"I know a bit about antiques myself," Tillman said. "Mom dragged all of us to estate auctions when I was younger."

Shelly inwardly groaned. Of all the rotten luck, Tillman actually knew something of the worth of these objects. She had brought a law enforcement officer right into their home and introduced him to her errant cousin.

Jet's business was strictly to black-market vendors on a cash-only basis. That way, she avoided the pesky problem of explaining how the finds were retrieved with no treasure excavation expenses, and no worries of state and federal agents questioning the finds. In other words, it was all extremely illegal.

Jet shrugged and lifted both hands in a what-ya-gonna-do gesture.

Tillman continued his inspection of the room. This time he picked up a restored brass pocket watch from an end table, a pre–Civil War artifact etched with the date 1842.

"Where—?"

"Family heirloom," Jet said. "We're the sentimental sort."

Shelly almost snickered. Jet and Lily didn't have a sentimental bone or scale on their mermaid bodies. Unless you counted Jet's unexplained preoccupation with Perry, her human lover and partner in shipwreck recovery crimes—who turned out to be a lying, self-serving scumbag, now serving time.

And good riddance, Shelly and Lily told each other. Unfortunately, Jet was still hung up on the guy, even if she refused to admit it. She probably mistook him for a swashbuckling pirate, à la Johnny Depp.

"Fascinating place you have here," Tillman said, eyeing the large brass porthole above the fireplace. Shelly couldn't help but feel a little surge of pride. That porthole had been a lucky discovery on her part when she was only sixteen years old and visiting the Bosarge family for the summer. She'd been swimming five miles from the house when her eyes picked up a reflective glint from a black sand bed. It had been a risky and difficult swim home with her prize, but she'd managed.

"I found that porthole myself," she admitted, ignoring Jet's warning glare. "It…uh…washed up on shore one day after a storm."

"I've lived here all my life and never found anything more interesting than broken beer glasses and rusted tin cans," Tillman said.

Jet swept up the stack of treasure maps. "Then you're not very observant."

Tillman turned and raised a questioning eyebrow at the sharp edge in Jet's voice. "Or you're very lucky," he countered.

"Treasure hunting is Jet's passion," Shelly said.

"I'll say." Tillman went to the now-vacated coffee table and drew out a fistful of baubles from a handblown glass vase. Its size alone made it a rare find. Most intact glass artifacts were tiny perfume bottles or handheld mirrors. "What is this stuff in here?"

"Brass buttons, some old coins and other trinkets that—" Shelly began.

Jet grabbed the vase from Tillman. "Do you always walk in other people's houses and rifle through their stuff?"

Tillman held up both hands. "Just making conversation."

"C'mon, Jet," Shelly said, face reddening. Why did she have to be so rude? Jet was ruining her date.

Jet glared at Shelly before leaving the room, arms stuffed with papers and the vase.

In the sudden silence, Shelly faced Tillman. "Sorry about that. Jet's kind of funny about her things."

A door slammed shut from an upstairs bedroom.

"No problem." His eyes narrowed. "How long did you say you've lived here?"

"About three or four years."

"And how long have your two cousins lived in this house?"

"Close to twenty years. They inherited the house from their family. I used to visit them in the summer when I was a teenager."

She half expected Tillman to whip out a notepad and write down the information. For heaven's sake, she had to remember she was talking to law enforcement. Which probably meant he had an overdose of curiosity and the resources to check out anything that came out of her mouth.

A diversionary drink was in order.

"I'm going to get a glass of wine. You said you wanted a beer?"

"Correct." His back was toward her again, checking out the shelves of colored bottles, several from prohibition rumrunner boats forced to dump their cargos before seizure from the vigilant arm of the law, and other rare pieces from— Well, she couldn't remember all the details. That was Jet's thing. Her cousin spent most of her days researching artifacts and poring over old captain's logs.

In the kitchen she poured the sparkling sangria into a crystal goblet and took a long swallow, for courage. Outside the octagonal window above the sink, the ocean's eternal rhythm pushed and pulled against gravity, a scene Shelly found hypnotizing as her body responded to the sea's cadence. She mentally shook herself.

When she returned to the den, Tillman had his infernal phone back out, which he quickly shoved into his pocket.

Much too quickly. "Got another call?" she asked, holding out a beer.

"Yep," he said, with no elaboration. He popped the lid and took a long swallow, looking past her at the oil paintings covering the stair landing. "Lots of beautiful women. Your ancestors?"

"Yep." If he wanted to play taciturn, so could she.

"Where are all the men?"

Shelly gave a puzzled frown. She'd honestly never noticed. Only mermaids presided over this house. Mom had explained that mermen were casual lovers who didn't share in childrearing and she'd never once heard her cousins mention a father. She smiled brightly. "Good question."

Tillman put his hands on his hips and surveyed the room. "A most unusual house. Marlena would love this place."

"Marlena?"

He quickly took another long swallow of beer. "Um, ex-girlfriend. She's an interior designer in Atlanta."

Well, wasn't that just hoity-toity wonderful. "How long ago did you break up?"

He waved a hand dismissively. "Years ago." Tillman started to set his beer can on a coffee table but hesitated. "Got a coaster? Don't want to ruin your furniture. I suspect everything in here is expensive or priceless."

Shelly slapped one of Jet's old catalogs on the table. "There you go."

She watched his arm and hands as he slowly set down the can. His skin was deeply tanned and the dusting of hair on his forearm had been lightly bleached from the summer sun. Both his arms suddenly wrapped around her waist and she smiled at the sight of her pale skin alongside his. His arms tightened as she closed her eyes and lifted her chin.

They were all over each other at once. Lips to lips, skin exploring skin. Shelly moved her hand up the back of his shirt, felt his muscles grow rigid beneath her palms. Tillman cupped her breasts, and then his hands moved down to her ass, pressing her against his erection.

Heat exploded in her core and she moaned with need. Nothing mattered outside of this moment, this desperate desire to couple and become one.

Tillman groaned and the internal heat became a consuming fire of lust.

Suddenly he stepped back and she blinked at him, bewildered and weak-kneed.

He groaned again and held up the phone before reading the screen. "Damn, I've got to cut this short."

"Your work again?" Shelly tried to keep the disappointment out of her voice.

"No." He crammed the phone in his pocket. "It's Eddie."

"What about him? Is he okay?"

"It's just..." Tillman hesitated. "Sometimes he's too much for Mom to handle. The least little thing can set him off—a change in routine, loud noises, hell, sometimes there's no telling what makes him flip."

Shelly nodded. "He gets overstimulated. It happens a lot in people with autism."

"I need to get back." He moved toward the door. "Another time?"

"Sure." Shelly touched his arm. "I hope this has nothing to do with Jet. She doesn't exactly have good social skills."

He laughed. "I'm used to dealing with people not well-versed in social skills. No sweat."

Tillman lowered his head and gave her a brief, hard kiss on the mouth. "Later," he whispered in her ear. "This isn't how I wanted our date to end," he added in a deep, sexy baritone. A flush of heat ignited her skin as she responded to his voice as naturally as she did the ocean's echo.

"Next time, it's my cabin."

Shelly raised her fingers to her lips as she watched him leave. Until now she hadn't realized how lonely she'd been these past few years, shut up in a house out in the bayou. As long as she was careful, she could have Tillman as a lover. Lily managed affairs constantly.

But Lily never falls in love. You might. She stifled the cautionary voice in her head. She knew only too well there was little chance of a future between them after being raised in a house full of strife and unhappiness.

Shelly climbed the stairs to her room and threw herself on the bed. This was not how she'd wanted the night to end. She sighed and turned her head to look at the framed photograph of her mother on the bedside table. Picking it up, she traced a finger over Mom's mouth, which turned up at the corners, but the smile wasn't in her eyes.

When Shelly had turned fourteen, Mom had stood up to her husband for one of the few times Shelly could remember. Dad hadn't wanted his daughter to leave landlocked Indiana and visit his wife's "wild" family in—as he called it—the Alabama swamp hellhole.

"She's going," Mom had announced in a firm voice that wasn't aggressive but brooked no argument in the matter. "Shelly needs to meet her extended family, needs to discover who she really is."

"Our daughter is an outcast there," Dad said. "She's safer here with us."

Shelly had flattened against the hallway wall. Shouting matches between her parents were common, but she normally wasn't the cause of friction. Or so she thought. Her heart pounded wildly at hearing she was an outcast. Warring emotions of anticipation and fear rooted her feet to the floor.

"My sister and nieces will protect her. They'd never allow her to be exposed to danger or name-calling," Mom insisted. "We can't hide the truth from her forever. She already knows she can hold her breath underwater longer than a human should."

"She doesn't have to know." Dad's voice dropped a notch and Shelly strained to make out the words. "We'll just keep her from the damn beach."

"She's a teenager. You can't control *her* life forever." The implication of *like you did mine* hung in the air. "Shelly's a young woman now. I've watched her at the full moon. Even here, hundreds of miles from the ocean, the sea calls her and she doesn't understand what her body craves."

Shelly frowned. Cravings? The only thing she suffered every month were cramps and PMS.

"If she goes back to Alabama your people will shun her."

"Don't be ridiculous. Hardly anyone shows up at the old place anymore."

"They'll be back. And they've never forgiven you for marrying a dirt dweller. I absolutely forbid it."

"Tough shit—"

Shelly cringed at the curse words. Mom must be really mad.

"—I'm taking her to Alabama. This is about Shelly and what's best for her. She's a mermaid and it's time she learned the truth."

Holy crap. Shelly's knees buckled and she sank down onto the hardwood floor. The bedroom door had suddenly swung open and she'd been caught eavesdropping. Which turned out to be the least of her worries.

Had her mother known just how much Shelly would later need her cousins? Seven years later, Mom and Dad had died together in a car accident. And even though she'd been in college by that time, knowing her family down South had made Shelly feel she had some mooring in her life. Jet and Lily were all she had now.

Jet. She needed to talk to her cousin, find out why she'd acted so obnoxious tonight, well, more obnoxious than usual. As Shelly returned the photograph to the table she suddenly realized that the black pearl necklace, a gift from Mom and normally draped over the frame, was missing. She jumped off the bed and scanned the floor, having dropped it there many times before. Not seeing it, Shelly went to her knees and lifted the bed skirt. Nothing but dust bunnies.

No. No. No. Shelly's hunt became increasingly frantic as she searched behind furniture, opened drawers and started to remove the bedding. She had to find it. Mom had given it to her on her fourteenth birthday, not long after Shelly discovered they were mermaids. It was one of her most cherished possessions, a memento. When Mom had given her the gift, she had tried to explain the beauty and freedom of ocean swims, the hidden, wonderful aspects of a mermaid's life.

Her eyes caught a scrap of red at the foot of the aquamarine bedspread. A slip of cheap red satin material—a pair of women's bikini panties.

Not mine.

Certainly not Jet's, who stuck strictly to boyfriend briefs. And not the expensive, lacy concoctions in pastel colors that Lily always wore.

Maybe they'd gotten these for her as a joke. If so, it wasn't funny. Shelly stepped closer to the panties, observed the sleazy fibers of the slippery fabric. She bent over the bed, closer, and then recoiled in horror and disgust.

They were wrinkled and...soiled.

Chapter 5

Footprints in the sand
Returning to the sea
Who do they belong to?
How did this come to be?

"Run a background check on Jet Bosarge," Tillman instructed the deputy working the night shift. "Check for any previous arrests, legal residences and history."

That out of the way, Tillman called home. Mom answered after the fifth ring. "I'm on my way. Should be there in about fifteen minutes."

Eddie's screams almost drowned out her voice. "Thanks, son, my nerves are kinda shot."

Shit. Not what he'd been expecting tonight. First, Shelly's cousin acts like a moron, he finds their house loaded with priceless artifacts and his brother picks tonight to have a temper tantrum on an epic scale. If he were a cynical man, he'd think the universe was out to screw him.

And what was up with those women? When he'd run his hands through the contents of that vase, he'd seen valuable coins. Jet wasn't the only collector in town. He knew enough about coins to recognize several pieces of eight, old Spanish metal coins that could be broken into eight pieces to make change. When Jet and Shelly had left him alone in the room, he'd taken several pictures of the coins and baubles with his cell phone. Maybe later tonight, if Eddie calmed down, he'd have a chance to identify some of them.

The only good thing tonight had been the feel of Shelly in his arms on the beach. Something about her was peaceful and calming, the same feeling he usually only got deep-sea fishing. He should have asked her out long ago, but he didn't want any emotional entanglements, particularly with a woman who worked with Eddie. If they broke up, it would be awkward to keep running into her. He didn't need to jeopardize Shelly turning against Eddie when his brother enjoyed the swim therapy.

The woman was damn exciting. But how could he ask her for only a physical liaison with no strings attached? Somehow, he would work it out. At the rush of heat in his body, Tillman banged his fist on the steering wheel. Living with his mother was hell on his love life but he couldn't see moving out anytime soon. Resentment roiled in his stomach as he thought longingly of his old apartment in Mobile. At least he had the fish cabin, primitive as it was.

Finally, he pulled in the driveway and raced into the house. The sound of shattered glass drew him into the kitchen.

"Oh, Eddie, look what you've done," his mom wailed. "Is that you, Tillman?"

Entering the kitchen, he took in the broken glass on the floor, the orange juice splattered on cabinets and the sticky puddles on the tiles. Eddie's face was red, hands clenched at his sides.

"Leave the room, Mom. You upset him when you yell."

"Fine. You deal with it." She huffed out with as much relief as indignation.

He and Eddie faced each other. Tillman spoke slow and even. "If you didn't want any orange juice, all you had to do was say so."

Eddie looked around for something else to throw.

"Whoa." Tillman wrapped his arms around his brother. "Can't let you do that."

Eddie struggled and pushed. Tillman stood a good four inches taller, but when Eddie got like this, his strength was a match for anybody. Tillman maneuvered his brother away from the glass, fearing Eddie would step on it with his bare feet and get hurt. He knew to watch for a sudden head butt, too. Those hurt like hell.

"What say we get a bath, Eddie?" Tillman carefully eased his hold, forcing himself to keep his voice conversational. "You've got yourself all worked up and in a lather. Look, you've got juice all over your legs."

Eddie reached a hand down and swiped at the sugary goo matting his leg hairs. "Yuck," he said. "Get off."

"That's right." Tillman led him down a hallway to the bathroom, still careful to keep Eddie at arm's length. "A nice hot bath, and we'll get you all cleaned up."

Eddie screeched a few times in protest, but appeared to have let off most of his steam. Tillman ran the water, checked the temperature and then dumped in half a bottle of Mr. Bubble.

Tillman relaxed and stretched out his feet. Eddie was calming down in the tub. It hadn't been too bad tonight. After the bath, he'd give Eddie his night meds in a plastic cup (no glass—just in case), fix a bowl of pop-corn for himself, a bowl of Cap'n Crunch for Eddie and watch *SpongeBob* reruns on television until his brother fell asleep.

Not the way he'd originally planned to spend his evening.

Portia knocked. "Everything all right now?" she asked. Tillman opened the door where she hovered, clutching a faded pink Calvin Klein bathrobe. Her fingers fastened and unfastened the knot on its sash.

"Crisis averted."

"Oh, good." She breathed out a gush of expelled air.

"What set him off?" he asked.

"I've no idea. Maybe because you weren't home at supper." Her note held the faintest note of displeasure. How often she'd used that same tone with Dad.

Tillman fought for patience. "I can't be here every night."

"Did you have a date?"

"Yeah." He volunteered no more information.

"Who with?"

"Shelly Connors."

Portia crinkled her nose. "The pool girl? Really?"

"She's an aquatic therapist. And yeah, really."

Portia frowned. "Don't know much about her, other than she lives with her cousins. Lily Bosarge does my hair sometimes, if I don't feel like driving all the way to Mobile."

"What do you know about them?"

"Lily has *quite* the reputation, let me tell you. The Bosarge name is a respected one in the bayou—some of the founding fathers were Bosarges. But she is a discredit to their legacy." She narrowed her eyes. "I hope her cousin isn't so tawdry."

"Tawdry? You sound like an outraged spinster from Victorian England or something."

Portia lifted her chin. "In my day, Southern girls were raised to be ladies."

Tillman refrained from rolling his eyes. Barely. "Know anything about the other Bosarge girl—Jet?"

"Not much. She keeps to herself and doesn't even try to act social. Why, in my day, gracious Southern manners meant something."

Portia blew a kiss to Eddie and left, leaving Tillman to get him ready for bed.

Once Eddie got to his room he pointed to the photograph on his bedside table. The picture was from the summer of 1988, taken by the shore. Dad was helping him erect a sand castle while Eddie was frozen in time, watching sand dribble downward from his fist. He could do that for hours. Tillman speculated each new handful of sand contained some slightly different composition of ground shells and rocks that when released in a cascade reflected subtle differences in color. Or it could be Eddie was merely entranced with the sensation of the warm sand slipping from his grasp in swirling patterns. He never really knew what went on in Eddie's mind; his brother existed on an isolated island of autism. Barely visible in the photograph, at its outermost border, Mom sat under an umbrella wearing dark glasses, a drink in hand.

Eddie placed his index finger on the image of their Dad—caught in a relaxed, happy moment away from work.

"All gone," he said.

The words always sent a pang through Tillman. He'd

been closer to his dad than anybody. And, if he was completely honest, angry that Dad left him to shoulder everything alone. The anger made him feel guilty as hell.

Eddie shot him an impatient look. "All gone," he repeated louder.

This was Tillman's cue. He had to repeat Eddie's words before he would be satisfied and move on to the next step in his bedtime routine.

"All gone," Tillman parroted.

Bored, Tillman mentally replayed Mom's words about Shelly as he went about the nightly routine.

No one measured up to Portia LeBlanc Angier's standards. Portia had married beneath herself when she ended up with Frank Angier, a policeman. A fact she never let her husband forget. Disgusted with the direction of his thoughts, Tillman absently picked up Eddie's sketch pad and rifled through it, surprised to discover Eddie occasionally drew people. There was Mom, her nose slightly tilted in the air; there was himself unsmiling, the badge on his uniform etched in perfect detail. But the picture that surprised him the most was one of a mermaid. Eddie must have switched from Sponge-Bob to *The Little Mermaid* movie one night last week.

He startled when his phone went off. He'd forgotten all about it in the home minicrisis.

Tillman listened thoughtfully as his deputy filled him in on the background check for Jet Bosarge. Sounded like a dead end until Carl mentioned Jet's association with known felon Perry Hammonds, currently serving a ten-year sentence in a Chilean jail for robbery and attempt to defraud the Chilean government.

Interesting.

* * *

It was only later that night, after Shelly had grabbed a Ziploc baggie, gone upstairs and sealed the vile evidence inside it that she lay in the bathtub wondering how the killer had managed to find her. The warm water soothed her tense muscles and she allowed herself to relax in its liquid caress. It was almost as good as a midnight swim in the salty sea. Shelly submerged her entire body, head and all, in the large Victorian claw-foot tub and stayed underwater, letting the pressure in her ears create a cocoon of comfort. Funny how she never knew she could do that until her fourteenth summer, when she'd finally found out her true nature. Even the few times she'd played in the pool as a kid and discovered her lungs were different, she hadn't tested the full extent of her freakiness. All she'd wanted to do was blend in with the vanilla-ness of everyone else. Lifting her head out of the water, Shelly pushed tendrils of long hair away from her face. At the loud ring of the landline telephone, she rushed out, put on a robe and hurried across the bedroom. Maybe Tillman wanted to whisper sweet nothings in her ear about their date.

"Hello?"

Static crackled in the silence.

Shelly frowned and said louder, "Hello."

"Did you like my presents?" came a raspy voice, slow and menacing.

Presents? *Oh, my God.* The semen on the panties. Her heart pounded painfully in her chest, her vocal cords locked up, as if a hand was clamped on them, squeezing.

She straightened her spine and forced a deep breath. *Play along.* "The panties. Yes, I found them. Who are you?" she whispered.

"You know." A deep chuckle. "Wish you'd been home earlier when I visited."

"What do you want?"

"You know that, too." The playful note vanished, replaced by what she recognized as an intense, barely controlled fury. "I want my knife."

Her eyes traveled involuntarily to the top shelf of her closet, where she'd buried the knife in the folds of extra blankets and linens. So he hadn't found it.

"I don't know what you're talking about," Shelly lied. Maybe she could convince him he had the wrong person. How in the hell did he find her?

"Bitch!" The tightly coiled fury in his voice erupted. "Don't lie to me unless you want me to burn down your house with everyone inside."

The phone almost fell out of her hands from her sudden trembling. "Please," she begged. "Okay, I admit I've got your knife. I'll give it back. Promise."

The static crackled between them again and the killer laughed. "So it *was* you that saw me get rid of that whore."

She'd been tricked. He hadn't been sure she was the witness until she'd cracked under pressure. He was smart; she'd have to be very, very careful. "When do you want to meet?"

"There's not going to be a meeting, bitch. What you're going to do is bring the knife where I tell you. Ever hear of Happy Hollows?"

Shelly's mind raced. "On the south side of town—off County Road 143."

"Go 5.3 miles past the welcome sign. You'll come to a dip in the road. On your right I'll have a piece of red string tied to a branch of an oak tree. Under that tree will be an empty plastic container. Put the knife inside the bottle and then untie the red string. Got it?"

"Yes."

"Do it before seven in the morning."

"Do you promise to leave me and my family alone if I return your knife?"

"That's all I want."

Liar. Shelly didn't believe him. But she'd have to play along for now.

The scared-witless part was true enough. "Okay. You won't hurt us then?"

"I promise." His voice was intimate, husky with meaning.

Shelly pictured him on the other end of the line, probably playing with his dick as he fantasized about raping and killing her.

"Did you find my other present?" he asked.

"There's more than the underwear?"

"Look under your pillow."

Shelly's eyes drifted to the bed. The right side was a bit rumpled, the bedspread not as neatly tucked in as she normally left it.

"Go on, look," he urged in what sounded like suppressed excitement.

She couldn't move. It could be a snake or a tarantula, something alive and deadly.

"I'm waiting."

Shelly's entire body shook uncontrollably as she glanced at the drawn curtains. Could he see her right now? What if he was still in the house?

Just look. Get him off the line. She kept her body a foot from the bed and grabbed an inch of the bedspread's fabric and jerked. The pillow, encased in its crisp white linens, didn't move. Shelly turned it over, jumping back before checking to see what lay beneath.

Against the white sheet lay something tiny and colorful. A doll, perhaps. Shelly edged to the side of the bed and peered closer. She picked it up, a three-inch plastic mold of a mermaid with long blond hair, a jeweled comb in her locks and a fish tail instead of human legs.

It was broken in half.

"Found it yet?" he asked.

He couldn't see her. The knowledge took her fear down a notch. "Yes," she whispered. "I see it."

She gently replaced the phone on its base and sat on the edge of the bed. Her bed. He'd actually been here, touched her things, lain on her bed. She jumped off, stripped the pillowcase and wrapped up the severed mermaid figure inside the casing. That out of the way, Shelly jerked off the bedcover and sheets, trembling in fear and disgust, frantic to get rid of the contamination. She would wash them clean of the killer's touch. Her stomach roiled and cramped, the taste of bile tainted her mouth.

After putting the soiled sheets in the washer, Shelly sat in the porch rocking chair, moving in syncopation with the gentle rise and fall of the tides. The moonbeams reflected on the ocean swells were liquid swirls before being swallowed by whitecaps—like a galaxy of fireflies in the swarming sea.

Her ancestors had been drawn to this bayou hundreds of years ago, following pirates as they landed their vessels in small coastal coves and hid their illegal booty. In the secretive, sheltering canopy of cypress and live oaks they'd slithered through tall salt marshes in pale moonlight and reclaimed the treasures as their own. What fell to the sea belonged to its own.

In the Deep South they found a place where humans minded their own business and were too busy eking out their own daily survival to delve into others' shady backgrounds. In spite of moving inland to profit from the black market in maritime treasure, they remained at heart water gypsies who returned to the sea over and over during their lives.

Her mother had been born too late. Had fallen in love with a human long after the merfolk realized their mistake and interbreeding was banned.

I'm a mistake. A freak caught between earth and sea. Shelly stood with a sigh and climbed the stairs back to her bedroom.

But long after the sheets were changed, the killer's presence lingered, a poisonous miasma that would cling until she'd dealt with him. Hard to believe that hours earlier she'd been so happy, so secure in Tillman's arms. She pressed her fingers to her lips and remembered his hot kisses, a moment she'd been fantasizing for months. And he did not disappoint—in fact he surpassed her high expectations. This wasn't how she'd imagined the night ending. She'd give anything to be held all night long in his strong arms, safe and warm. Shelly hugged a down pillow to her chest, but it was a poor substitute.

She impulsively picked up her cell phone off the nightstand and found the phone number Tillman had input on her contacts page. Dare she call him? She hesitated. How in the world could she explain why someone was stalking her and how she had possession of a knife used to kill at least two women? Not to mention, Jet and Lily would be furious at the secrecy breach. Humans were not to be trusted, and Tillman's job as sheriff made him doubly risky as a confidant. She snapped the cell phone shut and tossed it back on the nightstand.

Shelly rubbed her forehead as she lay in the tainted bed and considered her other options.

In spite of the lined uniform jacket, Tillman shivered as he looked out the window of the utilitarian office and observed dozens of workers gutting fish at the seafood processing plant. Most of them were Laotian and Vietnamese women who eviscerated shrimp, crabs and fish with amazing speed and precision, despite the fourteen-hour days and the frigid temperature necessary to keep the sea harvest from spoiling. By far, the most undesirable job at the plant. The brief walk to the supervisor's office had left him chilled to the bone.

The door slammed and a heavyset man in khakis and a flannel shirt shook his hand. His grasp was strong, probably from years of hard labor at Trident Processing and Packing before promotion to management.

"What can I do for ya, Sheriff?" He was direct but not unfriendly.

Tillman dug a photo out of the inside pocket of his jacket. "Take a look at this." He slid it across the battered steel desk. "Are all employees issued these company baseball hats?"

"Anyone who wants one. Most do." He handed the photo back. "What's the deal?"

"It was found next to the latest victim's body."

The manager shrugged. "Hope you got more clues than that. We have hundreds of employees here."

"That many? How many employees do you have now?"

"About three hundred. That's counting the new waste facility. Luckily, we've been able to hire back most of the people laid off. The ones that wanted to come back, anyway."

"I know it's probably a long shot, but I need a list of all the employees at Trident so I can run their names in the computer and check for violent priors. Have you had any employees, current or old, that were fired for fighting at work or for any sexual misconduct on the job?"

The manager crossed his arms. "There's plenty of men go at it from time to time. Nothing we ever had to call the law to break up. Jobs in this town are mighty hard to come by and they know it. Gives them incentive to behave."

Tillman nodded. "Besides the names of current employees, I'd appreciate a list of all employees fired or laid off in the last nine months."

"You got it. I've got a wife and a daughter scared to get out at night since the killings. Myrtle Hyer in HR can set you right up." He picked up an old phone and pressed a number. "Myrtle? Grimes speaking. We've got the sheriff out here. He needs names of all current employees as well as recent fires and layoffs. I'm sending him over now."

It took ten minutes to walk from the main processing area to the administrative offices.

Myrtle awaited, documents in hand.

"Impressive," Tillman said, taking the thick manila envelope.

"No problem, Sheriff." Myrtle wore dark-rimmed spectacles and bore a no-nonsense attitude. "We always cooperative with law enforcement."

Tillman shook his head. His ears still rang from the

clanging of large equipment in the plant. He opened the folder and skimmed its contents. The list of fires and layoffs consisted of nearly thirty names. Of that number, only five were outright fires.

"Any way I can find out why these folks were fired? I'd really appreciate any help."

"Grimes didn't say you needed that, too." Her voice was laced with impatience and she pulled open a file drawer with a bit more force than necessary.

Tillman took out a pen. "Don't mean to make you go to a lot of trouble. If you could just briefly tell me why for each one, that's good enough." Working in Personnel, Myrtle should be familiar with the former employees. He read aloud the first name on the list.

"Earl Johnson?"

"Earl and Harold Dawes, also on the fire list, were terminated for fighting. It was their third offense."

"Gary Bradshaw?"

"Failure to show up for work for three days without calling in. Automatic dismissal."

"Lester Jones?"

"Drinking on the job. Also grounds for automatic dismissal."

Tillman scribbled notes next to each name.

"And the last one. Melkie Pellerin?"

"Insubordination."

Tillman looked up from the papers. "That's a fireable offense? Sounds a bit harsh."

Myrtle pursed her thin lips. "He objected to his new female boss, Kathy Albright. Called her names and refused to obey any orders she issued. Pellerin undermined her authority to the crew and hampered their ability to be productive."

"What kind of names?"

Myrtle hesitated. Despite the pink flush that crept up from her neck she repeated the words: "Cunt, bitch, whore—whatever you can think of, he said it."

Tillman stuffed the papers back in the envelope. "Thank you, ma'am."

Tillman got in his patrol car and called Carl for two addresses. He'd start with Earl Johnson and Harold Dawes.

Chapter 6

Inside the heart of Happy Hollows
Resides the bleakness of the gallows
Broken houses with broken dreams
Rotted by sighs and tears and screams.

Shelly held a stiletto knife in the palm of each hand—one used, the other new. Jet was right, this type of knife was common. She'd raced to the nearest sporting goods store in Mobile, bought a new knife and worked to manually age the new knife well enough to fool her enemy. Satisfied with her initial efforts, Shelly turned her attention to the finer details. She slipped on latex gloves, withdrew the original knife and studied where its handle was irregularly grooved with nicks and bumps. With the precision of a surgeon, she used the fine tip of a Swiss Army knife to carve similar markings on the new stiletto. Satisfied at last with the effect, Shelly again used the fine-grained sandpaper, dulling the sharp edge of the new knife.

She surveyed her handiwork. Would it be good enough to trick the killer? Her body broke out in chill bumps. She had to do this, scared or not.

An enraged scream rang through the upstairs hallway. "My rings! Someone stole my rings!"

Jet's door opened across the hall. "What's going on?"

Shelly stepped out of her bedroom. Lily's face was flushed with anger, ocean-blue eyes flashed in outrage. In her hands was an open jewelry box empty of all its contents. "They're gone. My diamonds, the fire opal, a ruby, the aquamarine, the citrine from my father, the pearls from our mama, and the—"

"Son of a bitch!" Jet dashed down the stairs. "What else is missing?"

Lily's eyes filled with salty tears. "They're all gone. All my treasures." She looked like a lost child, broken. Shelly had never seen her so upset.

"Oh, honey, I'm so sorry." Shelly put her arms around her cousin. Guilt stabbed through her. She had brought this on her family, had exposed them to the killer. If only she hadn't broken surface with that dead body.

"Who?" Lily's gaze penetrated Shelly's. "Who's been in our house?"

"The killer." Shelly's throat closed up, felt raw.

From below came the sound of objects falling, furniture scraping against the hardwood floor and Jet's muttered cursing.

"How can you be sure it's him?" Lily asked.

"He left me a message." Shelly led Lily to her bedroom and showed her the broken mermaid figurine and the bagged-up panties.

Jet's footsteps hammered up the stairs before she barged in. "I think the robber got some coins from the den, but I can't be sure." She stopped at the sight of the baggie. "What's that?"

"A present from the robber. Who also happens to be the killer," Lily said.

"Yep. Evidence." Shelly squared her shoulders. "I'm

going to take care of this. I'm giving this—" she held up the bag "—to Tillman. He might be able to get fingerprints."

"He'll want to file a police report on the robbery." Jet sighed, hands on hips. "Not a good idea. They'll probably send officers over here to scour the place. We don't want that."

"We need to file some kind of report. Otherwise, when they're recovered we can't claim them. I'll speak with Tillman about it and show him what the killer left."

"Did he steal anything of yours?" Lily asked.

"I don't have a lot of value other than Mom's emerald, which I always wear, and the black pearl necklace." Remembering her loss, Shelly felt a searing anger replace the fear. If the killer wasn't caught soon, he might pawn their treasures. More jewelry could always be scavenged undersea or bought with their enormous stash of wealth, but the memories attached to each piece were irreplaceable.

A few hours later, Shelly drove down the shady bayou roads, past tangles of saw palmettos and moss-laden live oaks with branches so long they spanned across the road and met in the middle. At last she saw the Happy Hollows welcome sign. Not much longer now. She checked her mileage—another 5.3 miles to go. Slowing the car, Shelly furtively looked down every dusty road she passed. Was he watching her now? Perhaps parked behind a grove of thick foliage? She tried to sustain the anger she'd felt earlier, but the fear was back with a vengeance.

Maybe she should just keep driving, all the way to Mississippi and beyond. Nothing held her forever to

Bayou La Siryna. She and Lily and Jet had enough
money to go anywhere in the world.

Tillman's image arose before her. His tall, strong
frame, the warm gray eyes that darkened to smoke when
he kissed her, the musky woodsy scent of him cloud-
ing her senses until she ached to be closer, ever closer.

If only he was with her now.

But as much as she wanted his protection, if she told
him about the killer she could be placing her family and
other mermaids in jeopardy. After all, she'd seen Melkie's face, could identify him in a criminal lineup, and
her cousins had dragged China's body to shore. By not
coming forward immediately, they were all, at the very
least, obstructing justice. Tillman wouldn't be likely to
overlook the deception if she told the truth now. And
any hope she had of exploring a relationship with Tillman would be over before it got started. No one wanted
a grotesque mutant that transformed into a half fish, half
human woman at a drop of seawater.

It wasn't fair. It was as if the fates were conspiring
against her just when she'd found someone that truly
excited her for the first time in years.

Shelly's fingers gripped the steering wheel so tightly
the muscles of her arms and shoulders knotted with tension. He wasn't here and she had to do this alone. Shelly
made an abrupt U-turn and headed back to the drop-off
spot. For the hundredth time, she patted the gun on the
seat beside her, the cool metal comforting. If the killer
was there waiting to get her, she would take him out if
she had no other choice.

At 6:55 a.m. Shelly did a second U-turn, coming to
a halt on the side of the road, only six feet from the
marked oak. Her eyes scanned the ground and found

the empty plastic container set only a foot away from a large shrub. It had an orange powdery residue inside, probably an old Cheetos container. She tried to peer between the green leaves and branches for a human form crouching in wait but couldn't make out anyone. But the man could be anywhere, watching her every move.

Shelly gripped the door handle with her left hand while the other held the gun, safety off.

Now or never.

She opened the door, pocketed the keys, hesitating, waiting to see if the madman would come roaring through a hidden ambush. At the silence, Shelly left the shelter of the car and emerged onto the road, quickly circling in all directions, keeping the gun up high, fingers on its trigger, letting him know she was armed.

What if he's brought an accomplice? The unwelcome question almost sent her back in the car and speeding all the way to California. But she was committed this far, and it would be over in less than a minute.

Shelly ran to the tree and prepared to scoop up the container before running back to the car. But as she bent over, hands reaching for the container, she came eye level with a clump of brown fur nestled amongst pine needles, sweet gum balls and oak leaves, only two feet away. Flies buzzed around the slit carcass of a squirrel, a pool of blood and gray matter staining the sandy soil around it. The squirrel's eyes were missing.

Her screams rent the morning air as she scrambled backward, sure that at any moment now the killer would attack. Quickly, Shelly grabbed the container and ran back to the car, locking herself in. Her hands shook so bad, it took three attempts before she could unscrew the plastic lid and drop the counterfeit knife inside. Once done, she slid down the passenger-side window, tossed the container back under the tree and hit the gas pedal before it had even touched the ground.

Two miles down the road, Shelly finally took a deep breath and tried to calm her nerves. *Remember your plan. Go back and try to get a picture of him. Nail that bastard.*

The car screeched loudly as Shelly spun it around, back to the place she'd just left.

It was 7:04 a.m. The deadline had come and gone. Would he be there? Shelly pulled her digital camera with its 200-millimeter telescopic lens out from under the car seat and unrolled the passenger-side window. At the dip in the road, she slowed in case there was an opportunity to catch him retrieving the knife. This time, she wanted him to be there, wanted to capture his face on the camera or at least the make and model of his vehicle so it would be easier to find out his identity. This would give her something to work with, maybe even to show it to Tillman—if she could ever trust him enough to confess what she'd witnessed. He could take it from there.

Shelly squinted. She couldn't find the tree with the red string, even though she was in the right place. She slowed the car and eased over to the opposite side of the road.

No string, no plastic container. But the dead squirrel still bled under the oak tree in its bed of pine needles.

The morning felt like a total waste with nothing but blind alleys. Tillman had visited most of the fired employees and returned to his office, completely frustrated. When his deputy wandered in for a chat, Tillman took the opportunity to quiz him on the Bosarge family.

"What do you know about Lily Bosarge?"

Carl scratched his chin. "Can't say I know much at all. Pretty girl, but distant."

"What about her sister?"

"She's a mean one, all right. 'Bout a year ago she went in Floyd's bar looking for Johnny Matthews. Seems she took exception to something he'd been saying around town about Lily." Carl chuckled. "Jet's a real spitfire. Told Johnny to keep his mouth shut or his new gal would get an earful about his sexual incompetence. Matthews has never lived it down."

Tillman remembered the SOB from high school. Always bragging on his supposed sexual conquests. He drove a rusted Camaro with an exposed muffler he thought sounded cool as shit.

"Couldn't happen to a nicer guy," he said. "Did you know either of their parents? According to the background check you ran, their house has been passed down through the decades in a matriarchal line."

"Can't say I do. They've always kept to themselves."

He probed again. "So you didn't know Adriana or Olivia Bosarge? Their names precede Jet and Lily's on the house deed."

Carl narrowed his eyes. "Why the twenty questions?"

"Just curious. Shelly, their cousin, lives with them and is Eddie's aquatic therapist."

"Is that what they call swim teachers now?" Carl snorted. "Aquatic therapists?"

"She's got a B.A. in exercise physiology and a master's degree in physical therapy."

"All that learning just to play in the water?"

Tillman fought down the hot need to further defend Shelly.

"Why did you want a background check? You never ask without good reason."

Tillman fidgeted. "I was at their house last night. They have lots of expensive stuff lying around."

Carl folded his arms. "Big deal. There's always been talk that the Bosarges were wealthy from trust funds handed down through generations. What were you doing there anyway?"

"I took Shelly out to dinner."

"No wonder you were so touchy about her being a therapist," Carl said with a wink.

Tillman pulled a file toward him, signaling it was time to get back to work. After his deputy left, he studied the photo of his father receiving an award for his many years of service. People remembered him with fondness. It wasn't fair that less than a year after this picture was taken, he'd had a massive coronary and left behind two people so dependent on him.

He resignedly turned back to his computer. Carl was right. He was making something out of nothing. If the Bosarge family was ridiculously rich, it was none of his business.

Still, he couldn't leave it alone. Once his curiosity was aroused, he had to find answers.

Tillman retrieved his phone and pulled up the pictures he'd taken at Shelly's. She had damn near caught him in the act. He downloaded the photos on the computer and enlarged them on-screen. Most of the vase had been filled with corroded coins, old buttons and bits of green-colored glass. Tillman had photographed a few of the more pristine, legible coins.

The first coin he examined was gold and engraved with lions and castles, dated 1617. To his untrained eye, it looked as if it might be Grade 1 with an estimated worth of nearly two thousand dollars.

Tillman let out a low whistle, trying to calculate how many identical coins were scattered in their home. The coins were recovered from the Spanish galleon *Nuestra Señora de Atocha,* which sank during a hurricane near the Florida Keys on September 6, 1622. The Grade 1 Atocha coins were salvaged from the innermost portion of a treasure chest that had protected them from salt-water damage. He skimmed an article on Atocha ship-wreck artifacts until he read about the color and clarity of Atocha emeralds.

No, it couldn't be.

Impatiently, he again pulled up the Bosarge photo-graphs and found what he had earlier thought were chips of green sea glass scattered in among the coins.

Emeralds. If he took one of the pieces to a gemologist, Tillman was sure the expert would confirm their value.

His mind jumped to Shelly at the restaurant as she ran her fingers through her hair, an emerald flashing on the right hand. The square-cut design and gold fili-gree band had an heirloom vibe. Was it made from a seventeenth-century treasure relic?

He paced the room and pondered what it meant, if anything. First, the stuff might only be antique replicas, not especially expensive. Second, the women's ancestors might have been wealthier than what anyone in Bayou La Siryna had previously guessed and Shelly and her cousins were living off that prior bounty.

He had no right to think anything illegal was going on.

But he did.

More startling, he recalled the silky feel of Shelly's

long hair—the color and length of which perfectly matched the strands recovered on China's body. The thought unnerved him. Had he become a jaded, cynical man who believed the worst of everyone? Shelly was kind, compassionate and worked hard to help the elderly and disabled. Hardly killer material. On the other hand, her cousin Jet was a piece of work. Too bad that woman's hair was short and black instead of long and blond.

Still, he had to consider everyone a suspect, even someone as sweet and innocent as Shelly.

I have to find him.

If she had the nerve to try to trick a killer, this should be a leisurely swim in calm waters. Shelly marched briskly into the Englazia County Sheriff's Office before she talked herself out of action. It wasn't really much of a deception after all, somebody *was* after her. No one paid much attention as she went down a few hallways and found his office. The door was ajar and, in spite of everything, her heart rate accelerated at the sight of Tillman. He was bent forward in his chair, staring intently at a computer.

If only she could tell him everything. As much as she hated deceiving him, it had to be done. She knocked smartly on the door and entered. "Sorry to interrupt. May I speak with you a few minutes?"

Gray eyes slammed into her own, inquisitive and probing. He stood and motioned to a chair. "Sure. Have a seat."

Shelly sat down, crossing and uncrossing her legs as Tillman rounded the desk and sat in a chair opposite her.

"What brings you here this morning?"

Shelly was disconcerted by his unreadable expression. His manner and voice were somewhere between friendly and professional, not at all like last night. Maybe it would be easier this way. "I need your help."

Tillman said nothing but continued to regard her searchingly.

Shelly fidgeted with the handle on her purse. Best to just get it over with. She set her purse on his desk and then froze at the eight-by-ten colored glossies spread across its surface.

The bodies of two dead, mutilated women lay exposed, both missing eyes. The redheaded woman she'd never seen before but the other—

Shelly inched one of the glossies closer. "It's her," she gasped, clasping a hand to her mouth as bile rose in the back of her throat. That heart-shaped, delicate face; the long black hair and scarlet lips… The last time Shelly had seen her was when she'd tucked her plastic-encased body between two rocks undersea.

"You knew this woman? China Wang?" Tillman's sharp tone broke through the morbid reverie.

Shelly shook her head at once. "No," she answered quickly. She scooted her chair farther from the desk to avoid seeing the photos again.

"But you said 'it's her,'" Tillman said.

"I meant it's her as in *the victim*. That's all."

His lips compressed into a single line. "There are two victims and photos of two different women there. Yet you singled out one of them."

Damn, he was far too sharp. Why did she have to be attracted to someone in his line of work? "I recognized China from the newspaper pictures. That's all." There, that lie would have to do. She rushed on, forestalling more questions. "I know you're busy. The reason I'm here is that I want to look at recent arrest photos of men."

He furrowed his brow and frowned. "What the hell for?"

Shelly went into the spiel she'd perfected while driving over. "I've been getting weird phone calls for several weeks. They're getting more frequent and in the last couple, he threatened me. And then this morning—"

"What did he say?"

"That he's watching me."

Tillman went still and spoke quietly. "Did he threaten bodily harm?"

Shelly thought fast. She had to make this convincing enough that he'd let her see those arrest pictures. "He said he'd get me and…and do things."

"What things?"

She waved a hand and brushed aside the question. "Anyway, this morning when I went to the grocery store some guy came up to me as I was getting in my car. He gave me this creepy grin and said he'd give me a call later. I'm sure it was him."

Tillman shot out of his chair. "Where did he go?"

"I don't know," she whispered. "I got in my car and took off."

"You didn't look to see if he got in a car so you could get the license plate number?"

Her back stiffened. "Don't shout. I've had a rough morning. Just let me look at the mug shots and see if one of them is the guy."

He ran a hand through his already-rumpled hair and let out a frustrated sigh. Abruptly, he strode to the door and stuck his head out, calling for someone to bring the arrest book.

She'd done it. She should be relieved. Instead, guilt pierced her sharp as a surgeon's scalpel. Beneath the anger, she knew Tillman was concerned and worried.

I had to. I have to find the killer. She tried to convince herself she was doing the right thing and perhaps Tillman would understand one day.

Shelly rose. It would be easier on both of them if she went to the records room alone to view the photographs. If she recognized the killer she could proceed with the plan to frame him. She would file a complaint and plant his knife in either his house or car. When the cops came to arrest him, they would find it and realize he was the serial killer.

As she rose and grabbed her purse from the desk, she caught a glimpse of Tillman's computer screen. Her mouth dropped open and she leaned forward for a closer look. A dozen photos from her living room were displayed: their coffee table with some of the contents from the vase scattered on its surface, the shelves with antique china and the fireplace mantel with its collection of rare swords. Several coins and pieces of jewelry were enlarged on the screen.

Her ears rang and she felt weighted down, as if she couldn't breathe, couldn't move. Tillman said something, but it sounded as if he was far away and she couldn't comprehend the words. Someone's hands were on her shoulders, guiding her downward. She was sitting in a chair again. Tillman's face wavered before her.

"Shelly? Take deep breaths."

She inhaled sharply and stared into those dark gray eyes. Anger and hurt, but mostly anger, broke through the stupor. "Why?" she asked hotly. "Why did you come in our home and take those pictures?"

His face hardened. "Because you have priceless artifacts lying around worth thousands and thousands of dollars. Because of the way your cousin got angry and acted secretive, gathering those maps and papers and sweeping out of the room. Something's not right with—"

"You had no right! If we're filthy rich and want to fill our home with expensive stuff it's none of your damn business." Of all the nerve. The man didn't even show a speck of remorse for being such a low-down sneak.

He held up a hand before turning his attention to the doorway. A young officer stared back and forth between them.

"Just leave the cart here," Tillman ordered.

"Yes, sir."

Shelly's face burned with a mixture of embarrassment and anger as the officer wheeled the cart to them and left. She drew up a chair and opened the first of two thick books, deliberately ignoring Tillman. He muttered something unintelligible and strode over to the window, his back to her.

Good. She could concentrate better without him crowding her. She scanned every photo carefully, sure she would remember those eyes, that beak nose and dark curly hair. By the end of the first book, hope trickled away. Shelly opened the second book and went through the same process until she'd turned the last page.

He wasn't there. All of this was for naught. She scraped back her chair and gathered her purse.

"You didn't see him?" Tillman walked toward her. "Describe him and we'll be on the lookout."

"Forget it," she snapped.

"C'mon, Shelly," he said softly, only a yard away. "I'm sorry about the pictures. You're right. It's none of

my business. Guess it's my cop training that makes me
so hard-nosed about getting to the bottom of everything.
You've got to understand. I'm trying to catch a serial
killer. Anything out of the ordinary catches my eye and
I have to check it out."

In spite of her anger, Shelly was dismayed to feel
the same old pull drawing her to this man. How easy it
would be to forgive Tillman and feel his arms wrapped
around her once more. But she saw now it would never
work. The lies would always come between them. Better to end it now.

"Don't call me. Don't ever come to see me again."

She turned away, but not before hearing his sharp in-
drawn breath and witnessing regret in his eyes. Good,
she hoped he felt as bad as she did, although that was
highly unlikely. Tillman Angier was too perceptive and
too dedicated to his sheriff job for them to have a relationship. More important, he couldn't be trusted. And
to think she'd felt guilty earlier about lying to protect
her shape-shifting. At least she hadn't invaded his privacy like he had done to her.

Too damn bad his kisses made her toes curl and heart
race. The risk of seeing him wasn't worth the pleasure
of his touch.

Or so she tried to convince herself.

Tillman erased all the Bosarge photos from his cell
and computer and dove into the pile of paperwork on
his desk with a hollow ache in the pit of his belly. He
tried to view the case objectively. What possible connection could Shelly have with the prostitute or a violent perp? She was educated, respected and financially
secure. If she had a hidden proclivity for violence or

sexual crimes, her name would probably have come to his attention at some point. But instead, he'd watched her for months, observed her many small acts of kindness with Eddie and other clients. No one had anything but good to say about Shelly Bosarge.

If she was now the killer's target, why would he switch the kind of victim he sought? Had Shelly witnessed something she shouldn't have seen? Was she being framed by a psychopath? None of it made sense. The most likely scenario was that the blond hair wasn't hers and the creep from the store wasn't the perp. The two events were unrelated and mere coincidence.

Too bad he wasn't the type of man to believe in coincidence.

Two hours later he grabbed his car keys, deciding he needed fresh air and a diversion. The thought of Shelly being in danger was driving him crazy. He'd check another name from the factory list.

Forget her. No big deal. But he couldn't stop remembering those accusing green eyes or worrying about her mysterious caller as he drove out for the interview.

At 1724 Sea Way Court he parked in front of the cheerless shotgun house and opened the background file for a quick review. No criminal record on Pellerin, but his mother had a string of prostitution arrests.

He swung open the cruiser door. Before his foot hit the crumbling pavement, people sitting on porches abruptly rose and went into their homes. Even a few children, kicking around a football in a yard of weeds and sand, regarded him with solemn faces of distrust.

Inside the sagging picket fence of the front yard was an old Chevy truck with an extended cab and faded blue paint. He glanced in the truck's window as he passed—

nothing but crumpled-up Cheetos bags and empty Coke bottles on the floorboard.

He knocked on the door and waited, eyes roaming over years of accumulated junk on the porch: old plastic buckets, a cardboard box of broken Mason jars, wire—you name it, it was probably piled here somewhere.

A mouse darted under a pile of old pillows and Tillman frowned. Chances were the place was likely infested with roaches and mice.

Glancing at his watch, he saw it was after 3:00 p.m. Pellerin was unemployed so good chance he was in. Tillman rapped sharply on the door and heard excited yipping from deep inside. He waited a couple of heartbeats but heard no other sound. He knocked again, more insistent, and strained to hear any movement from within.

A faint scraping noise, like a chair pushed against the floor, came from the front area of the house.

"Melkie Pellerin?" he called out in a booming voice. If he had to fetch his bullhorn and use it to shame the guy into opening the door, he would.

Approaching footsteps, the creak of a latch lifting, and Pellerin appeared wearing a rumpled white T-shirt and jeans, disheveled, wiry hair and the disoriented eyes of someone just awakened. His black-brown eyes sharpened as they focused on the sheriff's badge at his eye level.

"May I come in to ask a few questions?"

Melkie hesitated, then grudgingly held open the screen door.

"Ain't got much time," he mumbled in a voice like rusty nails scratching together.

The yipping sound advanced and Tillman looked down. "What kind of dog you got?"

"Chinese crested." Melkie pointed to a worn sofa. "Have a seat."

Tillman schooled his features not to react at the filth or the smell of stale grease and fried bologna pervading the cramped quarters.

Melkie sat in an old recliner across from him. "Here, Reb." He gestured and the dog flopped down at his feet, still baring a mouthful of yellowed stubs at the stranger invading his territory.

Tillman stared at the tooth stubs yellow as Chiclet candy.

"Whatcha want?" Melkie leaned back in the recliner, arms folded across his chest.

"Need to ask you a few questions, if you don't mind. Wanted to talk about your firing from Trident back on the first of June."

Melkie sat up. "Did that old bitch Albright send you here? I ain't never touched the woman and she got me let go by the company. For nothing." The veins in his neck stretched and bulged with the violent pounding of blood.

"I take it you're referring to Kathy Albright, your former supervisor?"

"She had it in for me from day one. Thought she was so much better 'n me and tried to boss me around all the time. I knew my job."

"Yet you were the only one fired for insubordination. Everyone else must have got along with the new female supervisor with no problem," Tillman noted, as if only mildly curious.

Jolene Babineaux had been murdered on June 3. Could this man have been so enraged at getting fired by a female boss that he'd taken it out on another woman?

Maybe too much of a stretch, he mused. He was desperate to solve these murders.

Melkie settled back, visibly trying to control his emotions. "So what? I don't need no woman telling me what to do every minute."

Tillman raised a brow. "You got a problem accepting women in positions of authority?"

Melkie glowered. "Why you asking me? I'm drawing my pennies fair and square."

Tillman raised his hands, palms up. "No one's questioning your right to draw an unemployment check." He scanned the room. Its most striking feature was the dozens of butterfly shadow boxes covering the walls. He went over to one and studied the specimens precisely pinned and labeled in carefully calligraphed specimen names—*Boloria bellona, Strymon acis* and *Papilio troilus.*

"You make this yourself?" he asked, not turning around.

"Yeah."

Tillman walked a few feet farther into the home's interior, the butterfly boxes giving way to other dead insect collections. The spider display sent itchy, crawly sensations up and down his arms. A bit creepy but not all that uncommon. A display of beetles with shiny metallic scales he could—almost—appreciate. But another collection stopped him short. He spun around to Melkie, who stood a couple of feet behind, arms crossed. "*Bats?* Where did you get them?"

"Got a bat house out front. Keeps the skeeters away." Melkie stared him in the eye. "You didn't come over here to look at my insect collection. What do you want?"

Tillman decided to go in for the kill, maybe catch

this guy off guard. "Where were you on the night of September fifth?"

Melkie's right eye twitched. "Home, I suppose. Why?"

"You read the papers? Watch the local news?"

"Sometimes."

The dog went over to the far left corner of the room, mewling and digging his paws at a spot on the floor. "Get over here, Reb." The scratching grew louder, more agitated. Melkie scooped the dog up in his arms and set him on the porch. He faced Tillman again, right eye twitching violently. "I don't want to talk to you no more, unless you're here to arrest me."

"I'm just here to talk. If you keep up with the local news, you've got to know the big story this week."

"'Course I do." Melkie scowled and remained standing.

He was clamming up. "We're going around the community, asking questions, trying to get to the bottom of these murders."

"You been talking to the neighbors, too?"

"A few."

"But why'd you ask me about my job? You running checks on everyone out here?"

Tillman hitched his uniform pants, drawing attention to the gun holster at the waistband. "I'm the one asking the questions here. Now, where were you on the night of September fifth?"

Melkie frowned. "Home. Where I always am." Again the right-eye tick.

"Anyone who can provide an alibi?" Tillman took out his notebook, pen poised.

"No. Listen, I know my rights. I told you I was home."

"Were you watching television that night?"

A crafty narrowing of Melkie's eyes told Tillman he wasn't going to fall into an easy trap of not remembering what shows played that day of the week.

"I drank some beer and dozed on and off that night."

"No girlfriend with you?"

"Don't got one."

"Why not?"

"None of your business," he snapped.

Tillman nodded at the corner of the room. "Why's your dog so interested in that spot?"

"He's a dog. How the hell should I know? Probably smelled a mouse or something."

"Mind if I take a look?"

"Hell, yeah, I mind! Look, I don't live in no fancy place. Every house 'round here's got mice."

"Calm down—"

"Go. I answered your questions. I ain't got nothin' else to say." He opened the door.

Tillman stepped in front of Melkie, inches from his face. He lowered his voice, just a hint of warning. "You hiding anything, I'll find out."

"You threatening me?" His hands fisted and the tick in his right eye went into overdrive.

Tillman shrugged at the outraged words. Good, he'd shaken him up a little. Maybe this guy had nothing to hide. Maybe. But if he did, Tillman would find out. "Enjoy the rest of your afternoon, Mr. Pellerin. Keep control of your dog as I exit your property."

Rebel bounded inside. Tillman scanned the yard as he slowly walked to the cruiser, searching for anything unusual, all the while conscious of Pellerin glaring from the doorway.

Before entering the car, Tillman punched in Dismukes's cell number. "Hey, Carl, I want to know everything there is to know on one Melkie Pellerin." Tillman spoke loudly so Melkie could hear every word. Inside the car, Tillman asked his deputy to see what they could dig up and put a tail on him for a few days.

Tillman watched Melkie from his rearview mirror until he turned onto County Road 143. His last image was of Melkie holding Rebel in his arms, eyes hooded and inscrutable. What a creep. The possibility of Pellerin, or a man like him, targeting and harassing Shelly filled him with loathing and anger. What if her stalker and the bayou killer were one and the same person? The sense of urgency in finding the killer intensified. This was personal now.

A few minutes later, he circled back and began knocking on the doors of some of Melkie's neighbors. At the fourth door down, he found someone home. It was opened by a man so skinny Tillman wondered if he might be eaten up with tuberculosis. The man coughed, sounding like his lungs were full of phlegm. Tillman resisted taking an instinctive step backward. "Billy Holcomb?" he asked.

"Yeah. Why you wanna know?" Billy's hand gripped the door's handle, as if deciding whether it would do any good to slam it shut on the law.

"Just asking a few questions about one of your neighbors. Do you know Melkie Pellerin?"

Billy relaxed and grinned, revealing a mouthful of unfortunate teeth. "Reckon I know him 'bout as well as anyone." He motioned to a rickety porch rocker. "Have a seat, Mr.—?"

"Sheriff Angier." Tillman sat gingerly atop the half-rotted chair.

Billy sat, reached inside dirty overalls and pulled out a pack of unfiltered Pall Malls.

"He's a strange bird, that one is. Keeps to his self most the time." Billy took a long drag, exhaling perfect smoke rings.

"You seen that dog of his?" He again continued without waiting for an answer. "We've had a few run-ins over that mutt. Every chance he gets, that dog goes after my Angel."

"Your wife?" Tillman asked.

"No, my cat," he said, opening the screen door where a fat orange tabby waddled out. Billy scooped her up. "She's a healthy one, my girl is."

"So I see." Tillman reached out to the tabby, who hissed and rumbled a growl of warning. Some angel. Billy laughed so hard it induced a coughing fit. "About Pellerin—" Tillman prodded.

"Like I said, we've had a few words. Guy's got a chip on his shoulder all the time. Don't talk to nobody unless it's some smart-ass remark."

"Ever seen him in a physical fight?"

Billy scratched the whiskers on his leathered face. "Nope."

"Does he have a girlfriend or entertain women at his house?"

"Only women I ever seen over there were his mom and two older sisters. Old lady died years ago and the sisters moved out long before that."

"Did you know them?"

Billie's lips curled and his eyes grew coy. "For the right price, anyone could get to know them." He slapped his knees and hooted, which brought on another coughing spasm.

"All three were prostitutes?" Tillman stilled, his mind absorbing the implication.

"You oughta talk to Sammie Broward." Billy pointed to a little pink house two doors down from Pellerin. "She used to be friends with the sisters."

Tillman nodded and stood. "You've been a big help."

Billy also stood, still holding the growling Angel. "If you take him away, make sure someone gets rid of that dog."

Tillman got up and headed over to the Broward house. A child finally answered and directed him to the back porch.

Tillman quickly went down the steps and headed around the side of the house.

"She going to jail?" the boy asked, sounding curious.

A young woman in jeans and a red midriff top raised her head. "Fucking kid," she mumbled. "Whatcha want?" She sat on a cement stoop and stared with eyes full of resentment.

"You're in no trouble," Tillman assured her. "Just a few quick questions. Heard you know Melkie Pellerin and his sisters."

"So?"

Tillman sighed. "The sooner you answer my questions, the sooner I'll leave."

Sammie shrugged. "Haven't seen Sissy or Mena in at least a couple years. They were pretty wild and left home soon as they could. Can't blame them with that freaky ma of theirs."

"Tell me why you think she was a freak." Damn, it

was humid; the September sun shone relentlessly. He eyed Sammie's beer longingly.

She took a long swallow and wiped her mouth on her arm. She threw a cigarette on the ground and lit another. "Mrs. P. was a whore. And a bitch, too. One day she slapped Mena so hard she had a bruise on her face for a week. All because Mena made too much noise when she got home from school. Three o'clock in the fucking afternoon and Mrs. P. still sleeping."

"How did she treat Melkie?"

Sammie scowled. "We hated that kid. Always wanting to tag along everywhere we went."

He tried again. "What was his relationship like with his mother?"

"Never saw them too much together. Their house wasn't much fun to hang around in." Sammie narrowed her eyes. "Who's in trouble?"

"Nobody. Yet."

"Right. You're just curious about the goings-on here in the Hollows." She took a deep drag. "My bet's on Melkie. Strange kid. Kept to himself, mostly."

"Maybe he had a reserved nature," Tillman said.

"And maybe he was psycho. Melkie had these 'killing jars' he used to trap and kill insects." Sammie stood and ground out the cigarette with her sandal. "We through now?"

Tillman withdrew a card. "You think of anything, or see anything unusual at the Pellerin household, call me."

Sammie went to the door, ignoring his outstretched hand with the card. "Do I look like a fucking snitch to you?" She went in, slamming the door behind her.

Chapter 7

They're coming to get you
You know it's true
And oh the price you'll pay
Forever, each and every day.

The smell of chlorine was getting to her. The graph
lines on the clients' progress charts blurred and Shelly
rubbed her eyes. After being unable to sleep last night
and the emotionally charged morning, she'd thrown herself into her job. It was way after hours, and everyone
had gone, but she shut the door of the cramped office
and changed into a swimsuit before gathering her things
in a tote and heading to the pool. She walked into the
shallow end, enjoying the water's liquid embrace as she
sank her body into its arms.

Heaven.

God, how she missed her ocean swims. The killer had
ruined that. She couldn't fathom the idea of another unexpected encounter. It didn't stop Jet and Lily, but they
hadn't seen the dead body. No, she wouldn't think of
that now. This time was hers alone.

Although the pool lacked the sea's vitality, Shelly
luxuriated in its warm comfort…so like a lover. She
floated, alone in the immense indoor pool. The back-

ground noise of the pump echoed like a lullaby. Only a few overhead fluorescent lights glowed and, through the high windows, Shelly made out the silhouette of a crescent moon. Maybe she should stay all night, sink to the bottom of the pool and sleep like a baby.

Shelly weightlessly relaxed mind and body, the water a cushion, soothing as a mother's embrace. She dozed, sinking into dreamless nether regions, floating in and out of awareness.

Wham. A loud metallic clang reverberated in the empty pool room.

Shelly jerked and sputtered in the deep end. Hadn't she locked all the doors after everyone left for the day? Heavy footsteps clonked ponderously down a hallway, coming closer.

Probably one of the staff coming back for something they forgot. Yet her body jazzed with adrenaline, mind racing in alarm. She had two options if the killer had traced her here—dive to the bottom of the pool and stay there, hiding, or run to the office and lock herself in.

At the creak of the pool room door, Shelly dove straight down and hugged the concrete bottom. Shit. She remembered her bag with her clothes and phone by the pool side. Maybe whoever it was would think it belonged to someone who had left earlier and forgot it.

The water pressure built in her ears; she could hear nothing from above. Shelly realized the insanity of staying under. If he was looking for her, he would see her in the pool. It wasn't like she was invisible. There was a third option, entice him to come in the water after her where she could have a fighting chance.

Shelly swam to the surface and raised her head like

a periscope on an espionage submarine confronting an enemy. A male figure stood at the end of the pool.

Brown pressed uniform, shiny star badge. Tillman. She let out a gigantic swoosh of relief.

"Shelly? Holy hell, woman, you about scared the shit out of me. I didn't know you were in the pool." Tillman's face held that curious expression of relief coupled with exasperation. He raked a hand through his sandy short-cropped hair.

"*I* scared *you?* I thought I'd locked all the doors." She swam to the shallow end where he stood.

"You did. I saw your car out front when I was driving home and decided to swing by. Jim Atkins was just leaving. Said to remind you to lock up again when you go."

The adrenaline left in one fell swoop and Shelly felt giddy as the tension left. It was so damn good to see Tillman. She couldn't help it, the man excited her like no one else had ever done.

He knelt down on one foot. "Any more phone calls?"

Shelly blinked. She'd been so relieved to see Tillman she almost forgot how mad she was at him.

Almost.

"Checking up on me?" She came out of the water and sidestepped his crouching body.

He rose and touched her arm. "No, making sure you're okay. I'm worried about you."

"I'm fine," she said coldly, averting her face. "You can go now."

"Damn it, Shelly, cut me some slack. I can't help feeling like you're holding something back."

"We all have our secrets."

"Not me," he denied, frowning. "What you see is what you get."

"Oh, really? If you're such an open book, why were you sneaking pictures of stuff in our house? Why didn't you question me more about it instead of acting like a jerk?"

He folded his arms across his chest. "I'm willing to let this matter drop. I'm in the middle of a murder investigation and don't have time to wonder anymore about your property."

"I'm not dropping anything," she countered, crossing her arms as he did. "You violated our privacy."

"I've already apologized for that. Besides, don't you have more important things to worry about? Like your stalker?" He looked around the vacant pool room and shook his head. "You shouldn't be out alone at night. At least not until the killer is found."

"Your concern is touching." Shelly jerked a towel off a poolside lounge chair and vigorously began rubbing it into her wet hair. She had to get rid of him. He was too close, too accessible in the empty, private area. Too much temptation. "Now go away and leave me alone."

Tillman's eyes narrowed as he watched her towel-dry her hair. "Is there something you haven't told me?"

She stilled. "What do you mean?"

"You were vague about the guy following you this morning. You felt threatened by him, yet you failed to get his license plate number or provide a detailed description."

"I was *scared.* I wasn't thinking clearly." What a colossal mistake this morning had been. Neither of them was any closer to knowing the killer's identity. At least she'd seen the photographs and realized the extent of Tillman's suspicious nature. She threw the towel back down on the chair.

He held up a hand. "Fair enough. I didn't come here to argue."

"Sure fooled me."

"Damn it, Shelly, I couldn't stop thinking about you today. Couldn't stop wondering if you might be in some kind of trouble."

His voice was rough with emotion and Shelly's own throat constricted involuntarily in response. Tillman cared. It was a start, something she could work with. Something in her face must have betrayed her emotions because he stepped closer, placed a finger under her chin and guided her face to his. "Let's start over."

"If we do, you have to promise to lay off my family. You can't come in our home and take pictures or question our lifestyle."

His gray eyes darkened with desire, just like last night.

He nodded. "Agreed." Tillman's gaze swept over her body and she closed her eyes, remembering the feel of his hard muscles and his hands cupping her ass, pressing her into his erection. She'd wanted him for too long to stop now.

As if sensing her weakness, Tillman rained soft kisses down on her forehead, her cheeks and the sweet spot on the side of her throat. "C'mon, baby." He gave a lopsided grin. "Hell, I've wanted you since the first time I laid eyes on you."

The admission warmed Shelly's heart, emboldened her courage. But did he really mean it? Had he fantasized about her like she had him? She took a deep breath. He obviously wanted her now. Maybe if she was careful and guarded her heart, she could enjoy an affair for as long as it lasted. She hadn't felt this way since college and she wasn't going to hold back with this man. Not physically, anyway. She smiled softly. "Okay, we'll start over." She pressed her body and lips tight against him, wetting the front of his uniform. "Hello," she said in a voice low and gruff with need, "my name is Shelly."

His eyes lit up. "Well, *h-e-l-l-o,* Shelly." His mouth descended again, this time meeting her lips.

Tillman felt warm and strong, a safe haven. At his low moan she corrected herself. He was an *exciting* haven.

This was what she needed, pure sex with no entanglements.

Tillman couldn't believe his luck. He hadn't expected a second chance or such a passionate reception. Shelly was so damn hot, so damn sweet. Her lips parted as he kissed her, her mouth wet and warm like her skin. He placed his hands on her lower back and squeezed, pulling Shelly hard against him, his hips pressed to hers. Their tongues met, hungry, greedy for more. Tillman ran a palm over her tight buttocks, smiling as he remembered the sight of her bathing suit slipping up her ass when he'd come to pick up Eddie. It had taken all his self-control not to grab her then, in this very room, in front of Eddie and the senior citizens.

His fingers pushed aside the wet spandex of her bathing suit to stroke her firm bottom, the way he'd been aching to do since he first saw her. Her soft gasp made him pause. Was he moving too fast? Shelly pulled him even closer, so close his erection throbbed against her abdomen.

Still not close enough. He lifted her up so that his arousal rubbed the apex between her thighs. Through a red haze of lust, he became aware that she was undoing his buckle.

"Do you think we're truly alone?" She hesitated, hands stilled on his belt.

"Jim's gone and I locked the door behind him." His voice was husky, strained. Tillman unzipped his pants and shucked them along with his shoes. When he turned back to Shelly she gave a mysterious smile and stepped away, one step lower in the pool. Her hands reached up and pulled down the shoulders of her bathing suit. She kept her eyes on his as she rolled it down over her hips and stepped out of it.

She was gloriously nude. Her breasts were full and milky-white in the dim light. His eyes traveled farther down to her dark patch of hair. Shelly crooked a finger. "Come play with me."

Tillman raced to get out of his shirt and briefs. When he stepped into the warm pool, Shelly backed up, enticing him deeper into the water. At his eager lunge forward, she laughed. "Catch me."

Three seconds later he did. "Come here, woman. There's no escaping me now." She shrieked playfully and splashed him as he scooped her to him, naked skin against naked skin.

Much better.

The playfulness died as he cupped her face in his hands. Shelly's green eyes widened, deepened, and he'd never seen anything sexier than the sparkle of water on her ivory skin. Tillman lowered his body, face level to her breast, and wrapped his tongue around a puckered nipple. He felt her legs wrap around his back and her fingers press against the back of his scalp, urging him to put more of her breast in his mouth. When he sucked, she moaned in pleasure. He inserted a finger past her swollen folds, into her core and felt a different kind of dampness, hot and ready for him. It had been far too long. Sex—the ultimate stress release.

Fever overtook him and all he could think about was being inside Shelly. He drew back his finger and slowly entered again. Tillman lost contact with his surroundings as he concentrated on the sensation of their intimate rhythm. He inhaled deeply, trying to make this last as long as possible. Hell, he wasn't a teenager on his first skinny-dipping experience and he wanted to pleasure Shelly first.

Her hands shifted from the back of his neck, pushed aside his hands on her and moved to cup his erection. Tillman gritted his teeth. This taking-his-time business wasn't going to work if she continued. He eased away.

"What's wrong?" she asked in that low, sexy voice of an aroused woman.

He clasped her hands and spun her body in a circle, letting the water form an eddy around them.

"Slowing the pace so I don't embarrass myself," he admitted.

She threw her head back and laughed. He marveled at how natural and free Shelly was tonight, as if the water had cleansed the inhibitions he'd sensed she had when they went to dinner. Even the sound of her voice was a sensual caress on his ears. He pulled her back against him and they kissed again, tender at first but quickly turning frantic. Shelly nibbled his ear. "Sheriff Angier, if you don't make me your prisoner immediately I'll have to file a complaint."

Tillman slipped an arm beneath her legs and picked

her up. "In that case, I hereby place you under arrest."
He carried her toward the pool steps.

"Where are you taking me, Sheriff?"

He paused, uncertain. He clearly hadn't thought this
all the way through. He was willing to have sex on the
cement floor if need be, but that was hardly the way he
wanted Shelly to remember their first time together. "Is
there a place we can go? I mean the water's great for
foreplay but maybe we need more privacy in case anyone comes back…." His voice trailed off. "We could go
to my cabin," he added, although he hoped she wouldn't
agree to that suggestion. He wanted her now.

Shelly slipped from his arm and took his hand. "I
can't wait that long. Follow me."

Curious, he let himself be led away, admiring her petite, shapely body. Firm in all the right places but curvy
like he appreciated. At the back of the pool room was a
small side door that she pushed open.

"This used to be a massage room."

"I had no idea the town of Bayou La Siryna afforded
such amenities." He looked around the tiny room, which
consisted of nothing more than shelves of white towels
on its back wall and a worn leather massage table in
the center. He picked up one of the towels and rubbed
Shelly down with it. When he was sure she was dried
off, he took the towel and rubbed it slowly across her
breasts, tantalizing her with its roughness as his mouth
nuzzled the side of her neck. "Don't want you to get
cold." He grabbed another towel and ran it through her
long, wet hair.

"I'm sure you'll keep me warm." She returned the
favor, getting a fresh towel and sweeping it over his

body. "Turn around and let me get your back," she ordered.

"Yes, ma'am."

She slapped his buttocks playfully. Tillman kissed her until they were both panting. She stepped away and found a white sheet with the towels and placed it on top of the massage table. She climbed up and lay on it.

He'd never seen such a glorious woman. Ever. Wet strands of honey-colored hair fanned the white sheets as she stretched out, eyes lit with feminine desire. Shelly raised her arms and he willingly did as she beckoned. He lowered his body over hers, leaned his elbows on the side of the table and hovered. "You're sure about this?"

She arched her hips upward. "Positive."

Thank God. He slid into her warm heat, watched her half-lidded eyes glaze in passion, her mouth part in a small O as her breasts rose and fell from sharp pants. He couldn't tear his eyes away as she whimpered her pleasure.

He withdrew and moved his mouth down her rib cage, pausing to lick a few drops of water that had pooled in her belly button before trailing his tongue over the salty, flawless skin of her flat abdomen. He didn't stop until his mouth and tongue were over the folds of her hot, moist core, tasting the very essence of her.

"Tillman."

Through the thick haze of lust he heard his name and looked up. Shelly beckoned him with her arms. "I want you back in me. Now."

Damn, if she wasn't the most beautiful and exciting woman he'd ever seen. Her blond hair curled in soft ringlets all the way down to her hips, framing fair skin that actually seemed to subtly sparkle like pixie dust. Her green eyes were the color of the deep ocean and just as mysterious. The curve of her hips and lushness of her breasts made him wild with need.

He slid back into her, as eager as she was for release. He rocked into her slowly, savoring the pulsating and throbbing of his swollen member. Shelly tried to quicken the pace but he held firm with slow, deliberate movements. Her fingers clutched his buttocks, frantically trying to push him to proceed faster, harder. At last, Shelly moaned and the sound clawed at his guts, made him lose the tight control he'd always maintained with other women. With Shelly, there was no holding back, and as her body spasmed and tightened beneath and around him, Tillman thrust into her deeply, furiously, lost in desire until he went over the edge and allowed his own release.

Afterward, as they lay together and he stroked the smooth, soft contours of her face and neck, he realized he didn't want the night to end. "Stay with me tonight," he whispered.

"At your cabin?"

At his nod, she lifted one of his hands and kissed the inside of his palm. "Yes."

Such a small gesture, yet his body tightened with desire again. Next time, she deserved the comfort of his bed. "Let's get moving."

They returned poolside, where he reluctantly put on his dampened uniform while Shelly pulled on the T-shirt and yoga pants that were in her tote bag.

Barefoot, no makeup and no artifice, Shelly was still a natural beauty. In her oversize Bama T-shirt, long blond hair drying in loose waves that cascaded to her hips, she grinned and patted his wet shirt. "Sorry about that. Hope you don't get cold."

"Don't be, it's raining outside and we'll both get wet anyway." But even if he had to go naked into the Antarctic, tonight was worth it. He looked around the room and grinned. "Don't think I'll ever view this place the same whenever I pick up Eddie." He glanced at his watch. It was 10:40 p.m. Eddie would be in bed by now, Mom would be either asleep or…indisposed.

They joined hands and strolled out of the building. Tillman tensed as a truck hurtled into the empty parking lot, bright headlights focused on the two of them. He pushed Shelly behind him and reached for his holster.

Shelly stepped up from behind him. "I think it's Jet."

A door opened and Jet spilled out. "Shelly! You okay?" Another door opened and a woman that could have been Shelly's twin emerged from the passenger side.

"I'm fine," she called out.

Jet stomped over. "Why the hell haven't you been answering your cell? Lily and I were scared shitless."

"Um, sorry. I was…busy."

Jet turned her anger toward him and scowled. "You again."

"Play nice," Shelly warned.

But he focused on the infamous Lily, who sauntered over, scooping a lock of her hair and draping it around her neck like a scarf. She had long hair like Shelly, but her eyes were blue instead of green and she was a good two to three inches shorter. Still, the resemblance between them was clear. She held out a perfectly manicured hand. "Tillman? Nice to finally meet you."

"Sorry," Shelly interrupted. "Tillman, this is my cousin Lily."

"Amazing." He shook Lily's hand.

"What's amazing?" Shelly asked with an edge of tartness.

"How much you two look alike." Tillman withdrew his hand and raised an eyebrow at Shelly, who looked a tad sheepish.

Lily shrugged. "Yeah, everybody says that. Looks like you two were having fun tonight." She winked at him.

"Why the hell is there a Sheriff's Office car parked in our yard?" Jet demanded.

"Shelly's been threatened, so I'm having one of my officers periodically check the area for signs of an intruder."

If he thought Jet would thank him, he was wrong. It was like she went out of her way to be nasty. "Have you got a problem with me?" Tillman asked, keeping his tone light. "Or is it that you don't like anybody from law enforcement?"

Jet's dark eyes flashed in challenge. "Only cops who run checks on me and take pictures of my personal property."

"Shouldn't matter if you've nothing to hide." He folded his arms, daring Jet to incriminate herself.

"*I* haven't been convicted of anything."

"True. But your boyfriend can't say the same."

He heard Shelly's quick intake of breath. Even in the darkness he could see her cheeks redden. "He's not my boyfriend," Jet said. Her shrill voice rang out in the night. "It's over. None of this is your fucking business, anyway."

Shelly tugged at his arm but Tillman stood his ground. So Shelly told them what happened. Good. Might as well get it all out in the open. "I've already apologized to Shelly. Can't blame me for being suspicious when I see thousands of dollars' worth of rare artifacts lying around."

"What are you saying? You think our stuff is stolen goods? All you crooked cops are the same. You're no different than your father."

Surprise rooted him to the spot.

"Wh-what are you saying, Jet?" Shelly whispered.

A soft hum arose, penetrating his disturbed thoughts. They all turned to Lily, the only seemingly calm one amongst them. He caught Shelly making a quick chop motion at her throat to Lily, who stopped humming abruptly.

"Only trying to take down the tension a notch," she said softly.

"That won't work with *me,*" Jet said in a clipped tone. "If the sheriff is accusing us of something, we have the right to know."

Tillman held up a hand. "Back it up. What does any of this have to do with my dad?"

"Because Sheriff Frank Angier was nothing but a low-down extortionist. Cops find something illegal, they figure they can turn a blind eye and make a little money under the table."

"Jet! Stop it." Shelly's eyes and mouth were wide with horror.

Jet's eyes softened a fraction. "Sorry, babe. It had to come out sooner or later with you seeing his son."

Tillman gritted his teeth to keep from losing it with Jet. "My father was a well-respected man in this community who served over thirty years as sheriff with no blemish of any kind on his record."

"He blackmailed Perry and me for years, right up until his heart attack."

"You're lying."

"Am I?" She regarded him coolly, challenging his beliefs.

Tillman briefly shut his eyes, picturing his dad. Always working so hard, always providing his family with a good life…therapy for Eddie, a private school for him and the opportunity for his wife to stay at home with the kids. *No!* Not his dad, he refused to believe it. For some reason, Shelly's cousin wanted to drive a wedge between them, that's all. He drew on his years of police training and experience to keep a calm demeanor. "That's pretty low, Jet. Making unfounded accusations against a dead man unable to defend his name. But for the sake of argument, what criminal activity were you and Perry involved in that you'd have to pay blackmail?"

"Your dad claimed we were stealing, running some kind of illegal black market for marine artifacts."

"Were you?"

"You expect me to admit guilt? Even if we were stealing—and I'm not saying we did—your dad should have arrested us instead of blackmailing us, right? That's what an honest cop would do." Jet compressed her lips, as if to stop from saying more, before storming back to the truck. Lily gave Shelly a quick, fierce hug and whispered something in her ear before joining Jet in the truck. Jet gunned the motor and they roared off.

"What did she say?"

Shelly's mouth twisted. "Something to the effect of 'family comes first.'"

Fury whipped through him. So they thought they could trash his father and Shelly was supposed to go along with them? "Had Jet told you this before about my father?"

"I swear, I didn't know anything about it. My cousins can be pretty closemouthed around me."

She reached out to touch him and he stepped back.

"Don't you believe me?"

"I don't know what to believe. But if there's one thing I won't tolerate it's someone lying to me."

Shelly's eyes narrowed. "I understand you're upset. But now I'm starting to get pissed, too. For the last time, I don't know anything about a blackmailing scheme."

His thoughts whirled in a jumble of anger and surprise. Best to find out the truth and say nothing more until he had proof one way or the other. "Maybe we should go our separate ways tonight," he said at last.

"Maybe we should," she agreed quietly.

Tillman watched as she got in her vehicle and drove off, already regretting his rash words. But something was weird about this family and he meant to find out what. As for Shelly…it might be over as fast as the passion had flared between them.

The realization left him cold. Somehow, the woman had got under his skin and he couldn't stop thinking about her, or worrying that she might be in danger.

Melkie squinted through the rain-splattered windshield. No mistaking it. An Englazia County Sheriff's car was parked in front of the mermaid house. The cops were on to him. First the visit this morning, and now this.

How? He gripped the steering wheel tightly, as if it

was one of those hookers' necks and he was choking the life out of it.

His first impulse was to hit the accelerator but he forced himself to drive the speed limit. *Never call attention to yourself.* He shouldn't have come out tonight. He left, expecting blue lights and sirens to flash behind him any moment. Melkie pulled Reb close and the dog licked his face. Despite his pet's devotion, each swish of the windshield wipers taunted Melkie.

You're screwed. You're screwed. You're screwed.

Chapter 8

Hide behind your dark sunglasses
While your son is taking classes
Don't think you're fooling anyone
You're one drink past the danger zone.

Eddie hesitated on the steps as two others walked in and splashed in the shallow end.

"These are your new pool buddies, Jason and Rick," Shelly explained.

Eddie stomped his feet a couple of times before plunging into the water waist-high. He pointed to the newcomers. "Out." He beat the water with his fists, splashing everybody. Jason and Rick mimicked his splashing and laughed.

Maybe this was a mistake. Shelly had thought Eddie was ready for a group session. She cast a quick glance in the bleachers. Portia Angier was tough to read behind sunglasses. She sat stiffly and swayed slightly, as if in time to some internal music. Jason's and Rick's moms were talking companionably. Their sons were part of a large Down syndrome class she held. She'd offered them free extra sessions as an experiment to help Eddie with his socialization skills.

Shelly quickly tossed a ball to Jason and Rick and

instructed them to play. She drew Eddie's attention, handing him a bright orange foam board. He grabbed it and kicked up a storm, occasionally casting backward glances at Jason and Rick.

Shelly moved on to a game of water basketball, Eddie's favorite. As the session wore on, Eddie started ignoring the others. Plenty good for the first group session, as he learned to either tolerate or accept their close proximity. Gradually, she would integrate their activities and draw Eddie into social play.

At precisely 3:00 p.m. she ended the session. Jason's and Rick's mothers collected their children, thanking Shelly for the free workout and promising to return the following week.

"You're welcome. Your sons were great," Shelly said, wrapping a towel around Eddie.

Two sets of hands clasped around her legs in a hug. "Thank you, Miss Shelly," they said in unison. Shelly rubbed the tops of their wet scalps, feeling a fierce tenderness for the boys.

Shelly ushered Eddie toward the locker room as Portia weaved her way over, clutching a Coach handbag in front of her body like a shield.

Shelly smiled. "Eddie did a good job in his first group session."

"His what?" Portia's trembling fingers pushed the sunglasses atop her coiffed hair.

"His first group session. Remember I told you about his long-term therapy goals?"

"Um, yes, of course. His goals."

A cloud of bourbon assaulted Shelly's nose.

"Thanks, Miss…?" Portia waved a hand, evidently trying to pull her name out of the air.

"Shelly."

"Shelleee. Pretty name. Shelleee." The words slurred.

A chill of dread ran up Shelly's spine. The woman was stinking drunk. Three in the afternoon, about to drive her son home, and she was smashed. She remembered Tillman's cryptic words—*she can't cope, I had to help out my mom,* the many afternoons Tillman fetched Eddie because his mom had a headache.

Portia was an alcoholic.

"Is Tillman coming to pick y'all up?" Shelly asked hopefully.

"No." She fumbled through the oversize purse, dropping her keys and wallet on the wet cement. Coins scattered everywhere. "Oh, dear. Look what I've done." She dropped to her knees and began picking up the spilled contents.

Shelly's mind whirled. She pictured the crashed shell of her parents' car after being hit by a drunk driver and the state trooper who'd shown up at her college dorm one perfectly normal fall afternoon with the news that they were both dead. No way she would stand by and let this woman jeopardize Eddie's life.

"Let me help you." Shelly leaned over, scooped up the keys and hurried to her tote bag that held the cell.

"Hey, Shelleee, help me get this up."

"Just a minute," she called over her shoulder. Retrieving her cell, Shelly speed-dialed Tillman's private number, which he'd entered for her on their first date, hoping he'd take her call even after the scene last night. Jet's revelation had nothing to do with her and Tillman had simply lashed out because of hurt and surprise. Now that she'd cooled off from the heat of the moment, she could hardly blame him for being upset.

"The number you are trying to call is not in service at—" Crap. She hit the number for his office but he wasn't in. She clutched Portia's keys as the dispatcher switched her to a deputy.

"Carl Dismukes. May I help you?"

"This is Shelly Connors. I need to speak to Tillman. Immediately."

"He's out of the office. Is there a problem I can help you with?"

Dismukes had a soft, grandfatherly kind of voice and she was tempted to tell him. Shelly wavered but decided against it. She didn't want to embarrass him in front of his employees. "No. Just have him call me as soon as possible."

What to do? The Water Babes and Buoys were filing in. She didn't want to cause a scene.

That left one option. Call Lily. Her cousin would help her out, even if it indirectly was for Tillman. Besides, when she'd returned home last night, upset, Lily and Jet assumed she had sided with them against Tillman.

Shelly was amazed that she was willing to risk her family's wrath by continuing to see Tillman. If he would have her. Despite her best effort to guard her heart and keep their relationship confined to the physical realm, Tillman had touched more than her body last night. His tender yet passionate lovemaking had touched her heart.

Shelly reined in her errant thoughts and phoned Lily at the Mermaid's Hair Lair and they worked out a plan. All she had to do now was stall Eddie's mom for five minutes. Shelly dropped the car keys in her tote and returned to Portia, still fumbling with the purse spillage.

They spent a couple of minutes collecting all her

paraphernalia. Portia stood, still a bit wobbly. "Where's Eddie?" she asked.

"I'll go check on him." Shelly went to the lockers, glad for an excuse to get away. As she passed Lurlene Elmore, Shelly asked her to get the class started on their warm-ups.

Eddie exited the locker room and Shelly stepped in front, blocking his view of his mom. "Hey, Eddie, good job in class today." They high-fived. "You deserve a treat." She led him to the vending area. "Pick any drink and snack." Shelly dug out some change and handed it to him while keeping an eye on the window for Lily's car to pull into the parking lot. *Hurry up.*

A loud clank of a soda can as it dropped, and Eddie moved on to the snack machines. He frowned at the selection and looked at her questioningly. "Cap'n Crunch?"

"No. How about some potato chips?"

He shrugged. "Okay."

Selections over, she sat on the uncomfortable wooden bench and patted the empty space next to her. "Have a seat while we wait for your mom."

Once Eddie popped the soda lid and stuffed some chips in his mouth, Shelly got up and peeked around the corner. Portia was scanning the pool area, frowning. The Water Babes and Buoys mimicked Lurlene's series of warm-up movements. Portia approached Lurlene and leaned over the poolside, talking. Lurlene pointed in her direction and Portia caught Shelly staring at her. She frowned and stood, tugging at her elegant silk blouse. She wobbled a bit and Shelly sighed in relief when she didn't fall in the pool. Portia was the kind of woman who would blame the YMCA for her fall and charge them a hefty bill for ruined clothing.

"All done." Eddie stood and searched for a trash can.

"That quick?" She pulled out more change. "Here, get something else."

Portia was bearing down on them. Another quick glance at the parking lot showed Lily hadn't made it. She needed to stall Portia a bit longer.

"Mrs. Angier." She smiled brightly as Eddie's mom halted in front of her. "We're having a little celebration for Eddie's good work. How about I get you a cup of coffee?"

"No, thank you." The bourbon breath was still strong. "We are ready to leave." She motioned to Eddie. "Let's go."

"But…I thought you couldn't find your keys?"

"I keep a spare zipped inside an inner pocket of my purse." She swayed in her three-inch high heels. "Don't know why I forgot about that."

Because you are stinking drunk. At least Portia wasn't slurring her words now. Perhaps she was coming around. But Shelly still couldn't let her get behind the wheels of a car. Time to improvise another lie. Maybe she was as conniving as Jet and Lily. The lies came too easy.

"Guess Tillman forgot to tell you. My cousin's giving Eddie a complimentary haircut today."

"Now?" Portia asked uncertainly. "I don't—"

Eddie yelled, "No cut!" and clasped his hands on top of his head, as if warding off a great evil.

"You're upsetting him. We're going now."

Shelly followed behind them helplessly.

"Where are you going, Shelly?" Lurlene called from the pool.

Portia quickened her steps, Eddie in tow.

Shelly willed her cell to ring. *C'mon, Tillman, where are you?* They were out the door now. Portia's high heels sank in the pebbled surface of the parking lot. Shelly didn't have on sunglasses and the sun felt like a laser on her pupils. Although not as sensitive to sunlight as her cousins, her mermaid eyes were designed more for the dark, murky sea than the midday sun.

Lily's red Audi S4 roared into the lot before coming to a screeching halt beside them.

"Here's Lily now for Eddie," Shelly said with brittle brightness.

Eddie dropped his gym bag and slapped his hands on top of his head again. "No cut," he said firmly.

Lily exited the Audi, hair blowing in the breeze, looking angelic as usual. She went straight to Eddie, humming a little tune.

His eyes widened, as fascinated with Lily as every other man in this town. Slowly, he lowered his hands to his sides.

Shelly was relieved Lily didn't try to shake his hand. Eddie cringed at contact from strangers.

Lily hummed again, slowly circling Eddie. "No major haircut, Eddie. I'm just going to snip a few of the scraggly ends off."

"Now wait a minute—" Portia began.

"Did you know the ice cream store is next to my shop?" Lily continued, as if Portia hadn't spoken. "What kind of ice cream do you like?"

"'Nilla."

Lily hummed a few more notes. "Tell you what, Eddie. I'm going to take you to my shop for a little cut and then you and I will get us some 'nilla ice cream.

That sound good?" Lily opened the car door and Eddie hopped in.

Beneath her dark shades, Lily winked at Shelly and climbed into the car beside Eddie.

Lily was going to leave Portia behind. Shelly eyed Eddie's mom, dressed in a peach linen pantsuit and blond hair coifed in a precise shoulder-length bob. But instead of the regal effect she sought, Portia looked vulnerable and awkward, like a child playing dress-up. They had to stop her from hurting herself or others. This was Tillman and Eddie's mother after all.

"Wait."

Lily paused.

"Don't you think Mrs. Angier could benefit from a trim?"

Lily sighed. "I'm really busy right now. I left Jet with two of my customers waiting for their color to develop."

"Please." Shelly pleaded with her eyes.

Lily sighed again. "Hop in, Mrs. Angier."

Portia stiffened beside Shelly. "I will not. I don't know who you girls think you are, but—"

Shelly gently laid a hand on Portia's shoulder. "Tillman will be so disappointed if you don't," she lied. "He arranged this as a surprise for both of you."

A flash of uncertainty danced in Portia's dark gray eyes, so like Tillman's. "Then I guess I should." She opened the back door and got in, her back ramrod-straight, eyes staring straight ahead, purse in her lap.

Shelly had a feeling Portia knew she was being bamboozled. Lily turned on the radio and started singing.

"Be there as soon as this class is over," Shelly promised. She headed back to the pool with a sinking heart, wondering how upset Tillman was going to be when he found out what she'd done. First, Jet had probably destroyed the illusion of the father he admired and now Shelly had exposed his mom's drinking. As maddening as he was, she cared about him.

More than she wanted to admit.

As soon as Tillman crossed over the county line, his cell went off. He checked his messages and saw Shelly's call. His breath quickened. Had she met her stalker again? Surely, if that was it, she'd call the police. He grimaced. This was probably about last night and he had no idea what to say except that he wanted—no, *needed*—to see her again. Damn those irritating cousins of Shelly's. He'd always imagined his family would be the one to screw up a relationship and not the other way around.

He wasn't sure how he felt about Jet's accusation, other than confused. Later today, he planned to examine his father's records and see if he could find anything to substantiate Jet's claim.

The sinking feeling of dread in his stomach told him it might be true. He knew the sheriff's salary. A decent amount, but hardly enough to keep up the kind of lifestyle of his youth. He'd always assumed Mom's rich relatives brought money into the family to supplement Dad's income.

He returned Shelly's call. It took almost five rings before she answered, out of breath. He heard the echo of splashing water in the background.

"Are you okay?"

"Yes." She hesitated a beat. "Just wanted to let you know your mom and Eddie are at the shop with Lily.

Eddie's getting a cut, and your mom's getting a complimentary one, too."

Irritation snapped through his temples—he'd been worried Shelly was in serious trouble. "I thought there was something wrong, you calling in the middle of the day like this."

"Well...the thing is, you need to get down there. Your mom isn't in any condition to drive. I...um...created a stalling tactic, hoping you could give them a lift home. Her town car is still in the parking lot at the Y."

Shit. "I'm on my way," he said tersely. "How long have they been over there?"

"About twenty minutes."

"Good deal. I'll let you get back to work." Tillman hung up and pounded the steering wheel. Mom was getting worse. He glanced at his watch. Christ, it was only 3:25 p.m. It was one thing if she wanted to drink herself to death, but damn if he'd let anything happen to Eddie.

He hit the accelerator. Less than ten minutes later, he entered the beauty salon.

The smell of ammonia hit him. A crowd of old ladies, pink perm rods covering their heads like helmets, dropped their magazines and stared at him, a foreigner in a strange land. Mom was under one of the dryers, eyes closed. Eddie was spinning in a beauty chair, ice cream dribbling down his shirt. Tillman headed toward him.

"Nice haircut," he said.

"All done," Eddie informed him.

Tillman turned to Lily. "He give you any trouble?"

"He's been a doll," Lily assured him.

He had to know. "How did you get him to keep still? I cut his hair at home with barber scissors and he has a fit whenever a single piece of hair gets on him. Then he has to head straight to the shower and rinse it off."

"Shower," Eddie said, stuffing the last of the ice cream cone in his mouth.

"I washed him in the sink area. He took off his shirt and I gave him a good rinsing down."

Lily hummed. Eddie stopped twirling and listened. It was pretty damn captivating somehow.

Out of the corner of his eye, Tillman saw Jet rinsing someone's hair. She gave him a frosty glare.

Fine. He wasn't looking to make conversation either. At least not until he'd checked out her allegation.

"You ready to go, Eddie?"

He jumped from the chair and gathered his backpack. Tillman went to his mom and turned off the dryer switch. "Time to go," he announced curtly.

"But my hair is still damp."

"Don't care." Tillman fought to keep his voice civil. No sense creating a scene, if she hadn't caused one already.

Lily began taking out the foam rollers in his mother's hair, pocketing them in a pink apron. "Dry enough. All you needed were some soft waves." She removed the last roller and ran her fingers through Portia's hair.

Portia crooked her neck to the side. "It's different," she said, as if trying to decide if she liked it. "It's... looser."

Tillman thought it looked better than the stiff way she usually wore it. But he was in no mood to bestow compliments on her today.

Jet sauntered past him with a basket of white towels, a challenging glint in her dark eyes. Tillman's hands fisted by his sides. He supposed he should thank them for the interference, but his throat closed up. Damn Mom for putting him in this humiliating position. He stiffly nodded to Jet and Lily on the way out.

Tillman leaned back in his desk, staring hard at the evidence before him. Last night he'd collected IRS income tax forms from previous years and gone through them today with a critical eye. For nearly five years, Dad had claimed over fifty thousand dollars in "consulting" fees.

Much as he didn't want to drag anybody else into it, he had to know. He rang his deputy.

Carl meandered in a good ten minutes later. "What's up, son?" His hands, scarred with nicks and knife cuts, held a small wooden carving, which he set on the desk's blotter. Tillman picked it up and dropped it into a collection of several dozen others in a plastic bag. Next time he was in Mobile, he'd drop off the donation.

He stared at his deputy, a man he'd known all his life and that had been a loyal friend of his father's. Carl was always unruffled, a result, he claimed, of his frequent deep-sea fishing trips. He could trust Carl to help him get to the bottom of Jet's blackmailing claim. "Do you know of any kind of consulting work Dad did in the last five years before he died?"

Carl ran a large bony hand through a shock of white hair. "No. Can't say I do. Why do you ask?"

Tillman tapped the IRS forms by the computer. "Because he claimed a little over fifty thousand dollars' income for consulting work."

Carl whistled. "Never mentioned nothing like that to me."

"Get me the financial papers so I can review expenditures from this office. Maybe the county set up some special compensation for him in lieu of an official pay raise."

Carl shook his head. "Nope. Even that would require a special vote by the city council. Everything's an open book in that regard."

Tillman's heart sank. But he would check into every possibility. He owed Dad that much. "I want to review those papers."

"Will do." Carl's homely face creased. "There's got to be an explanation. Your dad was one of the finest, most honest men I've ever met."

"That's what I thought. Look, I'd appreciate it if you kept this information between us."

"Of course. I'm sure it's nothing. I'd forget about it if I were you."

"I have to know." Tillman shoved the offensive papers aside. "Anything interesting turn up on the background interviews for Pellerin?"

"Nothing exciting. He dropped out of high school in the tenth grade. Teachers described him as average, except in biology, where he excelled, even winning several science fair awards for insect projects."

Tillman recalled the mountings on Pellerin's wall. "Wonder why he didn't finish high school. Any reason given?"

"They suspect it was because he couldn't get along with others. He was bullied during middle school. By high school, his peers pretty much ignored him. He sat in the back of the room, never talking or participating in the usual teenage activities like football and dating."

"What about after he left school? Did he get along with coworkers?"

"No, it was pretty much like school. He's worked a series of jobs. Bosses and coworkers described him as a quick learner and a hard worker, but had trouble taking criticism or being told what to do, especially from women."

Tillman nodded. "He's smart but in a crafty way. My impression is that everything has to be on his own terms, preferably with him having control. What about the tail we put on Pellerin?"

"Langham followed him last night. He wandered around some of the county back roads for almost an hour, not stopping anywhere before returning home."

"Let's keep a record of what streets he travels on, in case it becomes important later. Did he go past Murrell's Point?"

"Returning to the scene of the crime?" Carl asked. "No. Actually, Langham gave me a summary of his activity." He pulled out a paper from his notepad and handed it to Tillman.

Tillman read it over until he saw Pendarvis Road. Where Shelly lived. Son of a bitch, had he been searching for a new victim? The thought of Shelly so close to danger made his skin crawl. And he couldn't erase the images of Pellerin's morbid collection of dead insects. Maybe it wasn't too much of a leap to think Pellerin's obsession with the dead, coupled with his control issues and contempt for women, made him a valid suspect.

Lily swiped her perfect lips with cotton-candy-pink lip gloss.

"Why bother with makeup when we're going to train for the games?" Jet asked. "We're out to build muscle, not catch a guy."

"I'm only exercising my vocal cords for the singing competition, not trying to outswim the other mermaids like you."

For once, Shelly wasn't envious of their annual pilgrimage to the mermaids' Poseidon Games without her. As a hybrid, she wasn't permitted to enter the full-blooded mer-kingdom located in the remote South Pacific. No way could she compete with the others, but she'd love to visit the undersea mermaid castles, perhaps meet some of her mother's kin. But this year, the danger kept Shelly from the usual wistful longing as the games drew near.

"Be careful." Shelly bit her lip. She couldn't help worrying. Each time she thought she had her fear under control, it crept up and refused to be silenced.

"We're fine together." Jet took a swig from her water bottle. "Join us—it'll help you get over this fear."

"Not this time. I'll start supper and do some cleaning while you're gone."

"Pussy," Jet said.

"Leave her alone, Jet. She'll swim again when she's ready."

Shelly shot Lily a grateful look. Once Tillman nailed the guy, she could let the fear go.

Tillman. She hadn't heard from him since the phone call yesterday. *He's busy. He's working a homicide. He'll call you later.*

Maybe when her cousins left she'd drink a glass of wine and get up the nerve to call him. She refused to believe the relationship was sunk just as it started. She'd been upset the other night when he didn't immediately believe she knew nothing about his father. She should have realized he was in shock over the news. And to top it off, she'd had to call him to pick up his drunk mother. Poor guy was probably embarrassed. She would explain to Tillman that he shouldn't be. Every family had its problems and she admired him for his loyalty and sense of duty.

"You never did tell us—" Lily laid the lip gloss on the mahogany foyer table. "Did your sheriff say what's going on with the murder investigation?"

"Only that they had some leads and he would have the killer soon."

Jet's face fell. "You couldn't get anything more specific?"

"If you hadn't showed your butt that night I would have had an opportunity."

A tiny wrinkle appeared on Lily's brow. "Dating a cop could backfire."

Jet grabbed Lily's arm and they headed outside.

"Dump him," Jet advised, banging the door shut behind her.

Shelly gazed at the shut door. Dump him? As if Jet had a right to give advice. She and Perry were physically separated, but Jet had never gotten over the black-hearted pirate, no matter how much she denied it.

Neither had the right to forbid anything. Shelly's anger rose, quick and hot, fed up with Jet's bossiness. She ran to the door, opened it and spied the pale outline of her cousins in the darkness as they were entering the shed hiding their portal.

"Don't tell me who to dump. You're the one who sulks around here waiting for someone who's never coming back."

Jet stiffened and turned. Lily held a hand to her mouth while Jet's fists curled at her sides.

Oh, no. What had she done? They never mentioned Perry in front of Jet. The first six months Jet had returned, alone, from her last shipwreck expedition had been a dark time. Jet had hardly eaten, never swam, and swung from spending days in bed to going on exercise splurges where she would run for miles or lift weights for hours.

Jet wouldn't say what happened until a year later. After too many tequilas late one night, she told them Perry had betrayed her in the worst possible way. Try as they might, Jet refused to ever speak his name or give more details.

And now Shelly had dredged it all up again.

She ran toward Jet, contrite. "I'm sorry. I had no right to bring him up."

"Do I ever bring up that ex-boyfriend of yours from college who broke your heart?"

Lily came between them. "C'mon, y'all." Her voice was light and melodic. "One human male is the same as the next. Do like I do, have your fun and then call it quits."

Jet and Shelly stared wordlessly at each other. Shelly was astonished to discover the two of them were more alike than Lily. Lily had never fallen in love and gotten hurt. Jet was vulnerable under that tough exterior while Lily's siren nature kept her invulnerable.

"Forget it." Jet spun on her heels and strode off.

"She'll cool down after her swim," Lily assured Shelly. "You know how she is."

Shelly returned inside and aimlessly paced the rooms, picking up objects and putting them back down. No word from Tillman, and now she'd pissed off one of the two people she had left in the world. Her cousins had generously let her in their home, at a time when Shelly was reeling from her bad breakup and the death of her parents.

Shelly flopped on the couch and turned on the television. Two mind-numbing sitcoms later, she got off the couch, disgusted with the self-pity.

The sound of exploding glass froze her. Shards of glass rained across her hair and cheeks like sleet. Something slimy thumped against her chest and slid to her feet. Shelly's gaze took in the gaping hole at the front window, before dropping downward. In the TV's flickering light, scales shimmered on an eighteen-inch Spanish mackerel.

The fish was mutilated. Its eyes had been cut from the sockets and guts spilled out from a knife embedded in the middle of its body. Pinned to the knife was a white sheet of blood and slime-stained paper.

Shelly saw it, but her mind refused to accept it as real. Her breath caught in her chest as her gaze jerked to the window. Through the sheer curtain was the pale outline of a human body.

The killer was out there, watching.

Shelly ran to the side of the window, away from his line of vision. *Get the gun.* In the foyer she withdrew the .32 caliber handgun stored in the top drawer of the entry table. It was more a collector's piece than a weapon, but it was loaded. She killed the lights and stood in the dark, heart skittering. The silence roared in her ears like pounding waves during a storm at sea.

She waited, ears strained for the faintest of noises. Nothing.

When she couldn't stand it any longer, Shelly crawled over broken glass back into the living room, the television providing enough light to spot the fish on the floor. She grabbed its slimy body and pulled it to her chest.

Oh, shit. Were the doors locked? She went to the front one. Locked. But she didn't remember locking the back door after Jet and Lily left. Grateful for her night vision, Shelly crept to the back and saw she had locked it earlier. She fled to the bathroom and locked herself in. Careful not to leave fingerprints on the knife or note, Shelly used a washcloth to dislodge the cheap switchblade knife and read the note.

I know what you are. You have something that belongs to me. I'll email in 48 hours for instructions on where to meet. You better bring it, bitch. Next time it's a knife through your fucking heart.

An odd noise cut through the low drone of the TV, a scraping and crunching sound followed by a creak from the wooden floorboards.

Shelly flipped off the bathroom light. Her breath came in painful jags that burned her throat, yet she couldn't suck down enough oxygen. The air pressed in around her and her vision blackened along the periphery until only the note remained visible. The black ink of the message burned her retinas like striking mamba snakes.

The killer was inside. Deep down, she had known this moment would come, had been expecting it ever since the night she'd caught him dumping a body. Footsteps sounded in the kitchen from rubber-bottomed shoes that slightly squeaked on the tile.

Closer now, he was getting closer.

Shelly pressed her back against the cold marble wall behind the door and raised the gun, finger on the trigger. If he entered, she would get the first shot off. Through the closed door she heard him stumble against the kitchen table. He was within a few feet of her hiding place.

She held her breath as seconds passed in silence. A slight movement from below caught her eye.

The brass doorknob turned.

This was it.

Something bumped against the door and the handle rattled as the killer tried to force his way in. She debated shooting him through the thick door, but was afraid the bullet wouldn't penetrate and might ricochet.

Wait. If he got in, she'd shoot.

Silence again descended but Shelly sensed him on the other side. Any moment now the door would crash.

"I know you're in there," he whispered. His voice was low and gravelly, the same voice from the earlier phone call. "Come on out. I won't hurt you." He sounded calm, as if cajoling a lover after a spat or coaxing a frightened child from under a bed.

She bit her lip, careful not to moan or betray her position. Her arms trembled from the strain of holding the gun at chest level.

A sudden crashing noise on the other side almost made her drop the gun. His fists battered the door with a steady pounding.

"Bitch! You fucking bitch."

His shrill scream made her clammy and nauseous. He drew in deep, ragged breaths, as if trying to regain control of his rage. When he spoke again, his voice shook with suppressed emotion.

"You better give me the knife next time. Because if you don't I'm going to get you when you least expect it." He paused. "You hear me, you fucking freak? You and your sister."

He slammed his fist against the door one last time and she heard retreating footsteps. The killer either threw or ran into something and the sound of crashing glass exploded from the living room.

Shelly lowered the gun as her body shook uncontrollably with surprise and relief. Not only had she put herself in danger, her cousins were also at risk. They were the only family she had left in the world and she had done this to them.

An even worse thought crept inside her mind. What if the killer was still outside the house and saw them returning from their swim? She had to warn them.

Resolutely, Shelly inched open the bathroom door. She refused to be reduced to a cowering prisoner in her own bathroom.

Gun in hand, she went outside, eyes and ears on alert. The shed seemed a mile away instead of a few yards. *Just put one foot in front of the other.*

A silly song from elementary school flashed through her brain and Shelly sang, "Row, row, row your boat," as if she was in kindergarten, drowning out her fear of the bogeyman. Her wobbly off-pitch alto had nothing going for it except volume, a childhood magical fallback to ward off danger. If the killer was out there, he was laughing his ass off right about now.

The sudden hoot of an owl interrupted the melody. Shelly froze, but heard nothing over the roaring of blood in her ears. "Row, row, row your boat," she sang even louder. "Merrily, merrily—" She paused at the shed door. What if he was inside waiting? "Merrily, merrily. Life is but a dream."

Shelly flung the door open and stood back, gun drawn, waiting for a dark shadow to emerge and attack. She entered cautiously, flipped on the light switch and bolted the door behind her. Quickly disrobing, she placed the gun under her discarded clothes and dove into the sea portal, fishtailing down the cave's narrow tunnel until she broke free to the wide expanse of the underwater world.

In spite of her fear, the transformation from human to mermaid felt damn good. The salty sea enveloped her body, and its wet comfort set every cell tingling and dancing. But there was a new wariness, too. Even here. The killer was with her no matter where she tried to escape.

"Jet? Lily?" Shelly pushed the words out of her lungs, sent them bubbling through the water's mass.

"Shelly—we're close," Jet answered. "Something wrong?"

"The killer's been here again. He got inside the house. Come home."

"Coming," Jet said. "Five minutes."

Shelly tried to take comfort in the water while waiting. But instead of relaxing, she lay on a bed of sand and stared at the ocean's surface. The waning coral moon rippled and shimmered over a patch of water as she waited for the sound of a boat engine to explode onto the serene waterscape, dumping another dead human into her open arms.

A disturbance in the sound waves and the trembling against her sensitive tail fin preceded her cousins' arrival. Jet appeared first, her face fiercer than when on land. She gripped a knife, at the ready. "Where is he?"

"Gone. I hope. Had to warn you before you came through the portal."

"You hurt?" Jet swam around her, searching for injuries.

Lily's long hair streamed unexpectedly in Shelly's face, blue eyes blazing.

"Shelly's okay," Jet said.

Lily laid a cold, clammy hand on Shelly's shoulder. "Let's go home. Whatever happens, we'll face it together."

They entered the house cautiously and systematically went room by room searching for the killer. Shelly looked under every bed, opened every closet.… Nothing.

"I wonder why he left without making you give him the knife," Jet said.

Or killed me, Shelly silently added. "That does it," she told them. "I'm going to see Tillman again. This time I'll describe the killer and tell him I was a witness."

Jet grabbed her arm. "You can't. You start blabbing and you put *all* of us in danger."

"I have to go with Jet on this one," Lily said. "Think of all the mermaids—"

"I'm nothing but a TRAB—a traitor baby—to other mermaids." Shelly jerked her arm away from Jet. "I'm not *good enough* for your pure race. I'm not welcome in your mermaid world." The bitter words tumbled out. "I'm a big fat nothing."

"That's not true." Lily stroked Shelly's hair. "We don't hold your human side against you. Can't you keep quiet for us? Your cousins?"

Shelly swallowed past the lump in her throat. "I'll

do what I can to protect you. But I have to make things right and help Tillman stop the killings."

Jet's dark eyes glistened like burning obsidian. "In other words, you choose a human over us, your mermaid family. Just like your mother did."

"Leave Mom out of this," Shelly snapped. "This is different and you know it."

"I'm outta here." Jet turned abruptly away.

"Think about it carefully," Lily said. "Look how unhappy your mother ended up. One day you will have to choose between our worlds. Remember *we're* your family. Not Tillman."

Lily left. Shelly hugged her arms around her waist and realized she'd already made her decision. No doubt she'd be unhappier than Mom, who'd had a man who loved her, at least in the beginning. But if she didn't pursue her feelings for Tillman, she might regret it forever. And if anyone could catch the killer, Tillman had the skill and the resources to do so. They didn't.

No matter what Shelly chose, she'd never fully belong on land or at sea.

Chapter 9

On the wall, pinned and mounted
Specimens all tagged and counted
Yet hidden in a secret cache
The eyes, they have a special place.

Someone was following him. A blue sedan with tinted windows had been on his tail all morning. *Damn, damn, damn.* Sweat popped out on his forehead and his head spun. Air. He needed air. Melkie turned the AC on high and sucked in the cold blast like a drowning person surfacing for oxygen. Rebel stuck his nose to the vent, competing for its bracing, cool draft.

Coward.

He'd wimped out last night, skittish that the cop car he'd dodged would show up any second. He should keep driving all the way to Mexico. Leave this stinking hellhole with its perpetual odor of dead fish rotting in swamp water. Nothing tied him here. No friends, no job and if he never saw one of his slutty sisters again, that would suit him fine. Melkie daydreamed about starting over. Him and Reb, living on the outskirts of some hot, dusty hacienda. Couldn't be hotter or more miserable than this Alabama bayou. And if they made fun of him and his dog, at least he wouldn't understand the jabbering.

Reality set in. He had no money to start over. It always came down to that. Ten years after her death, and Mom was still screwing him. At least the ramshackle house she'd left provided a rent-free existence. Without it, he'd be homeless.

Better the streets than in prison, the paranoid voice in his head taunted. *You gonna live a life of crime, you should be robbing for money and not sticking whores.*

Melkie checked the rearview mirror. The sedan followed behind at a discreet distance. He wondered if the mermaid reported his break-in last night. Were the cops trying to keep hidden or were they fucking with his mind on purpose? Just messing with him, Melkie decided. If they had anything concrete, he'd be facedown in the dirt in handcuffs. He felt marginally better.

"Wanna treat, ol' Reb?" Melkie abruptly turned into the hamburger shack. If he was going down, he'd do it drinking a chocolate milk shake and with Rebel gobbling a cheeseburger. No such luxuries in prison or a hacienda. He dug out a thin wallet from the back pocket of his faded jeans and scraped together change from the console. Yep, his new motto should be Live Big or Bust. This was life on the edge in the bayou.

Rebel drooled as the drive-through window girl handed over the wrapped meat with an expression of amused disgust, as if she was some beauty queen. Why he ought to choke some humility in her, make her... Melkie suppressed the thought, glancing at the sedan parked on the side of the lot, motor running.

The first slurp of the chocolate shake restored a little cheer. Time for some fun with the mystery man behind the tinted windows. Melkie went to the nearest convenience shop and made his purchase. Coming out, he went to the sedan idling nearby and rapped on the window. It mechanically lowered, revealing a thirty-something male wearing dark sunglasses and a brown uniform. Melkie shoved a pack of glazed doughnuts at him.

"Just in case you're hungry," he said with a smirk, walking away. He wanted the cops to know he was onto them. They were so stupid they couldn't find a biscuit in a gravy bowl.

"Hey, you," the cop yelled. "You forgot my coffee."

Melkie tipped his baseball hat at the officer—as if this was all a big joke.

He continued home. Melkie pulled into his driveway, refusing to give the cop the satisfaction of looking back. But once inside, he peered through the window. The sedan had parked about twenty yards down the road. Poor sucker must be blistering in the heat. The thought cheered Melkie as he sucked the last of the milk shake.

Maybe this was a sign that he needed to move on from his past. There wouldn't be much to pack up. Mainly his insect collections and his special prizes cached under the den floorboards.

His prizes. Melkie hadn't fondled them for days. He went to the far right corner of the den and lifted the rotted floorboard, pulling out several pint-size Mason jars.

Sets of eyeballs, preserved in formaldehyde, stared back at him. Rebel pawed at a jar.

"Get back, boy," Melkie growled. Rebel scooted backward.

The murky liquid held the eyeballs in suspension like

a lava lamp. Melkie picked up each jar and twirled it, remembering how he came by each.

"I want those glowing ones," he said aloud. "The freaky ones that light up and swirl." If—no, *when*—he captured the mermaid he'd also preserve that glittery fish fin he'd glimpsed before she'd disappeared into the sea. His collection wouldn't be complete without it.

He retrieved two more Mason jars from the secret niche. One held the mermaid's rings and necklaces, a separate one held the coins. He sifted through the gold and silver disks, convinced he was holding booty from sunken shipwrecks. Too bad he couldn't sell it now.

Later. He had to be patient, wait it out a bit. No more hooker-trawling nights until Alabama was hundreds of miles behind.

Lie low, keep your cool. His mermaid encounter might turn out to be for the best—if he kept the rage at bay. The need to kill, to take control, grew stronger with each bloodletting.

Just a couple of weeks, he consoled himself, and there would be new women, new opportunities.

Tillman set his chin in his hands, dismayed at the evidence spread before him: tax records and payroll and disbursement statements, all dating five years preceding Dad's death.

Prior to the infusion of "consulting fees," their family had been plunging in a downward spiral of debt. Eddie's therapy, Tillman's college tuition, Mom's town car and jewelry. Loans and interest payments lay hidden beneath the comfortable lifestyle, like an army of worms feasting on decay.

The pisser of it all was that the amount claimed to

the IRS probably didn't represent a fraction of the cash-only payments from Jet Bosarge.

Just yesterday, had anyone asked, he'd have sworn Dad was the epitome of honesty, the person in the world he most trusted.

"What are you still doing up?" Portia stood in the doorway, knotting the cord on her robe. "You'll be exhausted at work tomorrow."

She swept past him, got a glass from the cabinet and poured some water.

Tillman stared at her back, resentment and frustration building like a storm inside. To hell with walking on eggshells. "Dehydrated from all that alcohol?"

She spun around, eyes wide, lips parted in surprise until she compressed them into a thin line. "Don't you dare speak to me like that. I won't have it."

"And I won't have you driving drunk with Eddie."

"I wasn't drunk. Just a little tipsy. Janelle Piers and I had a couple of cocktails at lunch."

"Bullshit. You were stinking drunk in the middle of the afternoon."

"Tipsy," she corrected. Portia lifted her chin. "I can't believe you're talking this way to me. I'm your *mother*."

"I know who you are." Tillman crossed his arms, stood his ground. "You're an alcoholic."

"No!" The glass of water fell from her hand and exploded around their feet. "Look what you made me do." Portia strode past him and retrieved a broom and dustpan from the pantry.

Tillman stepped back as she angrily began sweeping up the broken pieces.

"How dare… Your father would never… Can't believe you…" She jerked the broom with each sweep, making an even bigger mess.

Tillman grabbed a dish towel by the sink and blotted up water.

Portia slapped his hand away. "I don't need your help. Get out of here."

With that bitter tongue, it was no wonder she had few real friends or people who cared enough to stand up to her. Shelly's face flashed before him. She had taken a stand and refused to let his mother drive drunk. Not only that, Shelly had done it in the kindest way imaginable and with the least amount of embarrassment possible for his family. If Shelly could do that, how could he, her son, do any less? So Tillman ignored the harsh words, squatted down, picked up the larger glass chunks and placed them in the towel. "I think you do need my help."

Mom glared at him, both on their knees on the hard floor. She wasn't so elegant now, without her makeup and fancy clothes. She looked like a tired, middle-aged woman who'd found life too hard. She wasn't an easy woman to love, but she was still his mother. "Mom," he said, as gently as he could. "Please. You need help."

She jerked as if he'd slapped her. "I'm fine. *Fine*. So I made a mistake today. Let it go."

Let it go. He'd been letting it go. Watched her get progressively worse as he found more bottles stashed around the house, more empty alcohol containers in the garbage, the length of sobriety shorten from late night until midafternoon. Dad's death had been the catalyst for her to stop trying. Tillman pulled out the big guns.

"Eddie needs you," he said.

She stood, emptied the dustpan in the trash. "Don't

tell me what my son needs." She put the dustpan and broom back in the pantry, started to sweep past him.

Tillman sighed. "Next time you're indisposed in the middle of the day, or have a cocktail party scheduled with your friends, I'd appreciate it if you'd let me know. I'll drive you."

"You're not around half the time," she snapped.

"Then call a taxi. Or ask Carl to help."

His mother ignored him as she went to her bedroom.

Tillman surveyed the half-cleaned mess on the floor. "Shit, that went well," he grumbled. He got back on his hands and knees, making sure to get up every tiny broken glass sliver. Thirty-one years old and still cleaning up Mom's messes. If he didn't watch it, he'd be doing it the rest of his life. Just like Dad.

Dad. The paper trail of deceit lay on the table. He wearily returned the financial records to the appropriate files. Separating and burying each incriminating piece. Had Mom known about it? He considered the idea briefly, dismissing it almost at once. Dad had shielded Mom all during their marriage. He wouldn't tell either.

Another secret. Each one wore him down a fraction every day. All he wanted right now was to find Shelly and bury himself in her hot body, feel her hair cover his naked skin like a blanket. Hell, even that was screwed up right now. If Shelly had her own set of secrets, which he highly suspected she did, that would be a deal-breaker. He'd had it with lies, even lies of omission.

Shelly stabbed her pillow and turned, trying to get comfortable. But it was no use. The alarm clock on her nightstand blinked the time, 2:10 a.m. She needed a good swim to relieve stress. Shelly smiled wryly. What she really needed was Tillman in bed beside her.

She flung off the sheets, went to the window and peeked through the curtain. Was the killer out there watching? Waiting for an opportunity? She shuddered, though the room was sticky with humidity.

No matter what, she would see Tillman tomorrow. She needed his help to catch the killer. He might be angry at her, and embarrassed she knew about his mother's drinking, but he was good at his job and would find the killer. Resolutely, she texted him a message that she needed to see him. Perhaps a lunch date?

Shelly went to the bathroom, filled the tub and submerged her entire head and body, letting the liquid weight calm and soothe. Beneath the water, the blue tile surrounding the tub appeared distorted and whirled, almost making Shelly feel that she was in the ocean.

After her bath she checked her cell. Tillman had texted despite the early hour. They were on for lunch.

"Appears we're at a standstill until the crime lab comes through with something." Carl sliced absent-mindedly at the wooden block in his hands.

Tillman sighed, frustrated. "Let's keep our officers knocking on doors and asking questions. Make sure we keep in touch with our informers."

"Snitches." Carl's lips curled. "Not any help at all when you really need them." He blew on the wooden piece, sending sawdust flying. At his feet was a growing mound of wood chips.

"You're not making me feel any better."

Carl chuckled.

"I meant to tell you thanks for getting those financial records for me yesterday."

His deputy looked up sharply. "Any help?"

Tillman nodded curtly. No sense dragging Dad's name in the mud.

"Mail call."

They turned as their longtime dispatcher entered with a stack of mail. "Same old, same old in here." She nodded at the deputy. "Carl's whittlin' and piddlin'—" her gaze swung to Tillman "—while you're pacing like a caged cougar."

Carl held up a hand. "I do my best thinking this way."

Tillman opened envelopes, glancing through the contents before sorting them into tidy stacks: bills, complaints, technical reports. He paused at a sheet of paper filled with large, childish handwriting.

Dear Sheriff,
You need to take a look at Lily Bosarge. She is a killer. She killed those women and cut out their eyeballs.
Yours,
A Concerned Citizen

"Holy hell." Tillman waved the paper at Carl. "Listen to this." He read it aloud.

"Lily Bosarge?" Carl asked, his voice skeptical.

Tillman's mouth twisted. If he had to pick a Bosarge, it would have been Jet. "Probably a hoax. Based on what you've told me about Lily, this could be from a jealous wife trying to cause trouble. I'll question Lily, see what she has to say."

"Your girlfriend's not going to like it," Carl said.

Tillman glanced at his watch. "As a matter of fact, I'm meeting her shortly for lunch."

"You going to tell her about this note?"

"Not before I question her cousin." He frowned. "I'm meeting Shelly in half an hour. Go to Lily Bosarge's salon and bring her here. That way, Shelly can't tip her off before the interview."

"That's some kind of trust you have going," Carl noted.

"I do what I have to do." Tillman waved a hand at the door, letting Carl know the conversation was closed.

After Carl exited, leaving a trail of wood chips in his wake, Tillman tapped a pencil on the edge of the desk, thinking. Damn it all, this latest development came just as he was ready to make amends with Shelly and tell her he appreciated and cared for her. This note changed everything. If it wasn't a hoax, if Lily was involved in the murders and Shelly was covering for her cousin, all bets were off.

He would drill Shelly at lunch and then interview Lily. "Follow the evidence" was his mantra and he would do just that—no matter what the personal cost.

"What can I get you today, Ms. Bosarge?" The teenage waitress waited, pencil poised over a notepad.

"I'm Shelly. You've mistaken me for my cousin Lily."

The waitress's mouth dropped open. "You kidding me?" She squinted at Shelly. "Oh, yeah, I do see a difference. Lily's more like, you know—" She shifted uncomfortably. "Like smaller or something."

She means prettier, Shelly thought with an inward sigh. Snapping her menu shut, she said, "I'll have a tuna salad, no bread and iced tea."

"And you, Sheriff?"

Tillman looked at Shelly with a speculative gleam she couldn't decipher.

"Sheriff?" the waitress repeated.

"A barbecue sandwich and sweet tea." Tillman handed the waitress their menus. When she left with their order, he faced Shelly again. "You get mistaken for Lily a lot?"

"All the time."

"Easy mistake. What with the long blond hair."

"I guess. Strange how she and I look more like sisters than she and Jet do." Shelly fidgeted with the silverware. Bringing up Jet wasn't smart. But since she had... "I'm sorry Jet told you about your father."

Tillman studied her in silence several moments. "How close are you to your cousins?"

"They're the only family I have. After my parents' car wreck, they let me know their home was always open for me." Shelly laid down the silverware. "I owe them."

"Family loyalty only goes so far."

Look who's talking, Shelly thought. *The man takes care of an alcoholic mom and an autistic brother, and defends his dead father's reputation.* "What's that supposed to mean?"

"That you have to protect yourself."

"Are you saying I have to be on guard against my cousins? That's crazy."

"I'm warning you more about Lily than Jet."

"I'm confused. What about Lily?" Shelly's face darkened. "You're not talking about her reputation, are you? Because if—"

"Here's your drinks." The waitress set down their glasses. "Your order will be here shortly."

This wasn't going at all like she'd planned. She thought of the disgusting baggie in her purse with the soiled panties. Better keep her temper in check if she wanted his help. Shelly leaned across the table. "I don't want to argue with you, Tillman. I realize things between us have been awkward because of Jet and then the incident with your mother."

He stiffened and a muscle worked near his jaw. "Thanks for keeping Eddie safe," he said flatly.

Shelly waved a hand. "No problem." So he was sensitive on that score, just as she suspected. "I see you have your own burdens when it comes to family loyalty. We probably have a lot in common."

His gray eyes studied her intently, revealing nothing. Shelly couldn't help the ball of hurt unfurling inside. He was so remote, so unlike the passionate man she'd made love with a short time ago. But maybe it had just been sex for Tillman.

"Why did you want to meet for lunch?" he asked abruptly. "You said it was important."

"One BBQ with fries and one tuna salad." Their waitress set the plates before them.

An uneasy silence fell as the waitress left. In the background, an Eric Church song played.

Shelly picked up her fork and bit into the tuna, too nervous to taste it. After a couple of bites and a sip of tea, she answered his question. "I need your help. Someone's been in our house."

He frowned. "You think it's the same man who bothered you at the grocery store?"

"I think so. We're out some jewelry, some coins—"

"When did this happen?"

Uh-oh. She shouldn't have mentioned the missing valuables. "A few nights ago, but the important thing—"

"You were robbed days ago and you're just now telling me? You haven't even filed a report yet."

"I was going to. But then you were busy with your mom and—"

"That's bullshit."

Several heads turned their way in the crowded deli.

"Keep your voice down," she hissed. "I have something to tell you and I don't want anyone else to hear."

Tillman raised a hand and signaled the waitress. "Two to-go boxes," he said. He faced her again. "In case you haven't noticed, there's not much privacy in Bayou La Siryna."

Five minutes later, they were seated in his cruiser.

"I feel like a criminal," Shelly said, watching people glance their way as they passed. "Everyone probably thinks I'm in trouble." She took a deep breath. "Actually, I am in trouble. What's scary isn't what's been stolen—it's what the man left behind." She pulled the baggie from her purse, hesitating slightly. She risked not only serious legal entanglements, but her lies and half-truths could also destroy a relationship that, so far, had only lasted all of a week.

Who was she kidding? It could never work out. She couldn't spend her life in constant fear of discovery. She took a deep breath and handed over the panties.

Tillman's eyes widened as he took it. "What the hell?"

"I found this on my bed. There's semen on them."

His face was grim, stoic. "Is this underwear yours?"

"No. And they don't belong to my cousins, either."

"You sure one of them didn't borrow your bedroom to fool around with some guy?"

"Positive. And—there's more. He left a note."

"Show it to me."

Shelly produced a second baggie from her purse. "It came speared on a dead fish."

"Jesus." Tillman smoothed the plastic and read it aloud.

"I know what you are. You have something that belongs to me. I'll email in 48 hours for instructions on where to meet. You better bring it, bitch. Next time it's a knife through your fucking heart."

"What the hell?" He turned the note over and held it to the light. "You say it was thrown in your window?"

"When I was home alone last night. I expect another email from him tomorrow."

He said nothing, just kept looking at her with those smoky-gray eyes as if dissecting her under a microscope. "Shouldn't you be doing something?" she asked breathlessly, waving an arm in the air.

He leaned back in the car seat. "Not until I get all the facts."

"What else do you need to know?"

"Everything." Tillman suddenly leaned forward, his face inches from her own. *"Everything,"* he repeated, with an intensity that made those gray eyes a darker shade of gunmetal. "Because you aren't even close."

Shelly licked her lips and her breath came out slightly above a whisper. "I'm not?" She couldn't help remembering the last time his eyes had darkened, as he'd laid his body over hers on the massage table. They'd been dark with passion then. Now they blazed with either anger or impatience. She couldn't be sure which. Maybe a little of both.

"No, you are not."

His words were too controlled, too neutral. What had she done to turn him from the warm, passionate man whose kisses had made her sleepless with longing these past nights? She thought he'd be beside himself with concern for her safety, despite their last meeting. If only she could trust him.

Shelly composed her features to betray nothing of the hurt burning in her gut. "What more do you need to know? I gave you the only things I have that are concrete." Shelly was astonished how easy the lies came. Self-preservation will do that for a person, she supposed, but she didn't want to become that kind of woman. Tillman either trusted her or he didn't. "Can't you trace him from the fingerprints on there? Or monitor our computers for his email?"

If he thought he could unnerve her with this silence, he was dead wrong. Still, she breathed easier when his attention returned to the note.

"My guess is we'll find that the email account is from an anonymous remailer website."

"What does that mean?"

"That we can't know who mailed it or from what computer it was sent."

A chill settled in her stomach. She glanced involuntarily at her watch and imagined the ticktock of the killer's deadline approaching.

"Just what kind of trouble are you in, Shelly?"

"I don't know! You saw the note." Shelly almost winced at the shrillness of her voice.

"I'm trying to help you," Tillman said.

"Really? 'Cause that's not how you're acting."

He let out a long sigh. "Let's take this line by line. First. 'I know what you are.' He doesn't say *who* you are but *what* you are."

"I know what it says."

"Unusual choice of words."

"Agreed."

Tillman raised an eyebrow. "Any idea what that means?"

"How should I know?"

"Let's just say your cousin Lily has a little—shall we say—*reputation* around town. Perhaps this person thinks you do, too."

"How dare you!" Shelly's fists knotted at her side. "Lily's the kindest, the sweetest, the—"

Tillman held up a hand. "Calm down. We're just getting started here."

She wanted to smack his hard, cold face. This was a side of Tillman she hadn't seen before. All cool professionalism with no hint of concern or warmth.

"Moving on," he continued in an implacable voice. "You must have some idea what he's talking about when he says you have something that belongs to him."

"No," she said at once, but realized she might have spoken a tad too soon when he scowled. She should have been prepared to answer such an obvious question, but she had been counting on his sympathy. He acted as if she was no more special to him than any of the other several thousand residents of Bayou La Siryna. The realization was like a sucker punch to the gut. Shelly closed her eyes so he wouldn't see her vulnerability.

Think, think.

"Could be the stalker believes I belong to him."

At his blank stare, she elaborated. "In a sexual way. In his twisted mind, I'm a sex object and he wants me to—you know—give it up for him."

"Jesus." Tillman stared at her intently, an undecipherable look in his eyes.

Shelly wasn't sure if he wanted to pull her close to him—or shake her.

"I need to have these tested right away. And I've got Lily waiting on me as we speak."

"What?" A burst of jealousy shot through her body like poison. All it took was one look from Lily and she could have any man she wanted. One damn look…

"I have to question her." He hesitated. "May as well tell you, she will, anyway, when you get home. I got an anonymous tip today that Lily is our serial killer."

"That's ridiculous! She would never—"

Tillman held up a hand. "I'm not saying she is. But I have to question her all the same. Now that you've given me this—" he tapped the evidence "—I have to wonder if your stalker is actually the serial killer and if his real target is Lily. Maybe he sent that tip to draw suspicion away from himself."

Shelly's breath caught. "Everyone confuses us. It's me. He's after me. He assumed my name was Lily." She bit her lip. *Remember who you're talking to.*

"What are you talking about?" Tillman grabbed her shoulder. "What's going on, Shelly? I want the truth. I don't know yet if the person who robbed and stalked you is the killer. One glaring loophole in my guess is that it makes no sense for the killer to leave incriminating evidence like he's shown me."

Shelly shuddered under his intense scrutiny. "Maybe he's plain crazy and sloppy."

"Let's slow down a minute. It may be that the killer and the person stalking you aren't the same person."

"But it's such a coincidence. The stalker was in our house last night and today you get a message about Lily as a suspect in the killings."

"I'm not a big believer in coincidence myself." His eyes softened, grew closer to the way she remembered him that night. "I'm worried about you, Shelly. I'm going to make sure your house is patrolled at night."

"Maybe you'll catch him when he comes back."

"You seem sure he will."

"He will."

Tillman drew back. "How can you be so sure of his behavior? The other victims weren't stalked before being killed. And they were prostitutes. I don't see any similarity in their cases and yours. The MO is different."

Shelly bit her lip. "Call it women's intuition."

"I don't believe in that, either." He raked a hand in his hair. "Damn it, Shelly, you aren't telling me the whole truth."

Shelly opened her mouth to speak, but this time the lies wouldn't come. "Please," she said, "try to have a little faith in me."

"Why should I when you won't trust me with the truth?" He growled in frustration before reaching across her and opening the passenger door. "I've got to get this evidence turned in and talk to your cousin. I'm going to swing by tonight. We'll talk."

Easing her legs out until she hit pavement, Shelly gave him a wobbly smile. "You make that sound like a threat. Is this when you warn me not to leave town?"

"Oh, it's most definitely a threat." He didn't crack a smile in return. "And you *will* tell me everything you know. No more secrets."

Chapter 10

Who can you trust
What do you believe
When faith turns to dust
And love becomes need.

Tillman entered his office where Carl sat at his desk, Lily across from him. He looked uncomfortable. Probably wanted to whittle but worried that wielding his knife in front of a person of interest could be construed as threatening, however casually it was done.

"Sheriff." Carl stood. "I believe you've met Miss Lily Bosarge?"

Tillman nodded at her. "Leave us, Carl," he said, taking a seat at his desk.

"Sheriff, why am I here?" She was composed, not at all shaken or surprised. She looked like a scoop of cool vanilla cream with her long blond hair and white linen skirt and blouse.

"I understand you had an incident at your home last night."

"Oh. So you've seen Shelly today?"

"I have." Best to take it slow, see what he could dig up. "She told me y'all were robbed."

"She wasn't supposed to—" Lily broke off.

"Wasn't supposed to what? Tell me all the details?" Tillman fought against showing his annoyance. What was it with these women and their secrecy?

Lily gave a delicate shrug of one shoulder. "So why am I here?"

He countered with a question of his own. "You want to file a robbery report?"

"No." She gave a small sigh. "I don't think it would do any good."

"Have that much faith in my office, do you?"

"Don't take it personally."

This woman's calmness was maddening. There was something a little off about Lily. She was too remote, too calm. She was beautiful, no denying that, and it was easy to see why she had her pick of men around town. But she didn't have Shelly's fire and passion. "You'll have to file a report for insurance purposes."

Lily gave another maddening shrug. "We'll see."

"But that's not why I called you here."

She looked only mildly curious.

"I got a letter this morning incriminating you in the serial killings around Bayou La Siryna."

For the first time since he'd met Lily, Tillman glimpsed real emotion. Her impossibly blue eyes widened and her glossed lips parted in surprise. "Me?"

Tillman picked up a paper. "Here's a copy."

Lily read it quickly. She crumpled it into a little ball and threw it in the trash can by the side of his desk. "That's ridiculous. You can't think I'm the murderer."

"Why do you think I got this letter? You know anyone who'd want to deliberately hurt you?"

She shook her head, golden hair flashing like a halo in the slit of sunlight from the window. About the same length as the hair found on China's body, Tillman couldn't help noticing. Was Shelly protecting her cousin? He'd find out tonight.

"Must be a silly prank."

"From a jealous wife or girlfriend, perhaps?"

She blinked. "I don't like where this is going."

"Just getting to the bottom of things. Is anyone angry or threatening to harm you?"

"Not that I know of."

Tillman leaned back, hands behind his head. He'd have to watch her inscrutable face closely for reactions. "Tell me, Miss Bosarge, do you recall where you were on the night of September fifth?"

She raised the tip of one long pink nail and tapped it against her lips. "I worked at the salon until six o'clock, came home, got ready for a date with Gary—"

Tillman took out a pen and paper. "Gary who?"

"Gary Armstrong. Then I—"

"Is he someone you're currently seeing?"

"No. I broke it off a couple of days ago. Too possessive."

"And how did Armstrong take the rejection?"

"Hurt, I guess. But no big deal. We hadn't been seeing each other long."

"He have a wife or a girlfriend?"

"Girlfriend."

"Her name?"

"Wanda something."

Tillman scribbled it down. He would check with Gary later.

"Any bad scenes between you and the ex-girlfriend?"

"She called me crying one night, all upset. I told

her Gary wasn't anything special, nothing to get upset about."

"And that's when you dropped your relationship with Armstrong?"

Lily smiled faintly. "No. I hadn't found a replacement for him yet."

Was she joking? Hard to tell. No wonder she did nothing for him. Lily was cold-blooded as a fish and ruthless as a shark.

Carl stuck his head in the door. "Coffee's ready. Can I get y'all anything to drink?"

"Water, please, Mr. Dismukes." Lily turned the charm of her smile on the old deputy. Carl melted like a marshmallow over a fire.

"What else can I get for you, Miss Bosarge? Anything you want."

"Water's fine."

Lily faced Tillman again, mouth upturned in a sly grin. Her long legs, crossed at the knees, began slowly rocking. He must have been the only man in the bayou not under her spell.

"Back to the night of September fifth. You'd come home, got ready for your date—"

"Right. I had a late supper with Shelly and Jet and then Gary picked me up to go to a nightclub in Mobile."

"What time?"

"It was pretty late."

"I'll need you to be a little more specific."

"About ten o'clock."

Carl returned with bottled water, presenting it with a boyish eagerness. Tillman waited until Carl left the room before resuming.

"Do you know Melkie Pellerin?"

Lily scrunched her face slightly. "Melkie Pellerin." She rolled the name around her mouth in slow deliberation before shaking her head. "Is that a male name?"

"Yes. Ring any bells?"

"It's an unusual name. I'd remember if I'd heard it before."

Tillman nodded and said nothing, hoping the silence might make Lily uncomfortable enough to want to talk and fill the void.

The silence stretched on. Lily kept her impassive eyes on his, never moving a muscle or showing any trace of wariness.

Lily was one cool customer.

Her glossy lips curved upward a fraction as she rose. "If there are no more questions?"

"That's all for now." He stood also. "If you don't mind, I'd like to get some fingerprints and hair samples from you before you go."

Lily retrieved her purse from the back of the chair. "No," she said simply.

"Why not?"

"I don't need a reason. Unless you arrest me, I have the right to refuse."

"True. But if you have nothing to hide I don't see why you won't do it."

"If that's all?" Lily asked, pausing at the doorway.

Tillman sighed. "Go on. I'll be by your house this evening to speak with Shelly."

The moment Lily exited, Carl returned.

"I want the Bosarge house watched 24/7. Effective immediately," he informed Dismukes.

"For their protection or for suspicious activity?"

"Both."

"That's stretching us pretty thin. We already have one officer tailing Pellerin."

They walked over to the personnel board and looked at the manpower available by shift. Most officers were dedicated to county jail posts, all positions mandatory for safe operation at the correctional facility. It didn't allow much leeway.

"Don't see how we can do both," Carl observed.

Tillman sighed. "Take the tail off Melkie. I don't really have anything on the guy. The collection of dead bugs in his house raised a red flag, but being creepy isn't a crime." Still, his gut told him Pellerin could be the killer.

Chapter 11

I've got a special checklist
One, two, three
Coming now to get you
All for me.

"Melkie Pellerin."

"Thanks, Lily. I'll take it from here." Shelly disconnected the call, booted up her computer screen and had the address less than ten minutes later. She glanced at the clock in her YMCA office. Plenty of time to shower and change and drive out before Tillman came over to the house. As a precaution, she'd stuff her hair in a baseball cap and wear dark sunglasses.

Melkie couldn't believe his luck. The cops had stopped tailing him. Now was his chance. He'd been crawling the walls while under surveillance and the blackness and anger demanded release. He would get the mermaid tonight. Hopefully, she'd be off guard, thinking his next move would be only an email to set up a meeting.

Methodically, Melkie collected supplies.

Killing jar with fresh chloroform and washcloth. Check.

Empty Mason jars. Check.

Phony stiletto knife from the mermaid bitch. Check.

Duct tape, kitchen steak knife, pint of formaldehyde. Check, check and check.

A duffel bag with a towel, change of clothes and baby wipes was already in his truck, as well as a large tarp cloth.

The dog ran to the door, expectant. "Sorry, fella. But Daddy's bringing home more for his special collection." Melkie gently pushed Reb back with his foot.

It felt great to get out of the tiny house and drive without being followed. *Free.* And if he intended to stay that way, he'd best play it smart. He would not be tricked again.

Melkie drove down streets laden with monstrously tall live oaks, their branches dripping with Spanish moss, like old men with long gray ZZ Top beards. And like old men, they were slowly dying, the parasitic moss eating away their life sap.

On Pendarvis Road, he slowed as the mermaid house came in sight.

Melkie's heart hammered as the Chevy's beam lit on an unmarked car twenty yards ahead, parked in a nest of trees and scrub brush.

Chill. Maybe someone had left the broken vehicle, planning to return later. He drove past the mermaid's house, scoping the potential threat.

That was no abandoned vehicle. Dusk hadn't settled enough to mask a man behind the wheel. Another couple hours, Melkie probably wouldn't have noticed. He recognized an unmarked cop car when he saw one—those hubcaps on the plain-Jane body were a dead giveaway. Melkie drove past, slightly under the speed limit. Could it be the same cop who had tailed him earlier? There were several pickups on the road; they were common as grits around the bayou. Adrenaline pumped through him, making him jittery and hyper-alert to the surroundings.

He held his breath, continually checking the rearview mirror, sure the car would emerge from its cover, blue lights flashing.

He was dizzy from lack of oxygen by the time he got on Interstate 10 East for Mobile. As the distance increased between him and Bayou La Siryna, Melkie sucked in long breaths. Nobody was after him. Disappointment at not being able confront the mermaid had subsided by the time he hit the city outskirts. Time enough for that tomorrow. The more he mulled over the cop stakeout, the more pleased he became. Could be his letter to Sheriff Angier had actually worked. It appeared the heat was off him and now focused on that freak of nature.

Perfect.

Melkie smiled as he crossed into the familiar territory of the Mobile docks. He was juiced and knew what would cool the fever.

It was time.

Shelly peered through the windshield at the man. He was the right height and body frame, and the curly brown hair also fit. Just a little closer, a little slower, and she'd know for sure. She had to get this right, couldn't pin this on the wrong person. She pulled the rim of her cap lower and watched him throw a cardboard box in the backseat of a truck.

She caught a glimpse of a hawkish nose and then the

dark brown eyes swept casually past her before he got in the truck.

It was him.

She quickly averted her eyes and drove on, keeping the same rate of speed. Had he recognized her? The truck backed out of the driveway. She held her breath, wondering what to do if he followed her. She pushed aside the handgun in her purse, grabbed the cell and selected Tillman's number from the menu. Her fingers poised over the send button, ready to hit Send if needed. At the end of the street, she looped around, twisting her head to keep an eye on Pellerin.

The truck swung onto the street and headed the opposite direction. Shelly let the phone drop in her lap, following him at a safe distance, another car between the vehicles. When Pellerin left Happy Hollows she got his license plate.

ALA3536.

Melkie ignored that the times were coming closer together and glanced at the dashboard clock. It was 9:06 p.m. A little early, but there should be some action by the docks. Pressure weighed his lungs and he was as antsy as a chain smoker trying to quit cold turkey.

Just a little longer.

Cruising into his lucky hunting area, Melkie surveyed the pickings. A few women were out, but he wanted one alone and not running with a pack of whores. He hit the accelerator and drove three blocks to a local bar and parked behind it, in a lot with only one working streetlamp. Melkie scrambled out of his truck and searched the crumbled blacktop for a small pothole with broken-up asphalt. He took a screwdriver from his belt and pried the pavement until he'd removed a sizable chunk. That ought to work.

Melkie flung it, crashing the bulb and casting the lot in darkness. It made a loud cracking noise, but music from the bar would drown the noise from the patrons inside. He crept back to the truck, using other parked vehicles as cover. He was dressed all in black and figured he blended into the shroud of night, especially considering the waning moon.

He took out a cold beer from a small cooler under the passenger seat and settled in to wait.

After a while, a batch of women rounded the corner of the bar. There were seven of them—pretty young things in tight jeans. Most likely they had all driven out here in groups. Four of them got in a Malibu and took off. He watched the remaining three closely. They stood in a giggling, chatty circle by a truck until two got inside it.

Melkie kept his eyes on the last girl. She had dark auburn hair and pale skin that glowed in the darkness. He couldn't believe his luck when, instead of hopping in the back of the truck with the others, she walked off alone, coming his way. He hastily dabbed chloroform onto a washcloth, folded it up and stuffed it in his pants pocket.

Showtime.

Shelly raced in the house, thankful her cousins were already home.

"I found him! I got the address for Pellerin, drove by his house and saw him come outside and take off in his truck."

Jet rose from the couch. "Did he see you?"

"I don't think so. And I've got his license plate number. He drives a Chevy extended cab truck so we know to be on the lookout for that."

"Now we can take him out." Jet smiled, a predatory gleam in her eye.

"No. We let Tillman get him." At Jet's frown, Shelly hurried on. "I still have his knife, remember? I'll carve his name on it and dump it in our yard for the cops to find. They'll think Melkie dropped it when he robbed us. That will directly tie him to the murders."

"I want my rings back," Lily said.

"You'll get them," Shelly promised. "I don't think he could sell them until the heat's off." She ran to the stairs. "I need to plant that knife before Tillman gets here."

When she returned to the kitchen, Jet and Lily were seated at the table. Jet wore a pair of latex gloves and held a bowie knife in one hand. Shelly dropped the baggie with the knife on the table and got a pair of gloves. She slipped them on and sat beside Lily.

Jet removed the killer's knife and started etching its blade. She glanced at Shelly. "M-e-l-k-i-e. Right?"

"Right." Shelly nodded. "And somewhere on the blade carve the initials of the victims—J. B. and C. W."

Jet kept carving. "Weird name."

"Weird *guy*," Lily said.

"By this time tomorrow, the killer could be in jail." Shelly felt almost dizzy with relief. Her cousins would be safe, and the killer couldn't hurt anyone else.

Jet finished and surveyed the handiwork. "It looks like a nine-year-old's scribble."

Shelly took it. "Who cares? It has a name on it. All that matters is that the cops find it and arrest Melkie." She scraped her chair from the table and went to the door. "Let me throw this outside before Tillman gets here."

Shelly stepped onto the front porch and tossed the knife by an azalea bush. The glint of the silver blade rested against the black soil. Easy to find when she asked Tillman to search the area. She'd tell him she heard a noise out front and then make sure he located it.

Everything was going to be fine.

"Officer Donnell, Angier speaking. You set up to watch the Bosarge house?"

"Been here just a few minutes, boss."

"Seen anything suspicious?"

"No. A few vehicles passing by, typical for this area."

"Don't forget to be on the lookout for a 1992 Chevrolet truck, license plate ALA3536, registered to a Melkie Pellerin, white male. If he stops the truck nearby or gets near the house I want you to approach and question him."

"Got it," Donnell said.

Tillman's senses hummed with energy. Finally, he'd have it out with Shelly tonight and question her about Pellerin. If she identified him as her stalker, and if the forensics lab confirmed Pellerin's DNA matched evidence from the previous murders, he could close this case. The murders had been eating away at him since the first body was discovered and now he felt everything was coming to a head and he'd get the killer. Until then, he had to watch Pellerin. If that meant the correctional facility might be short a man, then that's what he'd have to do. "I'm en route to your location, should be there in less than fifteen minutes. Consider Pellerin—"

Donnell cut in. "A woman is exiting the house and

she appears to be holding a— Wait, let me get the binoculars."

Tillman waited.

"Looks like a knife. She threw it by some shrubbery on the porch. Want me to go look?"

Tillman hesitated. "No. We'll retrieve it when I get there. Describe the woman."

"Long blond hair, slender."

Tillman frowned. Could be either Lily or Shelly.

"Describe her clothing."

"She's gone back inside, but she wore white shorts and a dark blue T-shirt."

"Thanks, Donnell. Call me back if you see anything else."

Tillman threw the cell on the passenger seat. A knife? What in the hell were those women up to?

At last he turned onto Pendarvis Road and dialed his officer. "What's your location?"

Even though Donnell told him where he parked, it took Tillman a few seconds to make out the shape of the vehicle surrounded by trees. "I'm right up on you. Follow behind me in your car and we'll check out the porch area."

He veered from the driveway and rode into the yard, aiming the headlights on the front porch. Before exiting the vehicle, he put on gloves and grabbed an evidence kit on the floor of the backseat.

The front door opened and Shelly, Lily and Jet came out.

"What's going on?" Lily asked, the faint raising of her eyebrows reflecting mild curiosity. He caught Shelly and Jet exchange a quick look before he turned his attention to finding the knife.

"Got it." Donnell picked up an object and held it up to the light.

A bone-handle stiletto knife. Tillman stood by his side and they examined it together.

"It's got an inscription," Donnell said. *"M-e-l-k-i-e."* His eyes caught Tillman's. "Pellerin." Donnell flipped the blade over and gave a low whistle. "Check this out."

Tillman's blood pounded as he read the initials.

"Isn't that the guy you asked me about today?" Lily called out.

Tillman combed his eyes over Lily. Blue jean cutoffs and a yellow T-shirt. He slid his gaze to Shelly. White shorts, blue T-shirt.

Shit.

"Think he's our stalker?" Lily tried again.

Tillman kept his eyes on Shelly, not bothering with the others. "You have some explaining to do, Miss Connors."

Chapter 12

In my truck, the killing jar,
You won't be going very far.
Don't think that you can get away,
I'm the hunter, you're my prey.

Stormy-gray eyes pierced Shelly as she stood on the porch. Her body felt heavy—as if a five-hundred-pound anchor rooted her to the spot. She couldn't breathe, couldn't move.

He knows what I did.

Why hadn't she thrown the knife out the back porch? She was so close to framing the killer and in a matter of seconds she'd ruined everything.

Tillman kept his eyes pinned on hers while he spoke to his officer. "Bag up the knife and return to your post."

The officer frowned. "But, shouldn't we—"

"I'll interview these women," Tillman interrupted. "Keep your watch, and when your shift ends take the evidence to the station."

The officer, clearly unhappy, did as instructed.

"Is there a problem, Sheriff?" Lily asked. Her tinkling voice betrayed no alarm.

Tillman climbed up the steps. "Everyone in the house."

Shelly's heart sank. He addressed them in the same clipped tone he'd used with his officer. She followed her cousins inside, weighed down with dread. Jet stomped over to the fireplace and leaned against the mantel, head held up in challenge, while Lily drifted to the piano and played a few notes.

That's not going to work, Shelly thought, settling on the sofa. They were in serious shit now.

"No music," Tillman ordered.

Lily gave a gentle sigh before turning to face him.

Tillman's presence filled the room. He folded his arms and didn't say a word. The silence became unbearable.

"You got a problem, Sheriff?" Jet asked.

"The three of you are my damn problem. What the hell is going on around here?"

Shelly kept her eyes down, didn't want to face him. He was on to her lies. And he'd never trust her again.

Lily twirled her long hair and gave a charming pout as she sensuously crossed her legs. "We're being stalked, Sheriff. We need your protection and understanding."

Tillman scowled. "I'm not sure who's stalking who. All I know is something fishy is going on here."

Jet snickered.

"What the hell is so funny? Framing someone for murder is no laughing matter."

Nobody spoke, nobody moved. Shelly watched the flickering play of the chandelier light against the black wood of the piano. She wanted to lose herself in the colors, be hypnotized by lavender, pink and white sparkles dancing and—

"Shelly." Tillman's harsh voice interrupted the trance. "Look at me," he ordered.

She raised her eyes and faced his, reading anger, accusation and condemnation.

"Officer Donnell saw you throw that knife in the shrubs. Explain yourself."

"It really is Melkie's knife."

Jet was at her side immediately. "Don't say another word, Shelly."

Tillman ignored Jet, his gaze fixed on Shelly. "How did it come to be in your possession?"

"Because I—"

"Shut up!" Jet stepped in front of her. "You don't have to answer his questions."

"I'm afraid she does," Tillman said. "I can charge all three of you right now with obstructing a murder investigation and tampering with evidence."

"Don't play big bad cop with me." Jet folded her arms defiantly. "You're all the same, your dad included. Why don't you cut to the chase and tell us how much we have to pay you to make all this go away."

Shelly stood. "Jet, stop it. Tillman doesn't want our money. He's not like that."

"How much?" Jet repeated.

"You can't buy your way out of this." Tillman's jaw clinched and his shoulders squared with determination. "Now sit your ass down and start talking."

Shelly held her breath as the two silently squared off. Even Lily seemed frozen on the piano bench, making no sound to smooth the tension. To Shelly's surprise, Jet unfolded her arms and sat on the sofa, back stiffened in anger.

"The way I see it," he began, "is that one or all of you has either been targeted by a killer, or you are in some way involved in the murders. Which is it?"

Shelly's heart hammered. She couldn't tell him the whole truth; he wouldn't believe her even if she did. But she had to tell him some of it. "Tillman, I saw Melkie Pellerin dump the body of the last victim. My cousins don't have anything to do with this."

"Shelly, don't—" Lily said.

"*I'm* the one who saw him, not —" Jet said.

"Both of you stop." Shelly shook her head and faced Tillman. "I witnessed it."

Tillman gave a curt nod to Jet and Lily. "Leave us."

Jet spoke low and quickly to Shelly. "Unless he actually he arrests you, don't say anything without a lawyer. I'll find you the best by morning."

Lily laid a hand on her shoulder. "We stand together. I won't let you face this alone."

Shelly's lips quivered. They had to be scared of exposure, had to be frightened their mermaid race might come to light, yet their first concern was to protect her, a mere TRAB, a traitor-baby product from the union of human and mermaid races. A contamination of the pure merfolk bloodline. "Go. I have to do this alone."

Jet opened her mouth to protest, but Shelly cut her off. "Go."

Lily gave her a quick hug and they left the den, casting anxious glances over their shoulders.

Tillman's face was set hard as marble. Shelly walked to him, raised a tentative hand and touched the hard plane of his jaw. But nothing in his somber eyes or rigid body softened. "How did you come to witness this, *Miss* Connors?"

Shelly dropped her hand and stepped away. She'd lost him. He would never understand or forgive her for not coming forward earlier, no matter what she said or did.

A chill settled in the pit of her stomach and she wrapped her arms around her waist. "I can't tell you everything," she whispered.

"You can and will."

Just tell him you were out on a boat. Why was this so hard? She'd been lying to him from the beginning. Trouble was, she'd grown to care for and respect Tillman more with each passing day. And the more she cared, the more it hurt to lie to him. Shelly looked down at the hardwood floor, unable to meet Tillman's penetrating glare. "I was out boating that night. I saw a man drop a large object wrapped in black plastic from the side of his boat. I was curious, so I motored over and he saw me. When he took off I pulled the object on my boat and slit it open to see what was inside." Shelly closed her eyes; a soft moan escaped her lips as she remembered the woman's maimed face with no eyes. Her stomach clutched with nausea and she doubled over.

Strong, steady hands guided her to a chair. She sank into it and put her head between her knees, taking deep breaths. Tillman's hand stayed on her back, gently stroking until she regained her composure.

"Shelly." His voice held the liquid depth of the ocean; it enveloped her whole body in its warmth, a comforting pool of affection she never wanted to leave. He put a hand beneath her chin and guided her face upward. "Most of what you just told me is a pack of lies—except for one thing."

He paused and Shelly studied his face. This was the Tillman she knew. The kindness in his eyes had returned, softened the harsh edges of his strong features. "What?" she asked in a rush of breath.

"I believe you found China Wang's body."

"I did." She nodded, relieved he at least accepted some of her story. "I wish I hadn't. Wish I'd never been out that night. I put all of us in jeopardy."

"Your cousins?"

She hesitated and then nodded in agreement. But there was so much more at stake. If humans found out the ancient myths of mermaids were true they would all be hunted like animals. Or fish. None of them would ever be safe again.

Tillman abruptly stood and put some distance between them. "What did you do after you supposedly—all alone—dragged this heavy body onto the boat?"

Shit. "I…um…took it to the beach at Murrell's Point and left it there to be found."

He raised an eyebrow. "All by yourself you managed to drag China's body out of the boat and onto land?"

"I'm strong."

He sighed. "Not that strong. But, moving on, explain why you're so sure Melkie Pellerin is the killer. Supposedly, you came across him after dark. How can you be certain he's the right man?"

"I have very good vision." Crap. That sounded lame even to herself.

He regarded her silently before letting that go. "What boat did you use?"

"We have one. Two, actually. They're docked in our boathouse about twenty yards down the road." She answered quickly and confidently, glad to be telling a small portion of the truth.

Tillman's eyes drifted to the boarded-up window behind her. "You think somehow Pellerin has discovered your identity and broken into this house."

"He has. Don't you have enough physical evidence now to make him give a DNA sample?"

"You may have destroyed any hope of a case against him by throwing that knife out the front door in the presence of one of my officers."

"Oh." She looked down at her clasped hands.

"How did you get that knife?"

"It was…stuck on that poor woman's body."

"Stop lying, damn it!" The controlled anger sprang back in Tillman's eyes. "A killer wouldn't leave his weapon like that. Is that really his knife or are you trying to frame Pellerin any way you can?"

Her stomach lurched again. "It's his. You have to believe me. He must be stopped."

"That's what I'm trying to do. But you have to tell me the truth so I can bring him in. Do you really want me to drag you to the station for formal questioning? Because I'll do whatever is needed to keep another woman from being murdered."

"I want him stopped, too." For the first time tonight, Shelly was angry. Maybe she shouldn't have gotten involved. Maybe it had all been for nothing. And maybe a half-breed like her had no business playing mermaid if she was too tenderhearted toward humans. "I'm doing the best I can, Tillman." Her voice rose and pitched higher, frustration boiling over.

"Not good enough."

Shelly stuck her hands out in front of her. "Guess you win. Go on. Handcuff me and take me in."

"At least I'd know you weren't in danger, you bullheaded, maddening…" He sputtered to a stop and threw up his hands. "What am I going to do with you?"

The spurt of anger died as quickly as it started. *He still cares.* She smiled, wanted to laugh in relief.

He frowned harder. "Why are you smiling? You obviously don't realize the trouble you're in."

"I realize you must still care for me. At least a little." Shelly stepped into his arms and laid her head on his broad chest, felt his heart beating against her cheek. He stood stiffly, unmoving for several moments before crushing her to him.

"Damn it, Shelly." He stepped away. "You need to trust me. I'll protect you. But if you don't tell me what really happened then we'll do this the hard way."

"Meaning?"

"You get to be questioned by cops who will be a lot tougher on you than me."

"I don't like being threatened."

"And I don't like being lied to." His face softened a fraction. "C'mon, Shelly."

She wanted to. Suddenly, she didn't know what the right thing to do was. Stay silent and keep her heritage a secret and protect her race, or tell the truth and possibly stop a killer. Either way, she would lose him.

He sensed her hesitation.

"Whatever you're hiding, we'll deal with it together. Now tell me."

"Can you keep a secret?"

He didn't jump to an immediate "yes." "Unless it means Pellerin walks."

Shelly shut her eyes, considered her options. *Just get it over with, the quicker the better.* "Okay. I'll do it." She opened her eyes to meet Tillman's steady gaze. She went to the front door, stopping at the entrance to pick up a set of keys hanging on a hook.

"Where are you going?"

"I have to show you. You'll never believe it otherwise." Shelly kept walking, her gaze on the dark waters ahead. Footsteps followed behind her.

"Shelly." Jet caught up to her and grabbed her arm. "Don't do it. You're making a huge mistake."

She shook off her cousin. "I've made up my mind."

"Let me get you an attorney. At least sleep on everything tonight."

"No." Shelly kept walking.

"He'll only hurt you," Jet said, her eyes savage.

No, not savage—hurt. Shelly stopped. Jet knew all about betrayal and loss. "Tillman is not Perry. He's kind and loyal with those he loves."

"Doesn't matter. Can't you see that? It won't work."

"Leave us." Tillman's sharp voice cut through the night air.

Jet walked off in a huff, calling over her shoulder, "We'll be here for you when you get home."

Shelly didn't look back—it was too tempting. If she did, she was afraid she'd run home, lock herself in the house and never come out.

Because once she got on that boat and jumped in the water, nothing would ever be the same.

"Where are we going?" Tillman shouted over the rumble of the boat cutting through dark water.

"Farther out," Shelly replied vaguely. All that really mattered was that it be out of sight of his officer's binoculars. Once past the oak shoreline, Shelly drove a few extra minutes. Circling mostly, buying a little time as she worked up courage, planning the easiest way to show Tillman, yet knowing he would be shocked whatever she did. She slowed the boat and the engine's noise decelerated.

"Is this where you found Pellerin disposing of the victim's body?"

Shelly cut the motor. "No. That was probably another quarter of a mile west of here."

Tillman's brows drew together. "Then why did you stop now?"

"This spot's as good as any." Water lapped gently against the boat, cradling them like a lullaby. Too bad it did nothing to calm her nerves. She stared at the wide expanse of the calm gulf, stretching onward, shielding beneath it a vast unmapped underwater terrain that held the roots of her ancestry, where mermaids lived yet were pushed farther and deeper each year from man's ever-probing eyes.

When she had first overheard she was half-mermaid Shelly had found it hard to believe. Sure, she had the unusual ability to stay underwater indefinitely, but she'd been warned never to speak of it. Mom had tried to convince her they were special. Being mermaid was a unique aspect of herself that would add joy to her life.

Only to realize years later that it was a curse. Life had shown that living on the boundaries of two worlds yet fully belonging to neither carried a huge burden of isolation and loneliness. Just once before had she broken silence and told a college boyfriend. They'd been partying earlier and Steve had been pretty wasted—wasted enough she chanced telling him, hoping his inebriated state might make him more accepting of the news. Alone in a hot tub, she'd even demonstrated her miraculous ability to stay underwater and not breathe.

It had not gone well. Steve had called her a freak.

Even now, the look of disgust on his face haunted her and she'd vowed never again. The next day, she told him it had all been a joke. Steve acted as if he accepted her explanation, but she'd seen the doubt in his eyes. He dumped her days afterward.

And here she was again about to do the same. Only this time, she had to let a man see her in merform. Tillman would never believe it unless he witnessed it with his own eyes.

"Shelly, let's get on with this." Tillman drummed his fingers along the dashboard. "I can't imagine what we're doing here."

Shelly went to the back of the boat and lifted the T-shirt over her head. She wore no bra. Tillman's mouth opened slightly and then closed.

"Not that I don't appreciate the view, but now is hardly the time for this."

She unsnapped her shorts and tugged them down, watching him reluctantly admire her body.

Her human body.

Oh, God, this would be the last time he'd look at her body with appreciation and not disgust.

Jump in and get this over with. Tears streamed in tracks down her cheeks. Shelly licked her lips and tasted their salty flavor. "One kiss for courage," she said, bending forward. She cupped his head in her hands and kissed his mouth.

I love you. Her mind silently screamed the words she wouldn't say aloud. She hadn't meant to fall for him, but Tillman's strength, loyalty and kindness, combined with his intense sexual energy, made the man impossible to resist. No matter what happened next, at least

Tillman might eventually appreciate that she'd helped him solve his case.

As his hands reached to encircle her waist, Shelly stepped away and climbed to the boat's ledge. "Whatever happens, however long I stay under, don't worry. I'm safe." With that cryptic advice, she pushed off and dove as far from the boat as possible.

The ocean embraced her like a lover, caressing every inch of skin, transforming her body to please him and only him. The shift from human legs to fish tail wasn't uncomfortable like the shifting from tail fin to legs upon land. The morphing into a creature of the sea felt natural and pleasurable. How Mom must have missed it all those married years in Indiana.

She glanced above, saw the boat's hull and Tillman's dark shadow bent over its side, searching. Flicking her tail back and forth in a mermaid's version of a dog paddle, Shelly waited. In seconds he called for her.

"Shelly?" He stood and circled, checking all directions for a sign of her.

She'd wait a little longer. Enough time for him to know it wasn't humanly possible to stay underwater so long, and then she would emerge the top half of her torso, reassure him she was okay. If that was enough to convince him she was a mermaid, she would swim home while he took the boat.

"Shelly!" His voice grew louder, the first stirrings of panic threading through the words.

"Where are you?" Tillman raised a foot and pulled off a shoe, preparing to dive.

No! She didn't want him in the water where he could see the tail. She might convince Tillman of her supernatural water abilities without him seeing it. With a mighty flick of her fin, Shelly broke surface, careful to keep her lower body hidden.

"Over here," she yelled.

She couldn't see his expression this far from the boat. No doubt he was surprised how far she had swum and how long she'd stayed under. Tillman motioned for her to return.

The next stage of her reveal would astound him even more. Still submerged from the waist down, Shelly glided toward him without swimming. Her tail swished furiously underneath, but all he saw was her body from the waist up, hands idle by her sides. Shelly imagined she must look like one of those old mermaid figureheads sailors used to mount on the bows of their sea vessels, the figurehead visibly parting the sea above the water-line. Twenty yards from the boat she stopped.

"What the hell? How are you doing that?"

With her enhanced night vision, his incredulous expression was clear at this range. Shelly moved nearer, taking her time, until she drew about ten feet from the boat. With the waning moon she figured the light was weak enough for her tail to remain hidden from that distance.

"Tillman. I don't want to scare you. But I knew if I didn't show you, you'd never believe what I can do."

"It's a trick. Got to be."

Of all the reactions, his calm dismissal of this as a trick wasn't one she'd imagined. "There's no trick. What do I have to do to convince you?"

He waved her closer. "Come on. I'll figure this out."

Damn. He was too stubborn. There was no hope for it—he'd have to see the tail. She swam up to the boat. "Now do you believe it's not a trick?"

Tillman bent a little farther over the boat, straining to see. "I can't make out what's underneath you."

"Tillman," she pleaded. He was going to make her say the words. "I'm a…uh…mermaid."

He drew up and folded his arms. "Okay, joke's over. Get back on the boat. I don't have time for this shit."

"No!" She wouldn't. She couldn't. Let him see her flop around on the boat seat while she waited for her legs to form? No way. "Will you believe me if I swim home while you drive the boat back?"

He gaped at her before snapping his mouth shut. "I'm not leaving you alone out in the ocean."

She considered turning tail and swimming home. But if she did, they'd be right back where they started—Tillman not understanding how she had found the killer and she still remaining a target of the killer.

Shit. She had no choice. But she would keep her eyes closed until the legs formed. She refused to watch the revulsion and shock on his face as he witnessed the shift. Shelly grabbed on to the boat's side and with a strong grip, pulled herself into the boat's backseat, immediately rolling her face downward to avoid Tillman's eyes.

Nerve synapses twisted and pulsed, rending its usual pain. Shelly muffled her groans. This pain would be nothing next to facing Tillman's rejection. Pain lessened to a mere tingling in her legs, as if they had been numbed and were reawakening. Inch by slow inch, Shelly raised her eyes.

Tillman staggered backward in stunned belief. His mouth was parted slightly, eyes bewildered. He shook his head as if to obliterate what he'd seen.

Shelly stood and held out her hands. "I'm so sorry."

She leaned toward him and he jerked back so far his body was pinned against the steering wheel.

"It's still me—Shelly."

He worked his mouth and cleared his throat. "No." His voice was gruff. "No," he repeated, harsh and cold, anger replacing shock.

Shelly dropped her hands.

"I don't know who you are anymore."

She flinched, waited for the insults to pound down like hammer blows. *Freak, animal, unnatural, cursed.* Instead, he sat down and started the ignition. The boat lurched forward and she tumbled into the backseat. The roar of the motor and the white foam churning in its wake as they sped to land matched the storm thundering in her heart.

It was so unfair. She wanted to scream and rail and whine like a five-year-old. If only she hadn't come across Melkie. He'd ruined everything.

The boat slowed and she cringed, not wanting to get out and see that cold look on his face again. He tied the boat to the dock, avoiding her completely. Shelly took a deep breath and commandeered as much pride and dignity as possible. Since he didn't offer a hand, she got out of the boat on her own and climbed up on the small wooden dock. At last he finished securing the boat. He joined her on the dock, pocketed the keys and walked toward the house. She fell into step beside him.

"Who else?" He spoke suddenly, his voice taut.

"Wh-what?"

"Are there more mermaids in Bayou La Siryna?" He waved a hand in disgust. "Besides your cousins."

"I haven't seen any others."

"You wouldn't tell me if you had. You and your damn secrecy."

Shelly felt her insides shrink. He was right, of course. A secret identity was a sacred tenet of the merfolk. "But that's not to say there aren't more mermaids," she hastened to add. "Maybe not half-mermaid like me, but I'm positive there must be others. How much merblood is in them I can't say. Some are probably so far removed they have no clue. All they know is they're drawn to the ocean."

Tillman stopped on the edge of her property and narrowed his eyes. "Tell me what physical signs a mermaid has on land. I never suspected anything different about you."

"I haven't noticed it on anybody lately, but Jet and Lily say to look for scars at the base of a person's fingers or toes. Sometimes hybrids are born with webbing between them and the tissue must be surgically cut."

"I've heard of people being born with that webbing."

"I've actually researched it. Webbing generally occurs once in every two thousand births. But here in Bayou La Siryna, it occurs one in every eight hundred births."

He folded his arms across his chest, waiting for more.

"We also have sensitive eyes, the bright sunlight irritates them. So we always wear dark sunglasses outside."

"Anything else?"

"We...um...have a third eyelid."

Tillman lowered his face until it was inches from her own. "Where? I've never seen it."

Shelly backed away. "They usually only come out in merform or in old age. It's a kind of protection against the salt and microbes. And there's another thing about our eyes. When we get really afraid or angry our irises swirl."

They resumed walking in silence.

"So what happens now?" she asked, staring straight ahead. "About Melkie, I mean, not us."

"First thing in the morning, I send off the knife and the note to the state crime lab. Their backlog is huge but since this is a high-profile case, we should be able to speed up getting results. It will prove to me he's the killer, but I don't know how the knife will hold up in court since you were seen tossing it."

She tried to match his all-business tone. "I'll testify that I found it and, in a panic, just wanted to get it out of my house. Aren't you going to arrest him or at least search his house for our missing stuff?"

"On what grounds do I have to arrest him?"

Her temper rose. "Because I told you how I saw him that night. I *know* he's the one stalking me. He got a good look at me when he dumped that body and now he's somehow figured out who—what—I really am."

Tillman snorted. "I saw you change right in front of me and it's still hard to believe in…mermaids."

They neared the house. The front porch light was on, Jet and Lily waiting.

Tillman jerked his head at them. "They're the same as you."

"Yes. Except they're full-blooded. I'm only half-blooded, on my mother's side."

"What's the damn difference?"

She wished she hadn't brought it up. "I can't stay underwater indefinitely like them, or swim as fast, or have a mesmerizing voice like Lily."

Tillman shook his head. "Knew there was something

weird about them." He came to a sudden halt. "Shit. So that's how Jet's collected a fortune in sea treasure." He gave a bitter laugh and walked faster. "And, of course, they helped you set China Wang's body on the beach at Murrell's Point."

Shelly said nothing.

A car door opened and closed to the side of them. "You went on a boat ride, boss?" An officer exited the lookout vehicle and stared at them in puzzlement. "What's going on?"

Tillman dismissed him without slowing his walk. "Later, Officer Donnell."

They were almost to the porch. "You do remember tomorrow's the deadline to respond to Pellerin's email?" she asked.

"That's why Donnell's parked out front."

"But—"

"Don't respond to the email. You don't know what you're dealing with when it comes to a psychopath. With the DNA evidence, I should be able to make an arrest in a few days." Tillman pulled her to face him. "What else are you hiding from me, Shelly?"

She gasped at the hard suspicion in his eyes. "Nothing."

"Are you protecting one of your cousins?"

"What do you mean?"

"What the Sheriff *means*," Jet drawled from the porch, "is that he thinks *we're* the bad guys."

"It's my job to consider all the possibilities."

Shelly looked back and forth between Jet and Tillman. "But that's ridiculous. You can't possibly believe we have anything to do with killing—"

"No. But Lily could have been the one that found China and you're protecting her."

Shelly shook her head. She had told him everything, risked everything, and he still didn't believe her version of what happened that night.

"Why couldn't I have been the one that found the body?" Jet asked.

"Because a strand of long blond hair was found on the victim."

Jet's mouth twisted into a sarcastic smirk. "Next he's going to tell us all not to leave town."

"Not a bad idea." He turned and strode stiffly to his cruiser. At the door he called back to them, "Pellerin may not be the only one required to submit DNA samples."

"Yeah, that's not going to happen," Jet smirked.

Lily shuddered. "The scientists would have a field day with us."

Shelly hugged her arms to her waist, chilled in spite of the humid, stifling night air. She'd screwed up everything. Pissed off her family, lost her shot at love, and possibly ruined any legal case that would put away a serial killer.

Portia lay sprawled on the couch, the TV volume set on low while a West Coast football game played. A gentle snore escaped and Tillman sighed in relief. At least he didn't have to face a scene on that end. He slipped off his shoes and went upstairs to check on Eddie. He eased open the bedroom door, eyes adjusting to the darkness. Tangled up in the white sheets, Eddie's face was completely covered. Tillman trod softly to the bedside and eased the sheet down from his head. Eddie's eyelids fluttered while Tillman noted the rhythmic rise and fall of his chest underneath. Satisfied his brother was okay, he made his way to the kitchen for a bite.

What a freaking hell of a day, emphasis on *freaking*. After Shelly's revelation, he'd driven past Pellerin's place, noted his truck parked out front and, without making a conscious decision, he'd wound up at Murrell's Point. He had parked with the car facing the ocean and stared out at the calm waters.

His own thoughts were far from tranquil. Who could have guessed what lay underneath the surface? He'd lived here all his life, fishing and boating, the quiet sea a backdrop to his daily existence of school, play and work. A perfectly normal life with a great dad, friends, a nice house and security. Sure, his mom had been a bit prone to drink in the early years—and then there was always Eddie. But it had been manageable.

In one short week it had been blown to hell. It had started off great when he'd finally asked Shelly out. He'd kept his attraction for her under wraps, not wanting to get involved. Fearful that if it didn't work out, she might not want to continue working with Eddie. And when they made love, the physical chemistry between them blew his mind. It had never been so intense with Marlena. He realized now that Marlena had been a safe, comfortable girlfriend until she'd decided her career was more important than him. But to be fair, it wouldn't have worked anyway. No woman wanted the baggage of his family responsibilities. He had begun to hope Shelly was different, but she had lied to him from the beginning.

He opened the fridge and stared at his options: leftover meat loaf or a sandwich. Neither appealed, so he settled for a beer instead. Maybe Mom was on to something. If alcohol could take the edge off a shitty mood, then hallelujah. To hell with always being the responsible Boy Scout. He reached back in the fridge and grabbed two more bottles. Arms full of liquid comfort, Tillman returned to the den, settled in the recliner and turned up the sound on the fourth quarter of the game.

Portia bolted up from the couch and whirled in his direction. "Oh, you're home." She rubbed a hand over her forehead and yawned. "What time is it?" She squinted at the grandfather clock. "It's late. Shouldn't you go on to bed?"

"Not tired." Tillman took a long swallow and tried to take an interest in the game.

"Aren't you working tomorrow?" She looked pointedly at the collection of beer bottles by his side.

"Yep." He took another gulp, eyes directed on the TV.

"Bad day, huh?"

"Yep." He could feel her studying him but pretended not to notice.

"I really don't think…" She hesitated.

Tillman fixed her with an icy stare, daring her to make a single comment.

Portia laughed ruefully. "The answer isn't in that." She nodded at the beer.

"You want to go there, Mother? Really?" The righteous anger felt good, allowed him to focus on something besides the woman he thought he'd been falling hard for.

She stiffened and lifted her regal nose an inch. "Sounds like you're spoiling for a fight."

"Then maybe you should leave me alone."

Portia rose in a huff, knotted the sash around her robe with a fierce tug and spun on her heels.

Good, he wanted to be alone. In this ugly mood he might lash out and say things he'd later regret.

She paused at the top of the stair landing. "It's that woman, isn't it? The pool girl?"

Pool girl, ha. Shelly was a fucking mermaid, for God's sake. "None of your business."

"You never used to talk to me like this." Her lips pursed together. "I don't appreciate it."

"Cut the crap. I'm not two years old."

"Humph." She disappeared in a twirling puff of pink silk.

Tillman finished the beer and unscrewed the cap off another. It wasn't helping yet. He could still see Shelly, see the fish tail morph to legs, slowly creeping from her toes to her waist. What else lay beneath that deceiving, sweet face? The strands of blond hair on China's body had nagged him from the start, but he'd dismissed the coincidence of it matching Shelly's hair, just as he'd dismissed the small footprints from the dead body to the ocean.

Was it too much to ask for one damn thing in his life to be normal and uncomplicated?

He doubted he'd ever view Shelly the same again. He'd look at those gorgeous legs and only remember them changing to fish scales.

Forget her. Walk away while you can. Sadness replaced the anger and he felt much, much worse.

Chapter 13

Words as weapons
Syllables as shots
And in the cold pauses
I know he loves me not.

Shelly lifted her face to the warm night breeze, inhaling the scent of brine and feeling the echo of the waves deep in her stomach. But the magic didn't lift her sadness for long.

The killer could be out there right now, watching, waiting for a chance to make her his next victim. She cut her gaze to the County Sheriff's car, nestled in the oaks on their property. Tillman might be shocked and furious, but she was grateful he left them with protection.

"You showed yourself to Tillman out there on the boat, didn't you?" Lily asked.

"He had to know," she answered quickly. "He saw me toss that knife."

"So now he knows *all* of us are mermaids." Jet's brown eyes were like chips of black ice in the Antarctic Sea. "Your secret was our secret."

"I had no choice. Besides, you exposed your merform to Perry."

"Perry." Jet screwed up her face. "Look how well that turned out."

Shelly flushed. "Tillman would never betray me, or any of us, like Perry."

Lily languidly twirled a lock of pink highlights. "He seemed pretty upset when y'all came back."

"Give him time," Shelly said with a confidence she didn't feel.

"He wants you to leave everything to him," Lily guessed.

Jet squeezed her shoulder. "After what happened tonight, you want to trust that man? No way. We'll take care of the killer ourselves."

"Take care of him…how?"

"He has to be silenced," Lily said in her velvet voice. "Don't worry. You draw him out and Jet and I will take care of the rest."

Shelly looked back and forth between them. "You're serious," she said in disgust. She put her hands on her hips. "No. Absolutely not. Give Tillman a chance to arrest him."

"Why?" Jet asked. "Because you think it's the right— the human—thing to do, or is it because you're afraid to cross Tillman and risk your relationship?"

Shelly slumped her shoulders. "He may never accept what I am, but he could at least realize I'm a decent person."

"If it's over between the two of you, his opinion doesn't matter," Lily said. "If Melkie Pellerin disappeared from the face of the earth, everyone would be grateful."

"Tillman would never let him just disappear," Shelly said, appealing to their ingrained sense of self-preservation. "He wouldn't stop probing until he knew what happened. And then—" she gave them both a significant nod "—he would come after whoever killed him. We would all spend the rest of our lives in prison."

Jet dug in her heels. "No body, no crime."

"I don't want to kill anybody," Shelly said, and sighed. "I just want to be safe again. Can't you see that if you kill him our lives would be ruined? A dark shadow would follow us everywhere we went. You two could leave and join your family at sea. But I can't do that. I'm not built to stay underwater for long."

A silent look passed between Lily and Jet.

"Please," Shelly said. "I don't want you to risk your lives."

"You placed us and every mermaid in jeopardy tonight," Jet said. "You're as dangerous to us as Melkie Pellerin."

Lily ran a pointed fingernail down Shelly's cheek. "Stop worrying. We'll talk later when you're not so upset. But I have to admit, I'm as disappointed as Jet by what you did tonight."

They left her alone on the porch. Shelly wrapped her arms around her waist and leaned against a railing. She had lost not only Tillman but also the only family she had left in the world.

Tillman retrieved the tagged pieces from the evidence lockbox and arranged a special courier service to the state crime lab in Montgomery. He'd pulled every string he had and got a commitment from the assistant director that the DNA from today's delivery would be checked against the sperm samples from Jolene Babineaux and China Wang. A few days, tops, and he would have enough evidence to obtain a search warrant for Pellerin's house and make an arrest.

He opened a desk drawer for an aspirin to ease the dull ache in his temples from lack of sleep and last night's beers. He downed a couple of the pills with a sip of black coffee. No wonder Mom looked like hell the morning after a binge.

A scent of cedar preceded his deputy into the office.

"Morning, Tillman." Carl laid two wooden sea turtles on the desk and pulled up a chair for their customary morning meeting.

"Good morning." Tillman picked up one of the sculptures and admired the grooving that precisely reflected the markings on a turtle's shell. These two were keepers. "How long does it take you to make one of these?"

Carl sipped his coffee and shrugged. "Don't rightly know. I whittle when I'm thinking or goofing off and next thing I know, it's done." He eased one leg over the thigh of another and changed the subject. "Tell me about last night."

"Donnell must have turned in his report already."

"He did." Carl's eyes sharpened.

Carl could pretend to be nothing but a slow-witted old man, but Tillman wasn't fooled. Nothing got by his deputy. Old family friend or not, he wouldn't have kept him on the force, otherwise.

"Donnell was a bit troubled about last night."

"The knife," Tillman guessed.

"And the mysterious boat ride."

Tillman dismissed the boating incident with a wave of his hand. "I only did that to separate Shelly Connors from her cousins. Figured she would open up more alone, especially if she was protecting them from something."

"And what did you find out?"

Tillman got up and walked over to the window. The water was calm today, although the sky was dark with the promise of rain and wind. Was she out there now, swimming underwater, feeling the undercurrents of a storm? He scowled. What Shelly did was no longer his concern. It was only natural to wonder about her, but with time he'd learn to forget that sunshine-colored hair, skin that tasted like salt, blue eyes that darkened to indigo pools when passionate. Shit, she'd almost turned him into a blubbering poet. Best to forget about that night in the pool, it meant nothing.

He spun around and realized Carl had been trying to get his attention. "What did you say?"

"Don't let this get personal." Carl tapped his temples. "Think with this head and not the other."

Tillman flushed but stifled a snippy comeback out of respect for Carl's age and his close relationship to his father. "I never let my personal feelings affect my professional decisions," he said evenly.

"Be sure you keep it that way."

Tillman's back stiffened. "Of course."

"Donnell said Shelly Connors tossed the engraved knife in the bushes. She give you a reason for that?"

He stifled a grimace. After learning Shelly's secret, he'd been too surprised to question her properly. Carl was right to get on his case. "She panicked when she found it and wanted it out of the house."

"Bring her in for questioning. If you can't do it, I will."

Tillman gritted his teeth. "I've got this under control. Let it go."

"One more day. That's all you've got. If the case hasn't broken, Shelly Connors has a date in the interrogation room."

"With all respect, I run this ship, *sir*. If you don't like the job I'm doing, run for sheriff next election."

If Carl was offended, he kept it well hidden. "Maybe I will. So what happens now?"

"I've put a rush on the crime lab to see if the DNA on the newest evidence matches the sperm samples from our first two victims. If it does, we can arrest Pellerin and search his house."

Carl nodded. "Do we switch our stakeout from the Bosarge house to Pellerin's?"

"Switch the focus to Pellerin. I'll drive by the Bosarge house every hour or so tonight. Hopefully, this case will be wrapped up shortly."

"It better be," Carl warned.

As his deputy pushed out of his chair and left, Sam, his old partner from Mobile P.D., called.

"How's it going in the boondocks?" Sam asked.

"'Bout the same. How's life in the mean city streets?"

"That's why I called. You told me to let you know if something came up with missing persons. I don't know if it's related to your cases, but we had a twenty-five-year-old Caucasian female reported missing by her friends."

Tillman felt his nerves tingling. "A prostitute?"

"No known record. But she was last seen at a dive bar close to the docks where prostitutes hang out. Name's Alice Hargrove."

"Thanks, Sam. Let me know when or if she's found,

okay?" Tillman rubbed his chin. If it was Pellerin, his crimes were falling closer together and he may have broadened his net. Not a good sign at all.

Melkie stood among a row of bookshelves, secretly surveying the computer room across the hall. This was the slowest time of day, between lunch and the after-school stampede. He bided his time, pretending to look at book titles, until he spotted an opportunity. An elderly woman left the room without signing out on the computer. Casually, Melkie strode into the room and sat down in front of the monitor, still displaying a *New York Times* crossword puzzle. The library's policy was simply for users to log in on a screen with a patron card number. No sign-in sheet required.

Melkie pulled up his Hotmail account and saw he had an unread message from mermaidchicka. After a quick glance to make sure no one was watching—they weren't—he opened it and read the message.

Boatman. The knife is yours. No tricks this time. Please. I just want to be left alone. How about we meet at Harbor Bay? You say when, I'll be there.

His lips curled upward. She was afraid now. He minimized the screen while he considered his response. He'd thought to end it this evening, but an arranged meeting tomorrow might be easier.

Harbor Bay. He couldn't have chosen better himself. Nearly a hundred boats of all shapes and sizes from commercial and family-owned shrimping vessels to sailboats and bass boats were anchored along a heavily wooded shoreline. Rows of small wooden docks were interspersed along the bay.

Melkie typed.

Meet me at the last dock of the bay that's closest to the Trident shipyard. 7:00 p.m. tomorrow.

He hit Send, erased the internet history and closed his Hotmail account before shutting down the computer. Keeping his head lowered and avoiding eye contact with the other patrons, he left the library and headed to the truck. A familiar dark blue sedan was parked across the street. A man inside wore dark sunglasses, but Melkie knew those eyes were focused on him.

Son of a bitch.

He backed out of his parking space and turned right on Shell Belt Road. Sure enough, the sedan followed. Melkie unrolled the driver's side window to flip him off, but stopped at the last moment. Stay cool. Take care of business tomorrow night and it would be over. Once the mermaid creature was laid to rest at the bottom of the sea, he would cash in the stolen jewels and coins and leave Bayou La Siryna forever.

"Throw the ball to Jason," Shelly said.

Eddie held the ball to his chest. "Mine."

"Jason will throw it back to you. We're playing a game."

Jason splashed in the water and held up both hands. "My turn."

Rick laughed. "Then me."

Eddie turned his back on all of them, ball clutched

possessively in his hands. "Mine," he repeated louder, walking away as fast as he could in the water.

"It's okay," Shelly told Jason and Rick. "I'll get you another ball to shoot in the basket." She swam to the pool steps and dug out another one from the plastic container. "Catch," she called as she tossed it.

Shelly snuck a peak at the bleachers as she made her way to Eddie. Hard to tell what Portia Angier was thinking behind her dark sunglasses. She sat several feet away from the other moms and rebuffed their attempts to draw her into conversation. The woman had emotional walls as thick as Eddie's, only hers were a deliberate choice to remain isolated.

"Let's practice our swimming," she said, catching up to Eddie. He cast a suspicious look over his shoulder, still guarding the ball. Shelly laughed. "I don't want it. Just put it over there for now." She pointed to the cement floor a couple of feet away. After making sure Jason and Rick weren't close enough to take it, Eddie put the ball aside and mimicked Shelly as she demonstrated arm strokes.

Now for the hard part. Eddie had down the arm strokes and kicking, but he refused to put his head in the water. "Watch me. Inhale." Shelly took an exaggerated deep breath and puffed out her cheeks before dipping her face in the water. Then raising her face out of the water and to the side, she loudly blew out the breath. "Exhale." She repeated several more times. "Your turn."

Eddie did a perfect imitation, inhaled with puffed cheeks and exhaled noisily with his head tilted to the side. Only he did it above water level, refusing to submerge his face.

She really should be discouraged, but she enjoyed a

good challenge. She studied Eddie, catching that indefinable something that marked them as brothers.

Tillman. Her thoughts always circled around to him.

Seniors from Water Babes and Buoys entered the pool area. As soon as Eddie spotted them he headed to the steps, knowing his time was over. Shelly gathered the ball from Jason and Rick and rushed after Eddie. She beat him out of the pool by a mere second, and draped a towel around his waist before he came out of the wet bathing suit.

Portia minced over in strappy high heels. Shelly exchanged pleasantries with the other moms as the seniors entered the pool. She eyed Portia nervously. When she'd dropped off Eddie an hour ago, she'd been an ice bitch. Which meant Portia was furious after the last session, when Shelly had prevented her from driving.

"Eddie, before you go, I've got a surprise for you." Shelly scrambled over to her tote bag and pulled out a snack-sized Cap'n Crunch cereal box. "Good work, today."

Eddie's face lit up as he accepted the gift.

"No." Portia snatched it from his hands. "This will ruin your appetite for supper."

Eddie bellowed and grabbed it back.

Portia glared at her. "What do you think you are doing?" Her shrill voice echoed in the suddenly silent room.

"I…I'm sorry. Guess I should have checked with—"

"Yes. You should have. I don't know who you think you are, young lady, but I don't appreciate your interference in either of my sons' lives."

Shelly's skin flamed scalding-hot from embarrassment and anger. Jason's and Rick's moms watched the display with mouths open. Lurlene Elmore's face darkened and Fred Gusset, one of the Buoys, climbed the pool steps, looking ready to do battle on her behalf.

"Maybe we should discuss this later."

"We'll discuss it right now." Portia's voice escalated a notch higher. Eddie clapped his hands over his ears and rocked back and forth on his heels.

Shelly cocked her head toward Eddie. "Your son is getting upset."

"That's *your* fault." Portia jabbed a finger near her chest.

Fred stepped between them. "Perhaps it would be best if you left, Mrs. Angier."

"I'm not finished! This…this *pool girl* had the nerve to call Tillman and make trouble."

"Enough!" Lurlene Elmore hauled her considerable girth out of the water. "You should thank Shelly for taking your car keys. You're a menace to the entire community driving that town car three sheets to the wind."

Portia gasped, mouth open in outrage.

As much as Shelly appreciated the defense of her character, everyone needed to stop. Eddie was on the verge of a major meltdown.

Eddie wailed.

Portia hissed at Shelly. "See what you've done? I'm going to have to call Tillman to help me drive Eddie home." She took out a cell and punched in a set of numbers, all the while shepherding Eddie to the bleachers. Once seated, he banged his head on the hard aluminum steps with a sickening thud.

Everyone rushed to help, but the noise and the close proximity of so many people at one time made Eddie worse. Shelly bent on her knees in front of him and sang.

She couldn't hit a note, but it distracted Eddie. Shelly motioned the Babes and Buoys back to the pool.

It seemed Tillman would never get there, yet she sang on, her voice more and more raw and raspy. Thankfully, Portia didn't order her to shut up. She sat close by, nervously twisting the handbag in her lap and casting anxious looks at the clock. After what seemed hours later, Shelly caught sight of a pressed brown uniform making its way over.

Tillman squatted down beside her, eyes locked on his brother. "Hey, buddy. Heard you're having a hard day." His tone was level and he smiled at Eddie as if nothing was wrong. "How about we get you in some dry clothes and go home?" He pulled a towel out of Eddie's bag and wiped the tears off his face.

Shelly's own eyes watered at the gesture. He was a wonderful man, a *good* man—even if his tenderness and understanding for her fell short of what he gave his brother. If only they'd had more time together before the killer had forced her to reveal her shape-shifting. Maybe then Tillman would have fallen in love with her the way she had with him. As far as she was concerned, the events of the past couple of weeks were so intense and extraordinary that it forced her to quickly recognize and acknowledge her feelings.

She'd probably been a little in love with Tillman before he'd ever kissed her, although she'd convinced herself it was a mere sexual attraction. Shelly had watched him for months, watched his interactions with his family, the seniors, the physically challenged clients and their families. Not once had he been anything but unfailingly polite and kind, often going out of his way to bring a smile to their faces.

Tillman stuffed the towel back in the bag. "You can take a hot bath while Mom makes a big pot of gumbo. Sound good?"

Eddie sniffled and nodded. "Home."

Tillman stood. "Dry clothes first."

Eddie obediently walked to the locker room, Tillman close by his side.

A collective sigh of relief came from the Babes and Buoys. Portia crumpled, burying her head in her hands. Shelly hesitated, then placed a hand over Portia's. "He's okay now."

To her surprise, Portia didn't pull away but pressed her fingers into Shelly's palm and held on. "I upset him. It's my fault." She raised her head and looked at Shelly with eyes the same shade of gray as Tillman's. "I know everyone thinks I'm a coldhearted bitch, and maybe I am, but I do love Eddie."

"I know you do."

Portia managed a wobbly smile. "We got off on the wrong foot. I'd like to invite you to dinner. Are you free tomorrow night?"

Everything was too volatile right now. "Maybe a later date," she hedged.

Portia nodded. "I'll have Tillman call you and make the arrangements."

Tillman and Eddie emerged from the locker room and Tillman raised an eyebrow in surprise at the sight of his mother and Shelly holding hands. For the first time since the fiasco on the boat, he looked at her. *Really* looked at her.

The steel edge in his eyes softened and she couldn't stop the stirring of hope that danced butterflies in her stomach. For her own sake, she had to find a way to stop hoping. Tillman had emphatically rejected her and been repulsed at seeing her in mermaid form.

All that mattered now was that he found Pellerin.

Chapter 14

Two feet under
In a shallow grave
Unmarked, undone
Past being saved.

Sleep eluded him. Tillman rubbed his face and threw off the sheets. A few hours of shut-eye before night-patrol duty would have been ideal, but he was too wound up for rest. Adrenaline and caffeine would supply the needed stamina for tonight. A shower and a clean uniform would also help.

In the kitchen he packed a thermos of coffee. The pine boards upstairs in Eddie's room creaked, which meant he was pacing.

"You're going to work in the middle of the night?" Portia sat at the table. "I'd have made coffee if I'd known." She propped an elbow on the table and rested her head in the palm of her hand. "I used to do that for your father."

"I remember." He pointed toward Eddie's room. "He's still up."

"I know." Portia sighed. "I probably should have asked Dr. Saunders to prescribe Eddie a sleeping pill when he examined him. That knot on his forehead must hurt."

Jeff Saunders, the retired doctor who also served as county coroner, was an old family friend who could be counted on to see Eddie when needed.

"At least he doesn't have a concussion." Tillman set a mug down in front of Portia and poured her a cup. "I'm not the only one with a long night ahead."

She added two sugars and stirred. "I owe you an apology." Portia kept her gaze on the coffee mug. "I've acted a bit…foolish this past week."

A bit? Tillman stifled his impatience. Apologies from Mom were rare and he needed to take advantage of the opportunity. He didn't want to have this conversation now, not when he had to leave for work in five minutes, not in the middle of the turmoil from his job and not when she was making an effort at control. At dinner, she'd had only half a glass of wine.

Too little too late. It had to be done.

"Mom." Tillman sat in the chair beside her. "You need to get help for the drinking."

Portia stiffened and drew away. "I am *not* an alcoholic. I don't need anybody's help."

"Yes. You do." He wasn't backing down this time.

"I deserve my occasional cocktails and wine at dinner."

"Occasional? No. When you start driving drunk I have to draw the line."

"Just that one time. So I made a mistake. Shoot me." She stood and lifted her chin. "It won't happen again."

"It *can't* happen again. You're putting your life in danger, Eddie's life, and whoever happens to be on the road at the same time with you."

Portia's eyes welled with tears. "Your father never spoke to me like this."

"There were a lot of things Dad never talked to you about," Tillman muttered under his breath.

She narrowed her eyes. "What's that supposed to mean?"

He stood and hooked his thumbs through his belt. "Never mind. You're getting worse. Admit it."

"I'll do no such thing. Whatever will people think of me if I—as you put it—'got help.'"

"Your true friends will be relieved. Anyone else doesn't matter."

She bit her lower lip. Tillman sensed her wavering. "Talk to Jeff and see what he recommends. No one else has to know."

"But if he says I need a—" she gulped and spit out the word "—*clinic,* what would we do? I can't leave Eddie that long."

"We'd manage. Dad left him some money in a trust fund. We'd use it to hire fill-in staff while I'm at work."

"But what will Eddie think if I'm not home? You know how he is about his routine. He might have a major episode every day."

Have Shelly and Lily come sing to him. Tillman shook off the whimsical notion. "Don't borrow trouble. Talk to Jeff and let's look at what we're dealing with." He placed a finger under her chin and forced her to meet his eyes. "Will you do it?"

"Oh, *all right,*" she conceded with a huff.

"Great." Tillman picked up the thermos and car keys, feeling much lighter. "I'll be in and out until morning. I'll try not to make too much noise."

* * *

After checking the Bosarge house and seeing no signs of an intruder, Tillman swung by Happy Hollows and parked the cruiser on the potholed road in front of Pellerin's ramshackle house. Officer Donnell's cruiser was across the street as it should be. Tillman cut the lights and ignition and turned sideways for a better view. Behind the drapes, a TV screen flickered and he made out the dark figure of Melkie sipping a can of something on the couch. His mutt barked and poked his odd face against the window for a moment.

A night owl. Well, why not? The guy was unemployed; he might as well stay up all night and sleep all the next day with no job demanding his presence.

He half expected Pellerin to come outside and demand to know why his house was being watched, and half wished he would. These cat-and-mouse games bored him. After unpacking the thermos and pouring a cup of coffee, Tillman sipped and drummed his fingers against the dashboard. For damn sure he would call the crime lab in the morning and pressure them some more on completing the DNA tests. He hoped to hell Pellerin had nothing to do with the missing woman in Mobile. Because if he did, that woman was dead.

After finishing his cup of coffee, Tillman left. Might as well check back in at home and see if Eddie had stopped his pacing.

"Here, Reb." Melkie called his dog away from the window and checked his cheap plastic wristwatch—1:00 a.m. on the dot. By this time tomorrow he'd be hundreds of miles away from the bayou.

And the only witness to his crimes would be dead.

He flipped the channel to CNN, disappointed there were no more local newscasts until morning. At noon, when a Mobile news station had announced a missing woman, shown her picture on the screen and then her grieving parents, begging for information on her where-abouts, Melkie had felt a jolt of electric energy travel up his spine. He'd studied her photograph closely, a smil-ing twentysomething with auburn hair and sparkling hazel eyes full of youthful energy. Her name flashed on the bottom of the screen, "Alice Hargrove." If she was such a good girl she wouldn't have gone to that sleazy bar in the red-light district. Bitch was a whore like any other woman.

All those people looking for poor Alice and only he knew where she lay buried. Boo-hoo. He grinned at Rebel before glancing in the left corner of the den.

Those sparkling hazel eyes belonged to him now.

"Boo-boo hurt." Eddie pointed to the middle of his forehead where a purplish knot had formed.

Portia roused herself from the couch and yawned, the half-moons under her eyes staining her pale face.

"Is it time to give him another ibuprofen?" Tillman asked.

"What time is it?"

"A little after two in the morning."

She rose on wobbly legs. "Yes. I'll take a couple, too. I'm not feeling so hot myself. Come on, son."

They went to the kitchen as Tillman sank into the recliner and stretched out his legs. "Wake me up at two forty-five if I'm asleep," he called out. The ability to catnap came with the job territory, but when his mom shook his arm thirty minutes later he felt worse for the shut-eye.

"Blue light."

Eddie jumped in front of Tillman's bleary field of vision, waving his arms. "Blue light."

Portia shook her head and sighed. "Your dad spoiled Eddie with that."

A pang of nostalgia caught Tillman by surprise. As a special treat, Dad used to take him and Eddie out in the patrol car late at night. Once they hit some lonely back road with no one around, Dad would turn on the sirens and blue light. They'd hoot and holler with excitement, pretending they were cops chasing the bad guys. Well, he did anyway. Eddie just liked the sound-and-light show. Tillman had outgrown it by his early teenage years, Eddie had not.

"It's okay, Mom. I'll take Eddie with me this round and you can get a little more sleep."

Eddie ran to his room to get dressed. Portia didn't argue. Around this house, you took sleep when you could.

Eddie reemerged in record time wearing inside-out green shorts and an Alabama Crimson Tide T-shirt with the tag at the front instead of the back. Good enough for the middle of the night.

His brother raced past him to the car while Tillman grabbed a couple of juice packs in the fridge. Maybe Eddie's energy would rub off on him.

Eddie buckled himself in as Tillman backed out of the driveway. "You buckle," Eddie said, pointing to his seat belt. Before they were even out of the neighborhood, Eddie reached for the switch to start the show.

"Not yet. A little farther out." By the time they got to

Dark Corners Road, Eddie was jumping up and down in the seat.

"Now?" Eddie asked, fingers extended over the switch.

"Go for it."

The dark silence erupted in a flash of blue and a wail of sound. Tillman studied Eddie's face as he grinned and erupted in laughter. Eddie rarely laughed, but when he did, he did it unreservedly and with total abandon. They continued for miles and Tillman wasn't sure who had the most fun, Eddie with his treat, or him watching Eddie being happy. Finally, Tillman switched it off, unable to bear the noise any longer. His ears would be ringing for a while as it was. Nothing to wake you up like a 3:00 a.m. siren.

"All done," Eddie said.

"All done. I've got to swing by a couple of houses and then it's back home."

Even Happy Hollows was quiet this time of morning. He slowed by Pellerin's house. Officer Donnell waved from a parked cruiser. A TV still flickered from the home and the dog appeared at the window.

"Ugly," Eddie commented.

Pellerin pushed aside the flimsy drapes and scowled at them. Before Tillman could stop him, Eddie's hand shot out and flipped on the siren switch.

Pellerin's jaw dropped while his dog howled—as did every other dog in the Hollows. Tillman hastily turned off the siren, but it was too late. Lights blinked on at each house, doors opened and people stumbled outside to see who had been busted this time.

He should be angry. There would probably be some complaints at the office tomorrow.

But what the hell. Shit happened. As Tillman looped out of the dead-end street, he unrolled his window and waved to the spectators. Eddie mimicked him and did the same.

"Let's drive around a bit," he said as they left. "I need to talk and you need to wind down."

Tillman rattled off facts about the Pellerin case in the rambling, free-association way he talked with his brother. Somehow, talking to Eddie helped crystallize his ideas.

"…and he had a tough upbringing. Mom a prostitute, older sisters who left home early, no friends. No telling what kind of bad things he saw growing up."

Eddie clamped his hands over his eyes. "No see bad."

Tillman looked at him thoughtfully. "No see bad, huh?" An image of the victim's mutilated faces came to mind with their empty eye sockets. "Think he got rid of the eyes because he didn't want to see 'bad things'? Or maybe," he mused, "he didn't want the women to see the bad things he would do to them. Doubt he'll ever tell us why. Could be he doesn't know the reasons himself."

Tillman drove by Pendarvis Road to check on Shelly. He gave Eddie a stern glance. "Don't hit the siren again." He kept one hand on the steering wheel and one hand over the switch—just in case.

Officer Langham was parked by the house. He'd offered to spot-check during the nights as he made patrol rounds. Tillman pulled alongside him and they both unrolled their windows.

"Seen anything?" he asked.

"Nothing, boss. A couple of them went out for a few hours earlier, came back with a bunch of shopping bags."

Langham smiled and waved at Eddie. "You riding shot-gun tonight? Donnell said you woke up half the bayou."

Eddie's hand went for the switch. "Blue light."

"Oh, no, you don't," Tillman said, stopping him in time. "Carry on, Langham." As they eased away, Till-man noticed a light shining upstairs. Unfortunately, he'd never made it to Shelly's bedroom so he didn't know if she was the one awake. He pointed at the house. "That's where your swim teacher, Miss Shelly, lives."

Eddie grabbed the door handle. "Go see?"

"No, it's too late—or early—depending on your point of view. Besides, I'm probably the last person she wants to see." The words tumbled out, spilling from deep within as Tillman wrestled with all his confusing thoughts and poured them out to his brother. He drove past their own home, wanting to keep talking.

"So you see…Shelly's different. Shocked the hell out of me, actually, when she came out of the water and onto the boat." Tillman dug in his pocket and drew out the bit of fish scale he'd salvaged. "What do you think?"

Eddie took it and twirled the scale close to his eyes. "Pretty."

"Let me see." Tillman examined it. Iridescent shades of silver, purple, pink, green and blue shimmered on its surface. "I didn't notice that before. But you've got to admit this whole thing is weird. I mean—it's not normal."

"Not normal," Eddie drawled out the words, testing them in his mouth. "Not normal." He cocked his head to one side and tapped his chest. "Like me?"

Tillman almost ran off the road. Damn, just how much did Eddie really understand? He hesitated, think-ing through his answer. "You're special," he said at last.

But Eddie's head lay against the car seat, eyes closed.

Evidently, his monologue worked as well as any sleeping pill.

Not normal. So what if someone wasn't normal? Who the hell was, anyway? No one in his family could be considered normal by the bayou's small-town standards. Normal was boring and predictable. All that was extraordinary and startling originated from the uncommon. And breaking with the familiar added a freshness and zest to life.

Tillman set the sliver of mermaid tail fin on the dashboard, where the moonlight reflected the multifaceted, twinkling pastels. The effect was magical and mesmerizing.

He again envisioned Shelly coming out of the sea and climbing aboard the boat. But this time, now that the initial shock had worn off a bit, he recalled the graceful curve of her hip where it joined her tail fin, the glitter of her merform rippling under the moon.

She was beautiful, perfect in her own unique way. No, she was even more beautiful and desirable because of her shifting, unlike any other women he'd ever known. Shelly had treated his difficult mom and brother with compassion and understanding. She had risked losing her only family by exposing her secret to him, and she had tried to lead him to the killer when she could have swum away. No doubt that's what her mermaid cousins would have done in the same situation.

I'm such an ass. Tillman slammed his fist against the dashboard. He had to get her back somehow, and hope she would forgive him.

One package of incredibly amazing microfiber cloths, three jars of skin-care miracle creams and a dozen pairs of bargain discount earrings later, the beam of a car headlight entering the driveway made Shelly pause over a selection of imported wines. Probably one of the cops. Even though she hadn't been sleeping and had been mindlessly shopping online, the buzz of her cell phone had her on full alert. She picked up the phone and sighed in relief when she recognized the number.

"Tillman? What is it?"

"I hope the light on is from your room and I didn't wake you."

"I'm up."

"Look out your window."

She pulled aside the curtain and saw Tillman exit a vehicle, phone to his ear. "Is something wrong?"

"No. Can you let me in the back so I don't wake your cousins?"

"Be right there." Shelly hastily pulled on a T-shirt and shorts and finger-brushed her hair into some semblance of order on the way downstairs. She opened the door for Tillman, taking care to lock up behind him. "If nothing's wrong, then I hope you're here with good news."

"It's nothing to do with the case." He stuck his hands in his uniform pockets and gazed toward the den. "I just wanted to talk."

Shelly silently led him to the den and turned on a Tiffany table lamp, casting the room in a soft caramel halo of light.

She could guess where this was going. Tillman regretted his ill-treatment earlier and had come to apologize. He still didn't want her but, being a Southern gentleman, he would try to end it graciously. She sat on the couch, folded her hands in her lap and tensed, preparing for the blow.

Tillman stood at the window, back to her. So he couldn't even look her in the face. Shelly stiffened her spine. "Go ahead and spit it out. You came to tell me it's over. A mermaid girlfriend is just too weird, too freaky."

He spun around. "Hell, no. I came to apologize." Tillman rubbed the back of his neck, looking uncomfortable. "It was a shock seeing you like…*that*. And it shook me that if you had a secret that huge, well, what did I really know about you?"

"I'm still the same person," she said quietly. "Can't help my genetics."

He sat beside her. "I realize that now. Actually, Eddie helped me figure it out."

A hand fluttered to her throat. "Really? How did he do that?"

"He reminded me there are different kinds of normal." He placed a large, callused palm over her hands. "What you are is…special."

She tried to read those dark gray eyes. "You don't find my mermaid form revolting?"

"No. I was in shock last night. Though I admit it will take some getting used to," he confessed.

"There's no reason for you to *get used to* anything."

"There's every reason. Unless you toss me to the curb." He ran a hand through his hair in agitation. "Couldn't blame you if you did. I've been a lousy boyfriend."

Shelly rose and took a chair opposite Tillman, needing distance. She seemed to lose her good judgment when he was too close. "You don't want someone like me. You may think you do at the moment, but our differences will only make us both unhappy."

"You can't know that," he argued.

"Yes, I can. I witnessed it twenty years growing up. My parents were both miserable. Dad stifled Mom and she resented it."

"But I wouldn't—"

"Stop. Just stop." Shelly put her hands over her face for a moment to regain her composure. "Don't give me false hope. Do us both a favor and get a normal woman. I bet Marlena never gave you this much trouble."

Astonishment swept the rugged planes of his face. "Marlena? Where the hell did that come from?"

"You mentioned her name the first time you walked in my home." Shelly's face warmed. "Forget it."

"Marlena means nothing to me. You're the one—" He stopped and looked down at his hands. "I don't know the right words, Shelly. All I can say is you're the most exciting woman I've ever met. The first time we touched at the pool when we both bent down to pick up Eddie's bathing suit—remember?—I wanted you then."

She nodded. The contact had been intense, immediate.

"I knew we'd be good together. I just had no way of knowing how great it would be making love to you."

Even from six feet away, erotic heat crackled between them. She took a deep breath. "The chemistry's hot. But it doesn't mean we're right for each other."

"Damn it, Shelly, don't let your parents' bad marriage convince you we would end up the same. I'm not your father, I would never stifle you."

"So you say. But if you insisted we move from near the sea, then—"

"I couldn't do that even if I wanted to."

Shelly's brow furrowed and then cleared. "Because you don't want to leave Eddie."

"Puts a real damper on your love life when you're responsible for someone with special needs. Not exactly a chick magnet."

She jumped to his brother's defense. "Eddie's wonderful," she said hotly. "Any woman would be blind not to absolutely adore him."

Tillman's mouth upturned slightly and his eyes sparkled with bemused wonder. "You might be the only woman on the planet to believe that."

She dismissed his opinion with a shrug. "If someone loves you, nothing else should matter."

He raised a brow. "Exactly."

Damn. Threw my own words right back at me. Shelly decided on a diversionary tactic. "Shouldn't we focus on capturing Pellerin—instead of us? I want to explain what happened that night, if you're ready to listen."

"I'm doing everything possible to get him. We'll have the bastard soon. And I can guess what happened. You saw him dump China's body while you were swimming and he saw you. That's why Pellerin is after you. Then you convinced your cousins to put Wang's body on the beach so it could be found."

Tillman leaned forward, eyes bright with curiosity. "But what I don't know is how you managed to get his knife."

Shelly grimaced. "It was nothing clever or courageous on my part. When I dove to escape Pellerin, he threw it at me and it lodged in my tail fin. I didn't even know it until—"

Tillman leaped to his feet, roaring. "He stabbed you?"

She put a finger to her lips. "Shh. You'll wake everyone."

"How bad did he hurt you?" Tillman's jaw clenched as he came and pulled her from the chair.

"Not bad. The knife lodged in the tip of my tail. When I got out of the water and my legs returned, I had a cut in the webbing of one foot."

His gaze shifted to her feet. "The day after China's body was discovered I saw you limping when you got out of the YMCA pool."

"Now you know why. I kept the knife, hoping it might be useful later. We carved his name and the victim's initials on it to help you link him to the murders."

"Shit. The bastard almost got you." Tillman roughly pulled her to him. "I can't wait to nail that psycho."

His voice was fierce and husky against her ear, his cheek stubble against the side of her face sexy as all get-out. Her body responded instantly. Before she lost herself in his touch, Shelly placed her hands on his chest and pulled away a few inches. His eyes darkened with desire, the pupils unnaturally large with only the faintest tinge of pewter lining them.

She couldn't deny him any longer. Couldn't deny her own needs. She loved him and wanted to fight to make it work. Tillman was right; her parents' fate didn't have to be their fate. "If we're going to…" She swallowed, her throat suddenly dry. "We have to be clear on two things."

He patted his pocket. "If you're talking about condoms, we're good."

She gave a throaty laugh. "Not that."

"Hurry up and say what you've got to say." He grinned. "I'm an impatient man."

"If we see each other again, promise me two things. First, and most important, you can't tell anyone we're mermaids. Not just for us, but for the safety of the entire mermaid race."

"I would never tell your secret. Number two?"

"Promise you won't try to change me."

His brows drew together. "Don't see how I could even if I wanted to."

"You could object to my ocean swims like Dad did with Mom."

"She didn't stand up for herself?"

Shelly nodded. "I think she always regretted it. Mom was sickly, pale and more depressed each year that passed. I won't let a man do that—" she lowered her voice to a whisper "—no matter how much I love him."

"I promise on both counts." His breath was warm against her scalp as he spoke.

He kissed her, slow and tender. She ran her hands up and down the strong, sinewy muscles of his back. It seemed like a year since they had first made love. But this time it would be even better, with no lies between them as they joined bodies.

Tillman rested a large palm over her breast and tugged at her nipple through the silk of her thin T-shirt. He lowered his head and sucked on the raised nub, making her whimper. She reached down and cupped his erection bulging against the uniform pants. He tore his mouth from her breast.

"Let's go to my cabin," he whispered urgently. "It's only five minutes from here."

She wanted to suggest the couch and then thought better of it. She didn't want any interruptions from her cousins. And she and Tillman deserved the privacy and comfort of his cabin since their first time had been on a narrow massage table in a room that reeked of chlorine.

"Okay," she agreed. "But what is the officer who's watching our house going to think?"

Tillman frowned. "He saw me enter your house at three o'clock in the morning. News of our affair will be all over town in about three hours."

"Will it get you in trouble?" she asked anxiously.

"We're arresting Pellerin as early as tomorrow. That will overshadow everything else."

Shelly bit her lip. "Maybe we shouldn't."

"The hell you say." Tillman suddenly picked her up off her feet in one fell swoop.

Shelly shrieked, lighthearted and happy. "You he-man," she said, playfully swatting his chest.

Jet's voice from the doorway was a douse of ice water.

"Shouldn't you be out *sheriffing* or catching a killer or something?" Jet glared at Tillman.

Shelly groaned as Tillman let her back down.

"A pleasure seeing you, too," he said irritably. "We were just leaving."

Shelly quickly herded him out the back door. "Do you think the two of you will ever call a truce?" she asked with a rueful shake of her head.

"I doubt it." He drew her to his side as they made their way to his car. "But let's not waste time discussing Jet."

"Agreed. Will you turn on the siren so we can go faster?" she teased.

"The siren's had enough of a workout tonight. We'll get there soon."

But the drive to his cabin seemed three times longer than usual. He worried Shelly would lose her passionate fervor, or come to her senses about giving him another shot and insist he take her home.

Tillman made it in record time, abruptly stopping the

car at the end of a dirt road and kicking up a swirl of white sand in the process. The rustic cabin, built twenty years ago by his dad, looked even more primitive than usual when he saw it through Shelly's eyes. Made of split-hewn logs and capped off with a tinned roof, the only thing the cabin had going for it at the moment was privacy. Dense pine trees blocked out what little light shone from the moon.

He needn't have worried Shelly's ardor would cool during the drive. She scrambled out of the car and unerringly made her way to the front porch without benefit of a flashlight. As he unlocked the door, she ran her fingers down the two fishing poles leaning against the porch railing.

"One of these must belong to Eddie?"

"Right. We always have a good time when I can get away from work. It's one of the few things he enjoys doing outdoors."

The door gave way with a loud squeal. Shelly brushed past him and entered. Before he could flip on the light switch, she again made her way through darkness.

Tillman flipped on the switch and she blinked at the sudden light. She looked around the tiny space, spotted an open door to a bedroom, then walked directly to it and sank down on the mattress, beautiful as a goddess with her long hair fanned beneath her willowy body. Sea-green eyes glittered at him with passion, wide and dark against her luminous skin. Tillman gazed down, hungry with need, before placing his body atop hers. His erection pressed against her thighs and every nerve in his body screamed for release.

Tillman rolled to the side, unbuckled his gun belt

and put it on the bedside table. He started unbuttoning his shirt, not wanting a scrap of clothing between them.

"Let me do that."

Shelly slowly undid each button. Tillman pulled out of the shirt and white T-shirt underneath. She explored his chest and then her hands dropped lower to his abs. He tried to hurry the undressing, hands at the zipper of his pants. But Shelly pushed his hands away and unzipped the pants slowly over his straining bulge, smiling in satisfaction at his low moan. She pushed down the waistband of his white boxer briefs and he kicked out of them impatiently until he was at last naked.

She slid down his torso, feathering kisses along his abs before taking him in her mouth. Her tongue lapped the smooth velvet of his engorged shaft and darted into the head's cleft. Tillman moaned and ran his hands over her scalp as she licked and sucked.

"Stop, it feels too good," he said in a gruff, harsh voice. "It's your turn." He peeled off the thin T-shirt and shorts, leaving her deliciously naked. He kissed the side of her neck and licked the salty sweetness of her skin. Down he went, giving each nipple a cursory lick as his mouth went lower still, kissing her belly button until at last he reached her hot core.

Shelly bucked, impatient for him to enter. Instead, Tillman shifted his mouth to her thighs, pressing hot kisses against the sensitive flesh. Shelly protested, guiding his face back to where she wanted it.

His tongue laved the folds of her core before entering its sweetness. Shelly arched her back and moaned, right on the precipice. When his mouth moved away, she groaned in protest. Tillman reached for a condom and tore open the packet.

She stopped his hand holding the rubber.

"I want to put it on you."

As she gently rolled the condom down his hard, straining erection, Tillman sucked in his breath.

He entered her moist opening with a full thrust. "Yes," he groaned. "Oh, God, yes."

Sweet Jesus. It was even better than the first time they'd made love. Shelly bucked her hips and met him with every thrust and he strained to hold his own release until her body stiffened, ready to burst.

Now.

Shelly had never experienced such intense need. Her body convulsed and she was swept away to new heights. Waves of joy pulsed all the way down to her curled toes. Dazed, she opened her eyes and watched Tillman's half-lidded eyes, his face contorting with his own release, now that he had brought her over the edge.

"I love you." The words came unbidden, her emotions of tenderness and awe equal to the physical passion that had rocked her moments ago.

Tillman rolled onto his back, tucking her against him. She breathed in his masculine scent, felt his heart pounding against her cheek. She wrapped an arm around his waist and sighed as he stroked her hair.

Shelly never, ever wanted this moment to end, had never enjoyed coming together with a man she loved and who accepted everything about her. It was liberating and sweet and unbearably tender. The only thing in the world that existed was their combined breath, the comfort of his hands in her hair and the stillness of the dark night outside the cabin.

Tillman turned on his side and gave her a lopsided

grin. "Everything about you is perfect." He stroked a finger down her cheek. "I'm the luckiest man in the world."

She returned the grin. "You're pretty damn fantastic yourself. In fact—" she maneuvered her hand to cup his balls "—I can't get enough of you."

Tillman threw a hand over his face. "Are you trying to kill me, woman? I'm not the eighteen-year-old kid I used to be."

She laughed and climbed on top, straddling him between her thighs. "I'll grant you a few minutes' reprieve, but no more. You're too damn exciting for your own good."

He sighed. "Never let it be said I got out of bed leaving a woman unsatisfied. But," he added with regret, "I'm supposed to relieve Donnell on his stakeout at six." He shifted to his elbows and glanced at his watch. "Shit. It's already ten till six." He gave her a quick pat on the rear. "We've got to go, babe."

"I understand." Shelly slid off him and helped gather his clothes lying on the floor. "Duty calls. Just promise you won't wait too long before we make love again."

"That will be the easiest promise I've ever had to keep."

They quickly dressed and she noticed him eyeing her curiously. He ran a finger across a few pale scars on her arms and shoulders. "What really happened?" he asked softly.

"An encounter with a fisherman's trotline during one of my first swims. It wasn't so bad," she reassured him after he winced. "And not near as scary as the time I got entangled in a tuna net. I quickly learned to be more careful and to always carry a knife belted around my waist."

He frowned. "I don't like the idea of you being underwater alone. How often do you swim in the ocean anyway?"

"Since meeting up with Pellerin, I've only been once. And it was just a few minutes. Normally, I swim a couple of times a week. When the moon is full, the compulsion to change is hard to resist."

He rubbed his chin thoughtfully. "Seems like it would be dangerous. Not just the danger of being seen by men, but from sharks and stingrays, too."

"They have a healthy respect for us, but have been known to turn on mermaids, especially if we're bleeding from an injury." She laughed at his pained expression. "It's no more dangerous than you driving a car every day on land."

It didn't occur to Shelly until she returned home that Tillman didn't also say he was in love after her own declaration. She shook her head. The words didn't matter. She knew what was in his heart. When they were alone, his gorgeous gray eyes gave away his feelings, as did every caressing stroke of his large, strong hands. And if he didn't realize he was in love yet, he would. She would give him so much love that Tillman would be unable to resist doing the same.

Chapter 15

The secrets that you keep
Will eat away at you
Make you scream, make you weep
Until it must burst through.

Despite a couple cups of coffee and a Red Bull energy drink, by late afternoon the dull throbbing in his temples made paperwork more of a drudge than usual. Tillman pushed away an incident report from the county correctional facility and leaned back in the chair, propping his feet on the desk.

But all in all he had no room for complaint today. His mind drifted to last night with Shelly, her long hair fanning over his naked body, the feel of her....

"Don't need to ask why you've got that goofy grin on your face."

Tillman quickly shoved the report back under his nose, ignoring Carl's jab.

"It's all over the office that you picked up Shelly Connors at three in the morning."

"And you call women gossips," Tillman said, signing the report and pulling another out of the in-box.

Carl laid a knife-nicked hand over the paperwork. "Be careful. That's all I'm saying."

"I know what I'm doing." Tillman allowed a touch of exasperation in his voice. "I'm not a kid anymore, in case you haven't noticed."

"I know, I know." Carl withdrew his hand and sank into his usual seat across the desk. "Curse of the old to always think of adults as the kids they once were."

"No need for the warning. I know you think I shouldn't get involved with Shelly until the murder cases are solved. But I spoke with my contacts at the crime lab this morning and they assured me all the evidence will be processed by close of day. By tonight, I plan to have Pellerin arrested and his house thoroughly searched."

And Carl, being Carl, had more to say on the subject, after all. "Most of your case against him, so far, is based on evidence from Shelly Connors. Yet one of our men witnessed Connors throwing the supposed knife used by the killer out in her own yard. Explain that."

"Pellerin's been stalking Shelly and her cousins. When she found the knife in her house she panicked and tried to get rid of it." It sounded flimsy, but it would have to do.

Carl finally let it go. "Moving on, then, I should tell you we're short a couple of officers today. David Ott's wife had the baby last night, so he'll be out at least a few days, and Hollinger called in sick with the flu. That doesn't leave us enough manpower to keep a tail on Pellerin."

Tillman sighed. "We can't leave jail duty short, too dangerous. It looks like our suspect is a night owl anyway and sleeps during most of the day. He should stay put a few hours longer."

"If it makes you feel better, I'll drive by a few times."

Tillman's office phone rang and he recognized the

caller ID number. "It's Sam. Don't leave. Maybe he's got some information on the Alice Hargrove case that connects it to Pellerin. I'll put him on speakerphone."

Sam got right to the point. "We've got a man in custody, name of Hoyt Snowden, who claims he killed Jolene Babineaux and China Wang."

"What?" Tillman sprang to his feet. "No freaking way."

"We went to his house this morning after receiving information he was at the bar where Hargrove was last seen and that he was one of the last persons she spoke with."

Tillman picked up the case file notes. "I'm on my way over. Give me thirty minutes."

"Figured you'd want to talk to him yourself," Sam said. "And a word of warning—news of this confession has already leaked to the press and it's a circus in front of headquarters. You'll face a barrage of TV cameras getting in."

Sam wasn't lying.

Tillman called him on the cell phone. "Any way to sneak in the back?" he asked.

"Nope," Sam said immediately. "We've tried that. There are a few reporters staked at the back door, too. You try that entrance and they'll alert the others who will be there before you can set foot inside."

Might as well get moving and get this over with.

Tillman took long, purposeful strides, head lowered, as he crossed the parking lot and headed into the Mobile Police Department building, where his old partner met him in the lobby.

"You should have given a few television interviews.

Keeping your face in the public eye might help you with the election next year."

"Reelection is the last thing on my mind right now."

The two men shook hands and smiled. Sam motioned down a hallway to their right. "I believe you know the way."

"Snowden can't be my killer," Tillman said as they walked to the interrogation room. "I've got my man nailed. I'm expecting a call from my deputy any moment that the lab results confirmed my suspect."

"Why did you come, then?"

"It's possible my killer had an accomplice. Could be Snowden."

"Or Snowden could be a total mental case," Sam added. "False confessions happen a lot with high-profile crimes."

"Has he admitted any involvement with Hargrove's disappearance?"

"Says he was drunk that night and probably killed her but can't remember any details."

"How long has he been here?" Tillman knew the longer someone was interrogated, the more likely they were to confess, guilty or not. Sometimes, it was simply a desire to be left alone from the questioning, other times because they craved attention and, most frequently, because of an underlying mental or learning disability.

They entered the small, cheerless room with bare, drab walls. The only furniture was six metal folding chairs surrounding a chipped Formica-topped table stained yellow from years of cigarette smoke.

Hoyt Snowden sat slouched and listless, occasionally sipping a can of Coke. He had thin, shoulder-length red hair and a bushy red beard. He raised his head at the entrance of the two detectives. Tillman took in his pale face and red-rimmed eyes.

"Hoyt, this is Sheriff Angier from Englazia County," Sam said.

He grunted acknowledgment, swiping thin, twitching fingers across a wrinkled camouflage shirt.

Tillman sat across from Hoyt, placed his closed file on the table and leaned in. "I hear you have some information on Jolene Babineaux and China Wang."

"I killed 'em." Hoyt's voice was listless, mechanical, his eyes tired and empty of emotion.

"How?"

"Raped and then stuck them with knives, threw them in the water." Hoyt looked up at the ceiling, seemingly bored.

"Where, exactly, did you dispose of the bodies?"

He made brief eye contact before lowering his head. "Huh?"

"Where did you dump them?"

Hoyt made a vague gesture with his hands. "The ocean."

"A little more specific would be helpful," Tillman said drily.

"Got rid of them both in some marshy area. It all looks the same to me."

Wrong.

"Did anyone help you with either killing them or disposing of the bodies?"

"I did it all myself." Hoyt acted as if he were spitting out a grocery list instead of confessing to a double murder.

"Why?"

Momentary confusion registered in those listless eyes

before he shrugged. "I didn't like the looks of them? Hey, the cops in here before y'all told me if I cooperated and told them what I know, they'd let me go home."

"Excuse us a moment." Tillman picked up his file and Sam followed him out. As soon as the door closed, Tillman raised an eyebrow at Sam. "I drove all the way over for this?"

"Got to cover all the angles, buddy. Maybe Hoyt's thought better of his confession and is playing dumb now."

"He hasn't asked for a lawyer yet?" Tillman asked.

"Nope. Not too smart."

"I don't think the dumb act is an act at all. Anyone checked his education level?"

"Ninth grade dropout," Sam said.

"Sounds to me like your department is pretty desperate to stick him with the crime."

Sam spread his arms, palms up. "You remember what it's like here. Exploring every avenue, no matter how unpromising. That's our job."

Tillman sighed. "Just a few more questions and I'm done with this farce."

He reentered the interrogation room and leaned over the table, six inches from Hoyt's face. "I don't know about Alice Hargrove, but you have nothing to do with the murders in Bayou La Siryna, do you?"

Hoyt scooted his chair back. "Yes?" he asked with a tremor in his voice.

"Don't waste my time with lies." Tillman banged a fist on the table. "Any of these detectives tell you that lying to the police is a crime?"

Tears filled Hoyt's pale blue eyes. "I just want to go home."

Tillman lowered his voice almost to a whisper. "You don't know anything about these murders, do you, Hoyt?"

"No." Hoyt shook his head. "I don't know nothing. I only want out of here."

"That's what I thought." Tillman walked out, Hoyt's muttering curses echoing behind him.

Sam matched his long strides to the front of the police station. "We've got fingerprints, blood and hair samples from Snowden. If it turns up there's any validity in his confession, I'll call you."

"Thanks. Hope you find Alice Hargrove—alive."

"Not much chance of that," Sam said glumly. "If we do find her dead body, I hope the DNA results show it's the same killer for all three women."

"Wouldn't surprise me at all. Melkie Pellerin is capable of anything. But if Hargrove wasn't a prostitute, she's atypical of his pattern."

Tillman grimaced as the reporters came into view. The slight misting of rain on the drive over had turned to a steady drizzle. Television cameras and other equipment were covered with tarp while reporters huddled beneath umbrellas. The distant rumble of thunder didn't deter them from a journalistic stakeout for information.

Sam laughed and slapped him across the back. "Just another part of the job, buddy. Want to go get a burger before heading back to Hicksville?"

"Another time. I want to be in Bayou La Siryna when the lab techs call."

Sam pulled the door open for him. "Don't hold your breath. They've been known to break promises."

As Tillman stepped out into the rain, the reporters

spotted him and hurried over. Sam said in a low, teasing undertone, "Don't forget your pretty-boy smile for the cameras."

Melkie studied the latest batch of specimens that arrived via mail order, a welcome distraction from thinking about tonight's business. With a pair of tweezers, he held up a Common Jezebel butterfly from India and carefully ran a finger down the nearly transparent chitin, observing its vein-like structures. The upper side of the wings was white, but the brilliant underside had sections of bright yellow outlined in black with red conical spots edging the outer band and outlined in white. The bright coloration served notice to its predators that it was unpalatable because of toxins the larvae took in from host plants.

The excited voice of a TV reporter interrupted the old Mayberry R.F.D. episode playing.

"There may be a big break in the recent disappearance of Mobile native Alice Hargrove."

Startled, Melkie dropped the Common Jezebel in his lap. A local news reporter stood in front of the Mobile Police Station, a crowd of people behind him.

"A credible source has reported that a man is in custody after confessing to the abduction of Alice Hargrove and the recent murders of two women, Jolene Babineaux and China Wang, from nearby Bayou La Siryna."

What the fuck?

Melkie raced to the window and pushed aside the curtain. He squinted through sheets of rain, but there was no sign of the familiar cop car parked on the street. He pumped his fists in the air. "Yeesss!" Rebel lifted his head where he'd been dozing on the couch. "We did it, boy."

Melkie paced, too excited to sit and examine the other new specimens. He was pumped, jazzed, on top of the world. He didn't have to worry about getting by the stupid pigs tonight. A new confidence buoyed his spirits. He could do no wrong. Maybe once he escaped his crappy childhood home, the nightmares would go away, too.

In two hours he'd take the truck, pulling his boat on a utility trailer, to a remote marshy area. He'd motor the johnboat to Harbor Bay and anchor to the dock, and then wait in the woods until the mermaid arrived. Not even the pending threat of severe thunderstorms dampened his spirits. Actually, it worked to his advantage. The less people out and about, the less chance of getting caught.

Three more hours and it would all be over.

Shelly ran by the Mermaid's Hair Lair after work, hoping to coax Jet and Lily to go out for dinner with her and declare a truce. At breakfast this morning they'd been secretive, still giving her the old silent treatment. She hated it when they joined forces against her like that.

After parking the car and grabbing an umbrella, she hurried to the shop before coming to an abrupt halt in the doorway. A closed sign hung on the door. She pressed her face to the glass, but the shop was dark and empty. Her stomach tightened. They wouldn't try to arrange a meeting with Melkie Pellerin without her.

Would they?

Under the shelter of the store's awning, Shelly called the house on her cell but got no answer. Her heart slammed against her chest. She had a bad feeling about this. "Don't panic," she mumbled, trying to keep some semblance of calm. Shelly ran to the car. She called them five more times before arriving home in record time. The house was as dark as the beauty salon, but both cars were in the driveway.

She ran, unlocked the door and pushed inside.

"Jet? Lily?"

Nothing but an ominous, pressing silence.

Not bothering with an umbrella this time, Shelly ran to their boathouse, seeing only water lapping the shore where the boat should have been anchored. *Shit.* They could be with him right now. But where?

She reentered the house and went to Lily's bedroom. The metallic sheen of her cousin's laptop gleamed in the faint light. Shelly picked it up from the nightstand and opened it. She knew the password by heart—techno-challenged Lily always had Shelly fix or load things on it. She opened the Sent email folder. Only one email remained, addressed to "boatman."

Damn them. They were going to get themselves killed. She clicked on the message.

Boatman. The knife is yours. No tricks this time. I just want to be left alone. Please. How about we meet at Harbor Bay? You say when, I'll be there. Mermaidchicka

Shelly went to the in-box and found Melkie's response.

Meet me at the last dock on the bay that's closest to the Trident shipyard—7:00 p.m. tomorrow.

It was already six-thirty, and Harbor Bay was a good twenty-minute drive under normal driving conditions.

She went to the kitchen, found the largest knife on hand and tossed it into her purse. Thank heavens, her loaded gun was already in there.

Back to the car she raced, adrenaline pumping. She'd make it on time if it meant driving ninety miles per hour to do it.

Lightning crackled in the sky, its flare creating a strobe effect against the windshield wipers as she gripped the steering wheel. Even with the wipers on high speed, visibility was poor. She imagined time tick-tocking away, like a bomb about to explode. Shelly cursed as she swung the car to the side of the road, hating to waste even a second, but she couldn't negotiate making a phone call while navigating through the downpour.

Busy.

She hit the accelerator, pulled the car back on the wet road and kept hitting the redial button as she flew toward the bay. At last it rang once, twice, three times before his voice mail picked up.

"Tillman, it's Shelly. Where are you? Call me immediately. Pellerin's meeting Jet and Lily at Harbor Bay at seven. I'm on my way out there now." Her voice broke. "Hurry."

Damn it to hell. For what seemed like the hundredth time, Tillman hit redial on his cell. It was almost six forty-five, but he knew damn well there was a second shift of techies working at the forensics lab until at least nine o'clock. They were dodging him, the sorry sons of bitches. They'd *promised* to have results today. He pressed a different programmed number on his cell, for Carl, who assured him no one had called from Montgomery, doubted it would happen tonight, but if and when it did, he'd let Tillman know.

He wanted to fling the phone out the window. Instead, he told Carl to go home and have the dispatcher call him directly with any news. Through the pounding rain, the sign for Collinsville flashed with a swish of the windshield wipers, marking the halfway point between Mobile and Bayou La Siryna. Maybe it was frustration with the delayed tests or lack of sleep or even the violent thunderstorm, but he couldn't shake a premonition of disaster.

He checked the cell again and saw two voice mail messages. Eagerly, he punched in his code. The first was from Lieutenant Crane with a technical question on an inmate's due process hearing, adding he'd be at the jail until ten that evening. He deleted the message and went on to the next.

As Shelly's message played, Tillman sat up straighter. By the time he heard the catch in her voice saying "hurry" he was frantic. What the hell did her cousins think they were doing?

It hit him. They meant to kill Pellerin. And Shelly was headed right into the middle of it.

He'd bet anything this was all Jet Bosarge's idea. If anything happened to Shelly because of her idiocy he'd make her regret it.

If anything happened to Shelly… No, he wouldn't let anything happen. He switched on the blue lights and sped faster. He tried to call Shelly back, but couldn't get a ring tone. Shit. He was out of service range for at least another ten miles.

Harbor Bay appeared deserted. Over a hundred boats in all shapes and sizes swayed in the gusting wind. Shelly checked the dashboard clock—6:55 p.m. Only two vehicles were in the parking lot, a blue Chevy truck and an old Dodge Charger. Nobody appeared to be in either. Shelly turned into the closed car repair shop across the street, parking behind an old pickup severely smashed on one side from a collision. She cut the engine off and peered out at the bay.

A thicket of pine, cypress and juniper trees lined the shore only twenty feet away from the last dock, and she immediately understood why Pellerin had chosen that location. It took a minute, but at last Shelly spotted her cousins' blue bass boat.

No surprise, it was empty, also.

She threw on a raincoat and slipped the knife in the left pocket, the loaded gun in her right pocket. It was now 6:58 p.m. She waited for someone to appear, her jagged breath filling the car's interior.

The sound of the cell ringing made her jump and she clamped a hand over her mouth to keep from screaming. She checked the number before answering.

Tillman.

Her lungs expanded and then exhaled with a relieved whoosh. "Where are you?" she asked.

"Are you at Harbor Bay?"

"Yes. I'm sitting in the car waiting for someone to show up."

"Shelly, don't get out of that car! Do you hear me? I'll be there in five minutes."

"Thank God. I was starting to think… Oh, no." A flash of long blond hair passed underneath the solitary lamplight along the bay's sidewalk where the boats were anchored. "I've got to go," Shelly whispered.

"Don't you dare get—"

Shelly flipped the phone shut and tossed it into the backseat. Quietly easing the car door open, she kept her eyes peeled for the killer.

A figure emerged from the darkness of the trees. Dressed in dark clothes, hands stuffed in a windbreaker, he looked quickly in all directions before walking to the dock. Shelly ran into the rain, hurrying after him. Lily stood at the end of the narrow wooden dock that jutted about twelve feet into the ocean. Shelly couldn't see the expression on her face, only the slight, determined lift of her chin. As she neared, Shelly was grateful for the rumble of thunder covering the sound of her sneakers sloshing through the parking lot's puddles.

She searched for Jet one last time. Even though she couldn't find her, she knew Jet was out there somewhere in the storm, watching and waiting with a cunning equal to Pellerin's.

Melkie stepped onto the deck. "So we finally meet again, bitch." He advanced another step. "You're a fucking freak of nature." His voice was low and dangerous, barely audible against the banging of the crowded boats against one another along the shoreline.

Lily's lips curled upward, but her eyes glittered like a patch of azure calm waters, and just as deep and mysterious.

Only a few feet separated her from Pellerin. "Wait," Shelly yelled. "I'm the one you want."

Pellerin whirled to face her, mouth dropping open in astonishment.

"Go away, Shelly," Lily said. "You're going to ruin everything."

Shelly kept her eyes pinned on Melkie's as he looked back and forth between her and Lily. His face was as she remembered. She withdrew the knife from the left front pocket of her raincoat and slipped her index finger into the trigger of the gun hidden in her right pocket.

"Goddamn it." Melkie threw his head back and screamed in rage. "How many fucking mermaids are there?"

Shelly forced herself to walk closer. "I'm the one who saw you that night. You stabbed me on the tip of my fish tail with this." She held up the knife. "And now I'm returning it. Just promise to leave me alone and I'll promise not to tell anyone anything."

"Liar." His face twisted in a grimace, black eyes flashing with anger. "You put that fucking body out on Murrell's Point for the police to find."

Shelly took three more steps, her sneakers slightly slipping on the wet floorboard of the narrow dock, until she got within a few feet of Pellerin. Close enough to feel the smoldering heat of his outrage.

His right arm rose, a small gun palmed in his hand. "Drop the knife."

Shelly hesitated, watching Lily from the corner of her eye. For the first time, Shelly saw the preternaturally serene expression fade. Lily's eyes were wide, mouth slightly ajar.

"Now, Jet!" Lily screamed. "Do it now!" Lily dove into the water, leaving Shelly behind.

A gunfire shot exploded at the same time a large *thump* rumbled from beneath. The wooden dock cracked and split apart under their feet. Shelly fell backward, hitting her head on the wood. Despite a haze of pain, she realized her only chance of surviving depended on getting undersea. She rolled off the deck into the black, churning waters.

Chapter 16

Jolene by swampland
China by sea
Look where you can
You'll never find me.

Tillman radioed the dispatcher, requesting backup at Harbor Bay. "Possible hostage situation, approach with extreme caution," he added.

He'd turned off the cruiser's blue lights, not wanting to announce his presence too soon and force Pellerin into drastic action in order to flee the scene. He entered the parking lot at the bay, the car's headlights piercing through rain and darkness.

Three figures stood on the last dock, two women with long blond hair and a man between them.

A shot rang out.

Sheer terror washed through him. *Not Shelly, please, God, not Shelly.*

He floored it to the sidewalk and then, brakes squealing and tires spinning, he exited the vehicle, gun drawn. But there was only a black void where the three had stood; he couldn't see anything or anyone. He ran an arm over his face, wiping away the rain from his eyes and hair.

And still saw only a jagged crack, splitting the dock almost in two pieces. The sea was too black and churning with foam to see what lay beneath. He quickly searched the surface of the water through the fog and the rain for some sign of what happened. Bits of clothing bobbed against the white crests. He holstered his weapon and laid the gun belt on the sidewalk before kicking off his shoes.

She's okay. The water is her safety net. She has the advantage over Pellerin. But it didn't stop his panic to find Shelly. The boom of the gunshot reverberated in his brain. No one was invincible to the deadly hot steel of a bullet at close range.

Tillman jumped into the sea and swam, thrashing his arms and legs, hoping to make contact with someone or something. But his hands grasped nothing solid; his long legs felt nothing but the churning water. "Shelly, can you hear me? Where are you?"

He grabbed the only tangible thing in sight—bits of material bobbing like flotsam. He made it back to the dock, resting one hand on its battered surface while he studied the torn clothing, a couple pairs of underwear, a pair of white shorts and a pair of gray shorts. The lighting from the streetlamp was enough to make out the lettering on the gray ones.

YMCA. Instructor.

The ground went out from under Melkie as if he'd fallen into a sinkhole, sucked down into an abyss of no return. Water engulfed his whole body. He strained to open his eyes, but the sea salt stung and scalded them. He kicked and tried parting the waters with his arms, instinctively aiming for the surface, lungs on fire for air.

Something pinned his arms from behind. He kicked harder and twisted his torso, desperate to escape. He opened his eyes—had to see what kept him trapped. A beautiful pale face floated before him, long blond hair streaming upward like an underwater cloud. His eyes traveled downward, already knowing what he would find.

Fish tails.

The mermaids had tricked him somehow. All they had to do was get him into the water and fight him where they were strongest, in their own natural element. He knew he couldn't breathe, yet an instinctive reflex to inhale sent a trickle of brine down his throat, making him cough, causing yet more sea water to fill his lungs. The burning need for oxygen worsened.

The fight left his body as his mind roamed to a distinct, long-forgotten memory—four years old and seated at the table for lunch. He must have done something right that morning, uttered some magical word or smile that had his mother laughing. Her eyes and lips were unpainted and she wore a white robe, hair still damp from a shower. She smiled and drew him to her. He inhaled the clean scent of shampoo, the warm skin smelling of Ivory soap, and the collar of her robe pressing against his neck held the freshness of linen dried in sunshine.

"My little boy," she had murmured, giving him a quick squeeze and a kiss on top of his head.

One perfect moment, catalogued and stored somewhere deep within, forgotten until now when only a mother's love could drown the horror.

Shelly's athletic shorts and underwear ripped apart as her legs fused into a fish tail. The sea churned, pounding her body with its force. Small eddies on the sea floor lifted chunks of sediment in an upward spiral of distress.

Below and to the right, several fathoms under the dock, she found the others.

Jet had Melkie's arms pinned behind his back. He struggled to open his eyes in the salt water. Bubbles of oxygen poured from his mouth.

Lily was face-to-face with Melkie, not even an arm's width separated the two bodies. The irises in Lily's eyes swirled, indicating extreme mermaid duress while in merform. She smiled slightly at the same time she raised her right arm. Shelly didn't know her intention until Lily's long, sharp nails plunged into Melkie's right eye.

A pool of dark liquid circled in smoke rings, the tiny tendrils pooling above his head in a cloud of crimson.

An eye for an eye.

"No!" Shelly screamed. "Don't kill him."

Lily hesitated, left arm drawn for attack over Melkie's remaining eye. Jet kept Melkie pinned despite his violent thrashing to break surface. Jet looked at Lily and raised her eyebrows in question.

Shelly couldn't stop staring at Melkie, couldn't help the surge of pity stabbing her heart. The bubbles dribbled out slower. He needed oxygen.

Melkie's mouth parted, opening and closing twice in two syllables—*Mama*. And with each syllable the sea poured itself inside Melkie, forced out the life essence. The bubbles from his mouth, which had spewed like a child blowing bubble rings, had dwindled to two, then one last bubble.

With a violent surge of her tail fin, Shelly sliced through the last six feet of water toward the gruesome trio. She grabbed Lily's hair and yanked a fistful of angel-blond fluff.

"Let him go," she pleaded with both of them. "Tillman needs to arrest Pellerin. He won't be able to hurt anyone else again."

Lily paused, eyes returning to their normal blue. "He's here?"

"If he's not here yet, he's on his way."

"Pellerin will expose us. He needs to die." Lily's voice was as serene and musical as an angel singing a psalm.

Shelly felt the pull of it, the magical notes of it tingling through her blood and drawing her to its will, strong as the ocean's undertow. She gritted her teeth as she stared at Melkie, limp and lifeless.

"No. You said yourself no one would believe wild tales of mermaids. Release him."

Lily paused, and then nodded at Jet, who released her hold.

Shelly grabbed Melkie's limp body around the waist and motioned for her cousins to leave. "Go home." Without looking back at them, she carried Melkie up toward air, fearing it was too late. She broke the water's surface cautiously, only allowing her head to emerge. If the bay was swarming with cops, she'd have to abandon Melkie and leave.

"Shelly!" Tillman bent over the dock and reached his arms out toward her.

"Anyone else around?"

"Not yet, it's safe. Is that Pellerin?"

She swam to him and Tillman took Pellerin's body, roughly lifting it onto the broken dock.

"Did he shoot you? I heard a shot." He grabbed her

arms and pulled her to him, cradling her head in his hands. The rain and wind beat down upon them, but Shelly didn't care. The nightmare would soon be over.

"I'm fine," she assured him, throwing her arms around his neck and holding on for dear life. He clasped her to his chest and she felt his heart slamming against her breasts.

A wail of sirens sounded in the distance. Tillman released his hold. "You have to go."

"But how are you going to explain—" she pointed at Pellerin's inert body *"—that."*

"Doesn't matter. Just get the hell out of here before someone sees you."

"No. Help me up."

He shook his head, looking past her to the road. "They're almost here."

"Trust me, Tillman."

He hesitated and then his strong arms pulled her out of the water. "You better know what you're doing."

Shelly bit her lips against the pain as fish tail and scales shifted to skin and bones.

Tillman rubbed her hands and frowned. "This hurts you?"

"A little," she admitted. "Do you have something to cover me?"

He gave her his raincoat and she put it on while he retrieved her ripped gray shorts. "Put these on," he said, thrusting them at her. He hurriedly unbuttoned his shirt as the shifting continued.

Flashing blue lights bore down upon them. Shelly stood and yanked up the shorts, deliberately averting her eyes from Melkie's lifeless body lying a foot away.

"I'll tell the police that Pellerin kidnapped me and

brought me here," she said as Tillman tied his shirt around her waist, protecting her from cops seeing the exposed skin through the torn shorts. "He planned to shoot me and push my dead body into the sea. We struggled, I clawed at his eyes, and the wooden dock split in the storm. Melkie fell in just as you came."

Cars screeched to a halt along the bay's sidewalk. Car doors opened, followed by footsteps and voices.

"Got it." Tillman nodded and bent to whisper in her ear. "Act like you're in shock and I'll take your statement at your house later. Don't talk to anyone else."

Everyone was upon them, shouting questions. Tillman signaled the medics to check Melkie's body. Shelly shivered, watching an EMT pump Melkie's chest with rapid compressions while another EMT kept a finger on the pulse at the side of Melkie's neck. When that yielded no results, they stopped the chest compressions and one of them swept a finger through Melkie's mouth before placing a respirator mask over his face. Paddles were applied to the chest, and the strong charge made Melkie's feet and head rise up.

A hand went over her shoulders, someone trying to lead her away, out of the rain and into a police car. She shook them off, unwilling to leave the medical drama. What if he lived and people believed his story of mermaids? What if he died and she was tried for manslaughter?

A stream of brackish water poured out of Melkie's mouth and he gagged and coughed.

She didn't know whether to cry or rejoice.

A voice close to her ear called out, "I think this one's in shock."

More hands pushed at her, this time toward the red

lights of an ambulance. *Oh, hell, no.* If they took her to a hospital and ran tests, no telling what abnormalities doctors might uncover.

"No hospital. I'm fine." Shelly dug in her heels, seeking Tillman in the crowd. He spoke with his men, pointing at the rotted wood. He sensed her alarm and looked her way. He left the group and headed over, shirtless, chest hair matted from rain. She wanted nothing more than to be held against that chest, shielded from the stares and questions.

"What's wrong?"

"I can't go to the hospital."

Tillman waved off the medical personnel. "She has the right to refuse treatment."

"She could be in shock," one of them said with a frown.

"I'm fine," she repeated. "No medical treatment. It's…against my religion."

"You heard the lady." Tillman took her by the elbow and guided her to his car. "I need a blanket," he called out.

Once they were alone inside his car, he spoke quickly. "I'll be busy here for quite a while. Carl will drive you home and I'll come by as soon as I can. Give Carl a short, preliminary statement, like the one you told me earlier."

An officer rapped on the window, holding up a blanket. Tillman opened the door and retrieved it. He wrapped Shelly in it and turned on the car's motor. "You need heat."

As he radioed his deputy, the ambulance raced out of the parking lot.

* * *

Carl pulled the cruiser out from the dozens of flashing blue lights and the swarm of officers milling around the dock.

He didn't speak and Shelly was grateful for the silence. *Thank God, it's over.* The image of Lily sinking her fingernails into Melkie's eye socket made Shelly shake all over again. She'd got there just in time to stop another murder—whether Melkie deserved to die or not. She couldn't bear to think of her cousins sinking to such darkness.

The cruiser passed by the closed shops on Main Street. The pounding rain had driven folks inside their homes, the roads practically deserted. Shelly kept her gaze on the passing trees, their branches tossing feverishly and the Spanish moss dancing in the Gulf wind. As the trees seemed to press closer to the car, Shelly realized the street had narrowed and they were on a sandy back road.

"Sorry, you're going the wrong way. My house is on—"

The car sputtered to an abrupt stop and she turned to the deputy in surprise.

A pair of swirling irises spun and glowed in the darkness.

Shelly couldn't breathe, couldn't move. Her entire body clenched in panic as she felt her own eyes begin to spin.

"I knew you were one of us." Carl's voice was tight and raw, not the grandfatherly tone she remembered from their earlier phone conversation. "Tell me what really happened back there."

Shelly slipped a hand behind her back, feeling for

the doorknob. "I gave my statement to Tillman. I've got nothing more to say on the matter. Ever."

"You've betrayed your own kind, haven't you? That's why Tillman never arrested you for tampering with evidence or obstructing an investigation. You broke the code of silence and told him mermaids exist."

She lifted the handle, but the door wouldn't budge. She was trapped in the car with a madman. No. Make that a mad *merman*. She bit her lip to stop a hysterical giggle.

"I know all about you and your cousins," he went on. "Who do you think discovered Jet's illegal operation?"

"You're the blackmailer." Anger replaced the fear. "And you let Tillman believe his father did it."

"Oh, his dad was in on it, all right. Money's tight when you've got a crazy kid and a princess for a wife. He didn't know the details of how the treasures were recovered though."

"Eddie's not crazy! Don't you dare say that about him."

"Don't let your weak human feelings blind you to the opportunities out there." Carl's eyes stopped spinning and he ran scarred fingers through his thick white hair.

Scarred fingers. Tillman hadn't made the connection with the mer-signs she'd described to him earlier.

"What do you want from me?"

"First of all, don't ever tell another human about us. There are more of us out here than you know."

"I won't," she agreed immediately. He wasn't going to hurt her.

"And second, our conversation tonight stays between us."

"Done. Can we go now?"

"One more thing. When Jet starts up her operation again, I get an exclusive cut for my silence. If you don't, I'll make life hell for you and Tillman."

Opportunistic scumbag. "What makes you think Jet's going to do that?"

Carl reached for the ignition and started the car back up.

"Perry's out of prison."

Shelly kept her face pressed against the window. She'd rather look at the live oaks mournfully shrouded with moss than the profile of Carl's lying face. Not only was he a threat to her cousins, but he pretended to be Tillman's friend and right-hand man, while secretly working against him. Great, yet another person she might one day be forced to reveal as a fraud to Tillman. He might come to view her as a bad luck charm that did nothing but expose humans, especially those he was closest with, as greedy liars.

Tillman didn't deserve this. Bad enough his father had led a double life and his mother was a selfish alcoholic. Not to mention the ex-girlfriend, Marlena, who'd dumped him after his father's death, just when he'd needed her most. Eddie was the only person in his world who was exactly as he appeared on the surface. No wonder Tillman loved him so much and was willing to shoulder caretaking duty.

Shelly vowed never to let Tillman down if she could help it. She would love him and support him the rest of her life. And she wouldn't let a sneaky bastard like Carl Dismukes come between them.

"Is he dead?"

Shelly asked the question as soon as Tillman sank

into the velvet wing chair. He leaned forward, resting his hands on his knees. The warm glow of the chandelier cast a flattering light on the trio seated opposite him on the couch. Shelly and Lily perched on either side, bookends of blond sunshine and jewel-colored eyes, with Jet in the middle, chopped black hair gleaming like onyx, dark eyes glowering. All had extraordinary skin, smooth and polished like marble. Now he knew their secret, it all seemed so obvious. Their unnatural beauty and perfection set them apart.

He glanced out the window. The storm had abated to a mist, the ocean calmed to its usual placidity, the morning sun hovered in the horizon. A fresh scent from last night's rain blew in from the open window.

"Well?"

Jet's impatient voice drew him back to their original question.

"Something worse."

Shelly's eyes widened. "How is that possible?"

"He's incoherent and alternates between babbling about mermaids and calling for his mother."

Jet jumped up and began pacing, while Lily showed no reaction.

But he was only interested in Shelly, who had buried her face in her hands. He went and knelt in front of her. "It's okay," he reassured her, placing a hand on her thigh. "No one takes anything he says seriously."

She uncovered a pale, weary face. "I can't help but feel sorry for him. When his lungs filled with seawater, he called for his mama. We all want our mothers when we're desperate."

The son of a bitch had gotten to her with that line. Shelly still grieved the loss of her own mother.

"You might not feel so sorry for Pellerin when I tell you what we found at his house."

Jet stopped pacing and Lily stared at him, but he kept his gaze on Shelly as he sat beside her. "When I first questioned Pellerin, I noticed his dog whimpering and digging at an area under the far left floorboard of the den. When we searched his house, we discovered a loose board, pulled it up and found everything we need to send him away for the rest of his life."

"What was hidden?" Shelly whispered.

"Mason jars filled with formaldehyde and the missing eyes of his victims."

"Jolene and China." Shelly took a deep breath. "I'm glad for their families that you can punish their killer."

"There are several more unidentified eyes. I can't tell you how glad I am to put this case to bed," Tillman said. "My biggest regret is that I didn't catch him before he got to the last victim."

"The missing girl from Mobile," Shelly guessed.

"Alice Hargrove. I suspect forensics will identify her by one of Melkie's preserved specimens." He sighed and took her hand. "But at least you're safe."

"Don't be so sure about that," Jet said. "Pellerin may be playing crazy for the moment, but a few weeks in jail might do wonders for his sanity and for building a court defense."

Tillman scowled. God, Jet was one annoying woman.

"Where is he now?" Shelly asked.

"At a secure psychiatric hospital in Birmingham for evaluation. After that, he'll be taken to a maximum security facility while awaiting trial." He faced Jet. "This case is foolproof. Pellerin will be lucky to escape the death penalty for capital murder. Stop scaring Shelly."

Lily spoke up for the first time. "I'm not worried a bit." She smiled at Shelly. "Everyone will think he's nuts."

Maybe Lily wasn't so bad, after all, Tillman mused.

"Did you happen to find anything else when you searched his house?" Lily asked. "Like some jewelry? I want my rings back."

No, his first impressions were right, Lily was that bad.

"I can't believe you're worried about your rings right now," Shelly said.

Lily lifted her chin. "You know you're dying to find out if your black pearls were under that floorboard."

Shelly pointedly ignored her cousin and turned to him. "Where's his dog?"

The sudden conversation shift momentarily confused him. "His dog?"

"You know, Rebel, the one you said everyone makes fun of."

"I've been a little busy tonight," he said drily. "It was missing when we got there." At Shelly's look of concern, he added, "I'll call the animal control officer tomorrow and have him take a look out there."

She jumped to her feet. "We need to find him now. You told me one of Melkie's neighbors dislikes the dog because it chases his cat. He might hurt Rebel."

"You've been through a shock. You need to get some rest, not run around after that mutt. We'll look tomorrow."

She leaned over, kissing him on the cheek. "No offense, but you look like hell." Her sudden smile lightened his mood. "You're the one who needs sleep. I'm perfectly capable of handling this myself."

He rose with an exaggerated sigh. "Oh, all right. What's a couple more hours of playing good guy when you haven't slept for two nights, anyway?"

"Shelly's right," Jet said. "You should get some sleep."

Tillman snorted. "Don't tell me you're suddenly concerned with my health."

"I've been…wrong about you." Jet crossed her arms, a sheepish expression on her face. "You're not so bad, after all."

He placed a hand over his heart. "Who are you?"

"When I'm wrong, I admit it." She went to him and held out a hand. "Why don't we start over?"

Tillman looked at Shelly in astonishment. She beamed her approval.

He shrugged and shook Jet's hand. "Done."

Jet rewarded him with a grin that stunned. He glimpsed the warm, vital person behind Jet's dark, sullen eyes.

Lily gave a loud yawn. "Y'all have fun. *I'm* sleepy and going to bed."

He watched her hips sway as she took her leave, unruffled and casual. That one, Tillman decided, he would never understand. He hadn't asked any of them—yet—how that dock had broken and why Pellerin was missing an eye. But he would bet Lily had zero compunction in meting out her own brand of mermaid justice.

Jet tapped him on the shoulder. "I'll help Shelly with the dog. Stop checking out my sister's ass and go home."

"I wasn't—"

He stopped protesting at their laughter.

Shelly tugged his arm, leading him to the door. "Go make sure Eddie and your mom are okay and get some rest. I imagine you'll have a ton of things to do later."

At the door he cupped her face in his hands. "If you're sure you're okay—"

She leaned her forehead against his chin for a second and pulled away. "It's really over, isn't it?"

"He can't hurt you anymore."

"Thank you," she whispered.

He abruptly crushed her body to his. "You saved yourself." He'd come so close to losing her, he was reluctant to leave.

"Good God, you two," Jet snorted. "Say goodbye already."

Shelly laughed and gave him a push. "Call me later."

"This is it."

Shelly pointed to the Happy Hollows sign and Jet turned her truck onto the pothole-riddled street leading into a neighborhood of decrepit old houses jammed close together.

It was a quiet Saturday morning compared to most neighborhoods, where home owners had the gall to run lawnmowers and weed eaters early in the day.

Jet slowed the truck to a crawl as they searched. "Have you ever seen this dog?"

"No. But Tillman said we'll know it when we see it."

"Meaning?"

"Apparently, it's most outstanding feature is that it's hideous and has practically no hair."

Jet cocked her head to the left. "There's a dog."

A black boxer stretched out on a sagging porch, head resting on his paws. He opened one eye at this potential threat to his territory and promptly closed it again.

"He won't win any doggie beauty contest, but I wouldn't call him hideous," Shelly said.

Jet stopped the truck in front of the Pellerin house, sealed with yellow crime scene tape.

Shelly shivered, remembering what was hidden under the floorboard. "All the commotion last night probably scared the dog off for a little while. Let's get out and call his name, could be he's hiding close by."

But after a good ten minutes of whistling and calling, "Here, boy," they conceded defeat.

"There's something." Jet hurried a few houses down, Shelly in tow. A small brown furry creature skirted into some shrubs.

Shelly crinkled her nose. "Ew, I'm pretty sure that was a rat."

"You said it was ugly," Jet grumbled. "Let's go. We'll try again in a few hours."

A loud, high-pitched squeal sounded in the distance, followed by laughter and shouts. They exchanged a worried look and ran down the street. Five bicycles lay abandoned by a path in back of a house. They hurried over, the whimpering of an animal in pain goading them on.

The dirt path led them through a cluster of pines. In a small clearing, a half-dozen young boys hollered and laughed, picking up pebbles and hurling them at a small dog tied to a tree with an old boat rope. The dog let out a howl as one of the pebbles struck him on the side of the ribs and he ran in circles, desperately tugging at the rope around his neck.

"Hey!" Jet grabbed the arm of a kid who had his elbow raised shoulder height, a rock palmed in one fist, ready to strike. "Leave that dog alone."

The kid, who looked to be about eight or nine years old, swung around in surprise. All of the boys stopped hollering and stood motionless, assessing the strangers.

Jet was red-faced with anger. "Get out of here, all of you."

Shelly stepped though the crowd and went straight to the dog. Kneeling just outside the rope's reach, she spoke softly and exposed open palms. "It's okay, Rebel. You're safe now."

"Fuck you, lady," one of the kids yelled, the rest snickering at the insult. Shelly came to her feet and rushed to protect Jet.

She needn't have worried. Jet grabbed the T-shirt of the closest boy. "Shut your filthy mouth and get out of here."

His pals took off in a mad scramble for their bikes and pedaled as fast as they could to get away from the crazy lady.

"Let him go," Shelly said in a low voice.

Jet snatched her hand away and the kid ran after his friends. At the edge of the clearing, he stopped and yelled, "I'm telling my mom."

"Go away, punk." Jet turned her back and headed to the dog. "Freaking kids."

They both knelt by Rebel.

"Tillman was right," Jet said. "No doubt this is Pellerin's dog."

"*Was* Melkie's dog," Shelly corrected.

He bared crooked yellow teeth and growled.

"We should have brought a biscuit or something," Jet said. "Maybe we should get help and come back."

"And let those kids stone him to death? No way." Shelly edged an inch closer to Rebel and held out her fingers for him to sniff. "C'mon, Rebel," she coaxed. "We won't hurt you."

He tentatively poked his nose forward and sniffed.

Straining at the rope around his neck, he licked Shelly's fingers.

"See? I'm your friend."

Rebel rolled onto his back in submission.

Shelly laughed. "I knew that growl was just for show." She petted the hairless body and untied the rope. Rebel bounded in her lap and licked her face before doing the same to Jet.

"Let's skedaddle before those precious little ones return with mad mamas in tow," Jet said.

Shelly carried the willing dog to the truck. Rebel whined as they drove by Melkie's house.

"You're going to be okay, boy," Shelly said soothingly. "Do you think Lily's singing will have a calming effect on Rebel like it does with people?"

"We'll find out."

Rebel jumped out of Shelly's arms and plastered his nose against the back passenger window at the sight of an orange tabby. The cat arched its back, fur bushing out, ready for combat.

Jet grinned. "Maybe this dog will keep all those damn cats from following us everywhere we go."

Shelly pulled away from the curb. "There's something I need to warn you about," she began. "I wanted to get you alone, away from the others."

"Sounds serious."

"It is." Shelly bit her lip nervously. "Have you ever met Tillman's deputy, Carl Dismukes?"

"Unfortunately, yes. He was the go-between on the blackmail money with Tillman's father." Jet's eyes narrowed. "What about him?"

"He gave me a ride home last night." Shelly took a

deep breath—there was no easy way to say this. "He wants a share of your profits when you start back trading."

"What makes him think—" Jet's words died on a sudden inhale of breath. "Perry," she whispered.

"He's out of prison." Shelly lightly touched Jet's shoulder. "Hey, you okay?"

She stiffened her shoulders. "Fine. Thanks for the warning, Shelly. What did you tell Dismukes?"

"To take it up with you."

Chapter 17

If you're in some dark bayou
And think someone is watching you—
An eye does lie in the sea sand
Gazing upwards through tideland
Searching for mama in Alabama
In a liquid panorama.

Shelly absently fingered her black pearl necklace, watching Tillman through the kitchen window. The scent of sizzling steak and shrimp from the grill drifted in the open window and she smiled at his absorbed pleasure in the task. Shirtless and shoeless, he took occasional sips from a beer and drummed his fingers along the edge of a platter in time to an old Lynyrd Skynyrd classic. In the weeks since Pellerin's capture, Tillman had gradually become less uptight and driven. Regular work hours combined with steady sleep at night did a lot for a man.

And she liked to think their healthy sex life played a major role in this new, relaxed Tillman. She remembered the way he'd held her last night, the feel of his hands against...

"Eat."

Eddie's sudden command pulled her abruptly out of the steamy reverie.

"Almost done." She handed him a large salad bowl. "Put this on the table for me, please."

Shelly observed him surreptitiously as they worked together setting the table. The first week after Portia left for rehab had been rough. Eddie couldn't understand why his mother was gone and they'd called Lily more than once to come over and sing to calm him down. Beat the hell out of Xanax every time.

"Who's hungry?" Tillman came in and put the platter of grilled food on the table. "I'll be right back, let me pull on a T-shirt before we eat."

Shelly threw him a mischievous grin. "Not necessary. I'm enjoying the view."

"Shirt at table," Eddie pronounced.

In his world, a rule was a rule, no exceptions—and it always paid to accommodate Eddie's world. But Shelly didn't mind. Rules and routine helped him make sense out of the chaos in his reality.

They all dug in. Shelly stuck to shrimp dunked in butter while Tillman and Eddie ate steaks with all the fixings.

"What's the latest on Melkie?" she couldn't help from asking.

"Still in psychiatric lockdown. You don't need to ask about him every day. If something changes with his situation, I'll let you know."

"Nice to have my own personal pipeline." She tried to keep her voice light, a smile on her face. But she remembered those angry, glittering eyes, kept expecting to turn a corner and see him, or wake up from a nightmare and hear him whisper in the darkness. She thought of him at the oddest moments, too, like when a butterfly hovered nearby, or in underwater shadows during ocean swims.

Shelly straightened her spine, determined to switch the conversation. "In town today I came across a strange woman," she said. "I heard people whispering 'witch' so I turned to see who they were talking about. There was this old woman in a loud purple dress and I caught her staring at me with the strangest look on her face. When she caught my eye, she winked and then left without a word."

Tillman nodded. "Had to be Tia Henrietta, our local crackpot. She lives way out near Coden and tells fortunes."

"She ever read yours?"

Tillman snorted. "As if I would pay good money for something like that."

He could snort all he liked, but Shelly resolved to have Tia read her fortune one day.

"Normal humans see only half the world," she said. "You might be surprised by all that's out there."

A smile lifted one corner of his mouth. "I've seen all I care to see." He took a long swallow of iced tea. "Has Lily left yet?"

Shelly pushed back the plate of discarded shrimp tails and sighed. "She's leaving tonight. Nothing Jet and I say will sway her. Once Lily gets a notion to do something, that's it." She couldn't imagine Lily wanting to leave the bayou for uncertain, deep waters hundreds of miles away from her and Jet. Sure, they had some distant relatives in mermaid colonies. And living undersea could be beautiful and exciting. But, for Shelly, it was also a mysterious, dangerous world—one to be tasted in small doses close to shore.

Tillman slipped his hand over hers. "She'll come back."

"I'm not so sure," Shelly said slowly. "I think the encounter with Melkie upset her more than she lets on."

"How can you tell with Lily? Your cousin has the biggest poker face I've ever seen." Tillman withdrew his hand to finish up the last bit of his steak. "As far as I'm concerned, Lily's missed her calling. She's wasting time running a beauty salon when she could be winning a fortune playing the Vegas casinos."

"Lily already has a fortune," Shelly reminded him. "We all do, thanks to generations of—" she hesitated, glancing at Eddie "—um, maritime reclamations."

Tillman grinned and slapped his brother on the back. "You hear that, Eddie? You could say Shelly comes from a long line of supernatural pirates."

"Cap'n Crunch?" Eddie asked hopefully.

Shelly laughed. "I promised him a bowl of cereal for dessert if he ate his vegetables first."

Later, as she and Tillman finished washing the last of the dishes, Shelly grew quiet and pensive. Tillman studied her as he put up the dish rag.

"Still upset about Lily leaving?"

"A little."

"Something else bothering you?"

"Well…" She hesitated. There was no nice way to say it.

He folded his arms and leaned one hip against the kitchen counter. "Go on. Spit it out. Remember our agreement? No more secrets or lies between us."

Carl's mer-eyes flashed before her and Shelly crossed

her fingers behind her back. One little secret. "It's just… your mom is coming home in a few days."

He frowned. "I don't see what that has to do with us."

"I know there's always my house for us to spend the night together. But you have to stay close to your brother and look out for Portia."

"No." He shook his head. "No more looking after her. She stays clean and sober or I'm done with it."

"But Eddie…"

Tillman froze. "I thought you liked my brother."

Shelly made a face. "I don't *like* Eddie, I *love* him. That's not the problem."

"Then what is it?"

"At the risk of sounding incredibly selfish, I won't have you to myself anymore. I've been playing house the last few weeks in a place that belongs to Portia."

"I hadn't planned on telling you until later tonight, but I'm moving out, getting my own place. It's way past time. Mom should be able to handle things around here, especially since I convinced her she can afford a part-time caretaker with the trust fund Dad set up for Eddie."

Tillman laid his hands on her shoulders. "I promise," he said, gray eyes intense with emotion, "you mean everything in the world to me."

She threw her arms around him and hugged him tight. "That's all I needed to hear."

He pulled away, a lopsided grin on his face. "Really? That's enough? Then I guess you don't need this, either." He reached in the pockets of his cargo shorts and drew out a small velvet-lined box along with a small sliver of something.

Shelly drew in her breath. "Is that—?"

"It is." He held the box out.

"Not that." Shelly took the other object in his hand. "This looks like a fish scale."

"Oh, that." Tillman shrugged. "I picked it up off the boat the night you first showed yourself to me as a mermaid." He tried to take the scale away from her.

Shelly stepped back a step. "Why did you keep it?"

"At first I kept it to convince myself the sight of you wasn't some hallucination. Later, I held on to it because…well, it's beautiful. Like you."

Shelly's heart somersaulted as she watched Tillman's cheeks redden slightly.

"Just open the damn box," he said gruffly.

"Is it what I think it is?"

"Yep. Time we made everything official."

"Then there's one more thing I need to hear."

Tillman knitted his brows in confusion. "What the hell?"

She crossed her arms. "Just three little words. The first starts with 'I' and the third starts with 'you.'"

He relaxed his facial features. "Oh, for God's sake, Shelly, you know I love you."

Finally, the words.

"You're quite the romantic." She smiled.

"I can do better." He cleared his throat. "Shelly, you're the best thing that's ever happened to me. You're beautiful, kind, smart—"

"Don't forget 'rich,'" she teased.

He gently laid a finger on her lips. "Let me finish. I knew from the first moment I saw you that you were special and gorgeous. And now that we're together, I realize just how special and beautiful you are on the inside, as well." He withdrew his finger and replaced it with his lips, giving her a tender kiss, before saying, "Now you can open the box."

She opened it and slipped the ring on her finger, holding it out admiringly. "That's all I'll ever need to know."

Eddie reentered the kitchen. He came over and touched the sparkly diamond. "Ring," he said in his deadpan tone. He promptly dropped his hand and opened the refrigerator door, already losing interest. "Want juice."

Tillman raised a brow. "Is the answer 'yes'? Remember, I'm nothing but a low-paid county sheriff with plenty of baggage."

"And you know what I am," Shelly said. "You still game?"

He grabbed her and kissed her lips until she couldn't remember anything but how right this man felt. She pushed against his chest to admire her engagement ring.

"I'm sure you have larger, better pieces," he said regretfully.

She hastened to reassure him. "None that can compare to this one."

The diamond ring sparkled on her left hand; the flickering prism of its colors matched the iridescent shimmer of her fish tail in the dark bayou waters.

It shone like a promise, a light against the darkness.

Epilogue

Jet breached the water at over thirty miles an hour, gritty determination etching her angular face. She tucked in her tail fin as she did a one-and-a-half back-flip before slipping back into the water headfirst.

Bravo, Jet! Shelly pushed the words out in a compressed sound wave. Her cousin was one of the fastest mermaids alive and Shelly watched in awe as Jet's muscles rippled in a perfect blend of athleticism and poetry. *Bet you take first place this time at the games.*

Jet grinned and gave a fist pump. She excelled at the annual Poseidon Games held in the South Pacific and was ready for the competition set to begin in three weeks. As a TRAB, Shelly was forbidden to attend. Only the pure, full-blooded merfolk were permitted to participate and visit the grand underwater caverns housing mer-treasure. Spawning with mermen at the games was encouraged to preserve what was left of their race. In mer-society, Shelly's kind were considered diluted aquatic humanoids, not fit for breeding.

Heading home, Jet called out before disappearing into the moon-drenched swells.

Shelly's heart panged for Lily, who used to decide when it was time to return to land. She knew Shelly couldn't stay undersea as long as them and always wanted to spare her pride. *Miss you, Lily,* Shelly sang into the liquid abyss, knowing there would be no answering reply today, only the eternal crinkling sound of sand and rock as they rolled and tumbled in the shifting tide. Lovely Lily with the siren's voice that carried for miles and which humans mistakenly took for whale song. *Have fun with your mermen.*

Shelly no longer feared her cousins would abandon her while in the South Pacific. They'd be back. Jet couldn't tear away the hope that Perry would one day return and Lily wanted to be with her sister. Besides, they loved her just as she was.

A school of aqua mackerel skittered within inches, sending air bubbles tickling along her torso. Shelly reveled in the lightness of the ocean's womb, secure and surrounded by its amniotic fluid of life-giving sustenance. After encountering Melkie, she wasn't sure she'd ever again swim without fear. But not only could she do it, she had found new joy, had come to terms with shape-shifting between worlds.

She belonged.

Her heart was on land with Tillman, yet she had the freedom to come and go as she wanted.

Shelly floated, let the undertow sweep her at will, hair rising straight up from her scalp like the tentacles of an octopus.

Just a little longer.

At last Shelly flicked her tail fin and propelled upward, eager for home.

Tillman awaited as she emerged through the portal and into the shelter. She laid her elbows on the sandy edges of the opening, keeping her body in the water from the waist down. He brushed a strand of wet hair from her face and cradled a large palm against the curve of her left cheek, as tenderly as if she was the most precious, most fragile woman in the world.

"Is anything wrong?" she asked, heart in her throat. "Is Eddie okay?"

He gave a bemused smile. "Sometimes I think you love my brother more than you love me."

Shelly opened her mouth to protest, but he laid a callused finger against her lips. "You know I'm joking. Nothing's wrong and I'm lucky you put up with the both of us."

"Package deal. So what are you doing here?" She made no move to exit. Tillman had only seen her metamorphosis from mermaid to woman twice. Despite his assurances otherwise, she couldn't forget his shocked look the first time she was forced to reveal her true nature to him. The second time he'd seen her transform, they had both been focused on apprehending Melkie Pellerin. Besides, after a lifetime of secrecy, shape-shifting in front of a human still felt wrong.

Tillman held up her terry robe in one hand. "Aren't you coming out?"

"I need some privacy," she said softly.

He arched a brow. "Really? After all the times we've seen each other naked, why are you turning shy on me?"

"You know why."

Tillman tossed the robe to one side and placed both hands under her armpits. The golden specks in his gray eyes shimmered. "Shelly," he said, voice husky with emotion. "I love every inch of your body in every shape and form."

She gasped as he dragged her out of the water in one quick movement. The night air was chilly against her damp flesh until he pulled her against his warm, fully clothed body.

A slight moan escaped her lips as tail fin split in two and fish scales dissolved beneath human skin.

"How bad does it hurt?" Tillman whispered in her ear.

"Only a little."

He tightened his grip around her shoulder with one arm while gently stroking her face with one hand. She wanted to bury her head in his chest, still somewhat embarrassed at this last bit of intimacy.

At last the pain subsided and was replaced by the overwhelming need to be at one with Tillman. He quickly shed his clothes and they kissed, tongues dancing in lust.

A sudden blast of chill swept across Shelly as Tillman pulled away.

"What—?" she began.

He impatiently retrieved the cast-aside robe and spread it upon the sandy ground. Before she could move, he easily lifted her and placed her carefully on top of the makeshift blanket.

"I love everything about you, Shelly. *Everything.*"

She gazed up at the face she adored and knew so well. "I believe you. And I love—"

Her words were cut off as his mouth landed upon hers again.

Outside, the wind kicked up the sand, which beat

upon the steel shed in a staccato drumming. But here, with Tillman's body pressed against her own, Shelly was protected and uncaring of anything but this man she would love all her life—and who loved her in return.

* * * * *

A sneaky peek at next month...

NOCTURNE™

BEYOND DARKNESS...BEYOND DESIRE

My wish list for next month's titles...

In stores from 15th November 2013:

❏ Dark Wolf Running — Rhyannon Byrd
❏ Nightmaster — Susan Krinard

In stores from 6th December 2013:

❏ Dark Victory — Brenda Joyce

Available at WHSmith, Tesco, Asda, Eason, Amazon and Apple

Just can't wait?

Visit us Online

You can buy our books online a month before they hit the shops! **www.millsandboon.co.uk**

1113/89

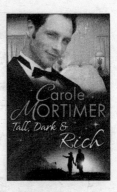

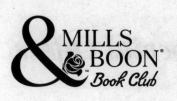

Join the Mills & Boon Book Club

Subscribe to **Nocturne**™ today for 3, 6 or 12 months and you could **save over £50!**

We'll also treat you to these fabulous extras:

- 🌹 **FREE L'Occitane gift set worth £10**
- 🌹 **FREE home delivery**
- 🌹 **Rewards scheme, exclusive offers...and much more!**

Subscribe now and save over £50
www.millsandboon.co.uk/subscribeme